BUT
HAVE NOT
LOVE

MW01038668

BUT
HAVE NOT
LOVE

MICHAEL EDWIN Q.

But Have Not Love by Michael Edwin Q.
Copyright © 2018 by Michael Edwin Q.
All Rights Reserved.
ISBN: 978-1-59755-494-7

Published by: ADVANTAGE BOOKS™
                  Longwood, Florida, USA
                  www.advbookstore.com

This book and parts thereof may not be reproduced in any form, stored in a retrieval system or transmitted in any form by any means (electronic, mechanical, photocopy, recording or otherwise) without prior written permission of the author, except as provided by United States of America copyright law.

Library of Congress Catalog Number: 2018961484
1. Fiction:: African American - Woman
2. Fiction: African American – Historical
3. Social Science - Slavery

Cover Design: Alexander von Ness
Edited by: Nancy E. Sabitini

First Printing: October 2018
18 19 20 21 22 23 24   10 9 8 7 6 5 4 3
Printed in the United States of America

Table of Contents

Part I

Her Story

One

A Blessed Event

Ravenna never wanted children. Now it looked like it was too late. Her husband, Azrael, felt the same. The life of a slave was hard enough without the burden of children. Besides, the world was too dark a place for anyone, least of all a child.

Being second generation slaves from Africa, Ravenna had her choice of old and new world preventions for not getting into the family way. Not wanting to take any chances, she used them all, only to find they were nothing more than old wives' tales, filled with ignorance and superstition.

After days of waking with the morning sickness, Ravenna was sure of her condition.

One night during dinner, sitting in their one-room shack, after a hard day's work, she told her husband.

"You're not eating?" Azrael commented, pointing his fork at her plate.

"I ain't hungry."

"What's the matter, ya sick?"

"In a way..." She hesitated, not looking up from her meal. "I'm goin' to have a baby."

Azrael dropped his fork, looking up at her as if she just announced the end of the world.

"Are ya sure?"

"Of course, I'm sure."

"I thought ya were takin' care about such things?"

"Well, they ain't worked!" she spit out her words at him. It always irked her how stupid he could be.

"What are we goin' to do?"

She looked up at him, her face twisted with anger. "We?" she said with strong sarcasm. "*We* are goin' to do everything possible to make this not happen. That's what '*We*' are gonna do."

They spoke not a word for the rest of the evening. Later, in their bed, in the dark, Azrael felt a strong urge to reach out to Ravenna. She rested on the other side of the bed, as far from him as she could possibly get with her back turned to him. He placed his hand on her shoulder. She grunted, shrugging him away. He realized then that if they had the child or not, their lives together would never be the same – a life of sadness.

As with the advice for prevention, the cures for ending her sorrows were of little use. She tried everything. She made Azrael fill their wooden tub with boiling water, not just hot water, boiling water. The result was painful burns on the skin of her legs and hips that would take weeks to heal.

A ride, standing in the back of a two-horse buckboard, at full speed down a rocky road yielded no results. There was sitting over a pot of steaming onions, jumping up and down for an hour, rolling on the ground, throwing yourself down a hill, all this did nothing.

She drank potions and teas made from potent herbs found in the forest. The effects of all these drinks did nothing about her condition, though often they left her feeling ill for days. Two of the potions brought her close to death's door, still she continued.

Finally, after many failures, she reluctantly accepted her fate, but not completely. She had a plan, one she kept to herself, telling no one, not even her husband.

The only good part of her being in this condition was that when she began to show the Master of the plantation took much of her daily workload off her plate. This was not out of compassion, but greed. Another slave born is another slave owned, adding to the wealth of the possessor.

In her last month, they treated her like a queen. All day long she sat sorting through tobacco leaves, placing them in stacks according to size. Extra food was sent from the main house of the Master, in hopes of keeping her healthy and strong for the oncoming ordeal.

For months, Ravenna turned down the services of every midwife on the plantation, even those who offered for free. The gossip was she was mad, foolish, or both. When the night came for what most would call *"A blessed event"*, save for her and Azrael, she was alone. She sprawled across the bed, reeling in pain. Sharp pains like no other came and went. Each time it came, it seemed stronger. More than once, she felt sure she would pass out. She hoped she would, but never did. Finally, close to midnight, the pains came more often with more intensity. She began to howl loud and long in her misery. Azrael stood at her bedside looking hopeless.

Suddenly, there was a pounding on their door. Azrael answered it. Standing in the doorway were some of the women from nearby shacks, some of them midwives.

"We heard her; we're here to help," said one of the women.

"Tell them to go away!" Ravenna screamed across the room from her bed.

Azrael rushed to a point in the room between the bed and the front door. "But ya might die!" he warned her.

"Get out of here, all of ya!" she shouted.

Azrael went back to the door. "I'm sorry, but she doesn't want any help. Thank ya, but…"

"Close the door, Azrael!" she hollered at the top of her lungs. "Now, Azrael…slam it!"

Azrael did as he was told, closing the door in the faces of their neighbors. He rushed back to Ravenna's side. "What are ya doin'? Why did ya send them away?"

"Shut up… does what I tell ya!"

Hours later, the time came. Though still in great pain, Ravenna was too exhausted to scream, she only moaned low and deep in her throat. So much sweat poured from her that her wet hair clung to her head. The blankets under her were soaked, as well.

Too weak to cry out, the child came into the world with a whimper. Azrael took some old rags, swaddling the child in them. To inspect the child, he carried it to the light of the moon shining through the window.

He turned to Ravenna, "It's a…"

"I don't want to know!" she struggled to push the words out. "I don't want to know what it is! I don't want to name it! And I don't want to see it!"

"But, Ravenna…"

"I want it dead! If anyone asks, tell 'em it died minutes after bein' born, and ya buried it out back."

"That's why ya didn't want any one of the midwives here. Ya planned it this way all along."

"Just do it, Azrael. Ya know I'm right."

He didn't argue the point. He believed as she did. It would be best. But she wasn't the one who had to do the dirty work. The thought of it chaffed him the wrong way. Holding the newborn in one arm, he opened the door and left.

Outside, the night was cool with a calm breeze blowing. Still holding the child, he fetched a shovel from under the house. There was about an acre of grassland behind their shack; beyond that was the edge of the forest. Carrying the child in his left arm and the shovel in his right hand, he stopped in the middle of the field. Ever so gently, he placed the baby on the ground; it was sleeping. Taking the shovel in both hands, he began to dig.

As he labored in the dark, he wondered what to do. It seemed so cruel to bury the poor thing alive. He shuttered at the thought. He would have to kill it first, but how? He could suffocate it, but that would take so long. Holding his hand over the child's face, covering its mouth and nose, might take minutes. The thought of slowly suffocating the child made him uneasy. No, it would have to be something quick. Perhaps, a quick, hard blow to the head with the shovel would be the most humane? He decided it would be best and much more comfortable for him.

When he'd dug the hole knee-deep, he believed it more than enough. After all, the child was so small, and he was so tired. He wanted to make quick work of it and get back to bed and try to get some sleep. It would only be a few more hours before he'd have to get up to a full day of labor.

A rustling sound behind him took him by surprise. He spun around to see the figure of a man standing a few feet away.

"Azrael, what the hell are ya doin'?"

He recognized the voice of one of his neighbors and fellow workers, Micah. Being taken off guard, Azrael didn't know what to say.

"Micah, what are ya doin' out here?"

Micah was a tall lanky man with willowy arms and dangly legs. His face was thin and long, looking like a great sculptor carved it, but midway ran out of marble. His eyes were bright, clear, beacons shining amid his dark skin. He felt it strange to find Azrael digging a hole behind his house before sunrise. What he found even stranger was that when he asked a question, Azrael came at him with a question.

"It's nearly sunup. I just stepped out for a moment and heard ya diggin' back here." He restated his original question. "Azrael, what the hell are ya doin'?"

"Ravenna had the baby last night. It was born dead. I was just diggin' a grave for the poor creature."

"Gee, Azrael, I'm sorry to hear that, I really am. Is there anything I can do to help?"

"Thank ya, Micah, but I got this well in hand. Ya can go back to whatever it is ya should be doin'."

Just then, the sound of a tiny yawn came from the small bundle on the ground. Micah rushed to it. Down on one knee he pulled the rags from the child's face.

"This child ain't dead. Here, Azrael, take a look-see. Praise the Lord! It ain't dead! It's a miracle!"

Azrael's mind raced. In that brief instant, he thought of a half dozen excuses. In the next moment, he realized how foolish they all sounded. He decided to tell it like it was.

"I wasn't straight with ya, Micah. Ya see it's like this. Ravenna and me don't cotton much to children. We never wanted any and never will. I was just goin' to bury it, and forget the whole thing. I wish ya would too. Now, just go back home, Micah."

"Ya gonna bury it alive?"

"No, of course not, I figured I'd hit it with this here shovel, merciful like."

Now, it was time for Micah's mind to race. He and Azrael were never close. He never knew anyone who could be so cold. Now he knew two - Ravenna and Azrael. His first thought was to chastise Azrael but he knew that would probably do no good. Beside, the welfare of the baby took priority. He had no idea where the words came from; they just came spewing out of his mouth like he'd thought it over for weeks.

"We'll take the baby. Lailah and I ain't got no kids of our own. We'll be glad to take it and raise it as ours. See…now ya don't have to kill it."

"I already got the hole dug," Azrael said stepping out of the grave.

"That's all right, Azrael, I'll fill it back in for ya. Ya can just go back to bed and forget about it all. I'll take care of everything."

This seemingly agreed with Azrael. He started to walk back to his home. Micah picked up the shovel and started to fill in the hole.

When he was few feet away, Azrael tuned to look back. "Ya can have the baby on one condition."

"What's that, Azrael?"

"Ya don't ever tell it that Ravenna and me is its parents."

"I promise we won't."

"Ya swear?"

"I swear."

Azrael was just about to leave when another thought struck him. "Oh, Micah, one last thing, when you're done ya can leave the shovel on my porch."

"Sure will, Azrael. Goodnight, Azrael."

"Goodnight, Micah."

Filling in the tiny grave was quick work, it was so shallow. Micah bent down, gently picked up the child. It cooed in his arms. He looked to the east. There was a dull yellow glow off on the horizon. The sun would be up soon.

He closed his eyes. "Dear Lord, it's Micah, again. I know I'm always askin' for things. Well, I'm askin' again. Only this time it's more important than usual. I'm gonna need your help real bad. I think I bit off more than I can chew, this time."

****

Sunlight was slowly making its way into the one room shack. His wife was still in bed asleep, her head sandwiched between two pillows. Physically, Lailah was the opposite of her husband. Short with robust and feminine lines, the face of a cherub and a heart that was part saint and part lion.

He sat on the edge of the bed staring at her. He placed the swaddled baby on the bed inches from her face, moving the rags aside exposing the child's face.

"Lailah…Lailah, it's time to get up," he whispered.

"Two more minutes…" she mumbled, her eyes still closed.

"Get up. I've got something to show ya," he said, caressing her cheek.

She opened her eyes slowly. The first thing she saw was the face of the newborn child. Her first reaction was to smile. Then when the image finally registered in her mind, her eyes went wide; she jumped up in bed to a sitting position, pointing at the child.

"What is that?" she shouted, scooting away from the bundle.

"It's a baby."

"I can see that. What I want to know is why it's here."

"It's Ravenna and Azrael's baby. She had it last night."

"But why's it here?"

Micah told Lailah everything. She listened, amazed, shaking her head in disbelief. She could not understand how any mother could reject their child. Micah and Lailah prayed for years for a child and had none. She could not identify with Ravenna who she believed to be insane, at the least, if not evil.

"Ya mean, they were gonna kill their own child?" she exclaimed.

"He already had the grave dug. So ya see…that's why I just had to take it."

"Of course, ya did," she agreed. "It was the right thing to do." She moved the rags away from the child. "What is it?" she asked.

"It's a baby."

"I know that. What I mean is it a boy or a girl."

Micah shook his head. "Ya know, I don't know. I didn't bother to ask."

"Well, we'll just see," she said, pulling the rags away. "Why, it's a girl."

Just then, the child began to cry.

"It's crying. What did ya do?" Micah asked.

"I didn't do nothin'; she's just hungry that's all. Take one of the bowls. Go around back and get me some goat's milk."

She wrapped the child again, taking it in her arms. "There…there, everything's gonna be all right." The child immediately stopped crying. Lailah smiled at Micah. "She likes me. Go on now, fetch the milk."

Ever so slowly and carefully, Micah returned with a bowlful of goat's milk. He looked to see the baby sleeping on the bed between two pillows. Lailah took the bowl, dipped a clean towel in the milk, cautiously letting it drip into the mouth of the child. Eventually, the child took hold of the edge of the towel in its mouth sucking in the milk.

"What about *my* breakfast?" Micah asked in a shy boyish tone.

"Can't ya see I'm busy? Ya have to get it yourself."

Micah looked around, finding an apple.

"Are ya sure they ain't gonna want her back?"

"Sure, I'm sure. They'd rather it be dead than have to raise it."

"I can't believe some people," Lailah said, dipping the towel into the milk again, and then returning the towel's edge to the child's mouth. "It's good, ain't it? Well, ya can just eat your fill. There's more where that came from."

Eventually, the child stopped feeding and fell asleep.

"I need to cut up some old sheets to put on this child," Lailah thought out loud.

Micah, with his half eaten apple started toward the door. "It's time I be gettin' to work. Are ya two goin' to be all right?"

"We're goin' to be just fine," she said, looking at the child and then smiling at her husband.

"Well, I'll be back at sundown," he nodded, his hand on the doorknob.

Lailah called him back, "Micah, there's one last thing we need to do."

"What's that, my dear?"

"This child needs a name."

The thought never crossed Micah's mind. "I don't know. I ain't never named any one before, cows, goats, and dogs, yes, but never any peoples."

Lailah didn't need to think much on the matter. "I've always been partial to the name *Angela*. After all, she looks like an angel."

Micah thought it over for a moment and smiled. "Sounds find to me. We got ourselves our own little angel." He turned and opened the door. When he took one step out the door into the world, his wife called him back, once more.

"Micah…thank ya for this, and bless ya. We is now a family," she said, her smile beaming at him.

He smiled back, "Yeah, I guess we is."

After the door closed and they were alone, Lailah picked the child up, holding her tightly in her arms. "Come here, Angela, momma loves ya so very, very much."

Two

The Seed of Hate

The Abernathy Plantation was famous, known as the largest grower of cotton in all the Carolinas. The owner, Aamon Abernathy was third generation planter. Aamon's grandfather started farming tobacco. The Abernathy Plantation continued this tradition until Aamon inherited the plantation after his father's death. He stopped tobacco production, trying his hand at rice farming, eventually settling on cotton as their main crop – being the most profitable.

Aamon was a bulldog of a man, short and muscular, stocky across the chest, dark hair and dark eyes that showed little expression except when angered.

It was a four-hundred acre plantation, self-sufficient in every way. His two-story mansion was dead center in the property, a ten minute horse ride from the main road. He lived with his wife, Amy, his two daughters, Lilith and Emily, six and five years old, respectively. Amy was a woman of quality and breeding with not a hint of a southern accent. Standing tall and slender, midnight dark hair and porcelain white skin. One would think her nose to be longer than it was instead of button size. For she spent most of her time and energy looking down it on everyone and everything, the entire world, including her husband. Lilith and Emily were apples that did not fall far from the tree – their mother, the greatest influence in their lives. At their young, tender age they were considered mischievous imps. It was clear to all that if they continued traveling the path they were on they would secede their mother in cruelty.

Slavery on a plantation in the south was never easy. Even if the master was considered a fair, decent man, it was a hard life. To labor for the profit of another and none for you is slavery of the body. Not to live your life in the manner you wish is slavery of the heart. To be born in the likeness of God, yet treated as a possession of another is slavery of the spirit. The slaves of the Abernathy Plantation were made to work harder than any other, always in a state of fear. Aamon was known for his cruelty, even to his white neighbors.

Though not a religious family, the Abernathys went to church every Sunday. It was expected of everyone within ten miles of the church. It was a social event for Amy and the girls. Every Sunday Amy could catch up on local gossip; Lilith and Emily could interact with other white children, which was seldom. As for Aamon, he'd keep in contact with other plantation owners. It was just good business.

The large family Bible constantly remained on display in the home library, always opened to the pages of Job. If looked at closely, it would reveal a thick coating of dust, for no one every read it – it was just for show. Not that it mattered; there were many men in the congregation who others considered to be *Good Christians*. They'd read their Bible daily, never considering slavery to be wrong, and would interpret passages concerning slavery as their justification.

The Abernathy family was respected by white folks in the county and feared by every black, even those who did not work for them. For the slaves of Abernathy Plantation life was a nightmare, and a dream for the Abernathy family. Yet, little did they know of the storm brewing north about to descend on them and that they would be the last generation of Abernathy planters.

****

Micah stayed true to his word. He and Lailah never spoke a word to Angela about whom her true parents were. Of course, most of the other slaves knew the truth, but they never said a word to the child. No one dared get on Ravenna's bad side. She was known to be a hard woman to deal with. Certainly not someone you'd want to be enemies with. Some even believed she had unearthly powers. A *Mchawi*, as they used to say in the old country – an enchanter, a witch.

When Angela turned seven, Lailah told her the truth, actually, only part of the truth.

"Though you're not of my flesh, ya are my daughter and I will always love ya."

Naturally the child asked, "Where is my mother?"

"She's in heaven, child," Lailah said. This was the lie she hated to say but felt it necessary.

Angela worked alongside her parents in the cotton fields. She was a lovely child, smart, kind, and obedient. She got along well with the other children; everyone thought well of her, and she of them. Still there was a dark melancholy cloud hanging over the girl that never seemed to go away. Often, Lailah wondered if Ravenna's rejection of her child played a part in Angela's makeup. Does an unborn child in the womb know it is not wanted? Does that rejection burrow deep into their soul to be carried with them all the days of their life?

****

When she turned nine years old, Angela's life changed. At nine a slave is no longer considered a child. They are given a quota of work each day that they must meet or face the consequences, which could be brutal. It was punishment for any infraction. As a child much was overlooked. Now she could face whipping, torture, or worse.

As well, no longer would she be free from viewing punishment brought upon other slaves, which was mandatory for all adult slaves. The veil of innocence would be torn away.

The first time Angela was forced to watch a whipping it was if the child herself felt every lash. In bed that night, Lailah held the quivering child in her arms till after long hours she stopped crying and fell asleep.

No one should *have* to witness a hanging, but to a nine-year-old girl, it was torment. They stood a man on the back of a buckboard, under a large tree with a noose around his neck. When the horses were whipped, the man fell from the buckboard, hanging from the tree like a one-string puppet. He kicked, choked, his eyes nearly popping out of his head. Before it was over, Angela fainted.

She woke to the tender slaps of her father. She was on the ground of the cotton field.

"Wake up, honey. Ya got to get up. If ya don't start working soon, there'll be hell to pay."

"What happened?" she asked in a daze.

"Ya fainted. I carried ya here. Now, come on, get up before someone sees ya."

Somehow she got to her feet and began to pick cotton, moving as one does sometimes in a dream, slowly and heavily.

By all accounts, she was still a child, but now she was forced into the cruel reality of slavery as an adult. At nine, her childhood was over.

As a child, Angela saw the world as a flat, one-dimensional picture. Blacks and whites lived separately; blacks worked all day and whites made sure they did. It wasn't the best of worlds, but it didn't seem cruel. Children have a built-in joy of the world, and then in time the world washes it away. No child knows or has hatred; it has to be acquired; it has to be learned. As an adult, it didn't take Angela long to understand the makeup of the world. It didn't take long for her to see the world as it was on a plantation. She acquired an *Us-and-Them* mentality. She understood it was the *Us* who suffered and it was the *Them* that caused the suffering. It didn't take long before she attained a growing hatred for *Them*, and started having truly wicked thoughts no child should have.

****

All emotions, be they love or hate, become more intense when the experience is personal. Over time, understandably, Angela learned to distrust and hate the plantation owner, his family, and his overseers. These feelings she lived with were only the seeds of what would grow in her as pure hatred.

In Angela's tenth year, she worked the backfields picking cotton with others of her own age. Two overseers mounted on horseback watched over their every move. By the afternoon the overseers became tired and sleepy from the heat. This allowed the workers to speak among themselves, one of the few pleasures of working together. As long as one spoke softly and no one laughed, they could hold a conversation. This made the workload lighter and the workday go by faster.

As the sun began touching the edge of the western horizon, the overseers called it a day. They walked to the storage house for their bags to be weighed. Calm was over them, as they were certain all of them made their daily quota.

After the weigh in, they started for their homes, as usual. Only this day would not be usual. The clang of the dinner bell could be heard coming from the Massa's house. Since they were never fed a late night meal, they would do their own cooking in their homes. This day, these precious moments at home were robbed from them. They knew what the clanging of the dinner bell meant. This was the call to gather at the main house. They were to witness a slave being punished. If it was a slight infraction, stealing food or not fulfilling their day's quota, they would be whipped. Depending on the mood of the master, would decide how many lashes. It was a horrific site to see – someone whipped till they are bloody and fall unconscious. No one dared look away or they'd receive the same punishment.

Though thankfully it seldom happened, it could be a hanging. This was the punishment for serious laws broken, running away, hitting one of the overseers, or if a black man touched a white woman.

Hangings gave Angela nightmares. She'd wake up sweating and crying in the middle of the night. The penalty for looking away from a hanging was lashing that usually left the offender crippled.

Angela walked to the main house with the others, everyone solemn and fearful of what they were about to witness. Aamon Abernathy was not present. He left such matters to his overseers.

Carl Bunter, the head overseer, stood atop the back of a buckboard wagon for all to see and hear him. Bunter was a tall, string bean of a man. He wore his black hair to his shoulders. His equally dark mustache was large and bushy, covering his upper lip. He always wore a black, large brimmed hat that kept his eyes in the shadows, the lifeless eyes of a snake. He took his work seriously beyond what was expected of him. He was a cruel a man as one would expect a head overseer to be – and more.

"I know what you're thinking," Bunter shouted for all to hear, "that I'm cruel and this is unjust. But if ya look long and hard, you'll realize this is for your own good. Understand your lot in life, accept it. It's not going to change. Fighting against it is like goin' against a flood. It will only wash ya away. Once ya come to terms with your life, ya want to take the easiest and safest path. That is what I offer ya. Take it!

"If ya do what you're told, filling your daily quota, life can be good. If not, a world of hurt will come down on ya.

"One of ya did not meet his quota, today. He's been robbing from all of ya. What he didn't do, ya had to make up for. Ya all lose! We are now goin' to teach him the error of his ways. May all of ya watch and learn."

So it was to be a flogging. Normally, they tied the poor soul to the back wheel of the wagon, facing forward. Angela moved forward, pushing her way through the crowd, to see who it was.

Standing at the front of the crowd, Angela saw one of the larger overseers, a big brute of a man, cracking his bullwhip in preparation. Tied to the back wheel of the wagon was a black man, his face turned from the crowd. The overseer ripped the shirt off the back of the man. At that moment, the man turned his head. Angela got a good look at his face. It was Micah.

"No!!!" she screamed.

Her first impulse was to rush forward, pull the bullwhip from the overseer, and cut her father free. Not caring if it was a foolish notion, she took a step forward. Immediately, she felt a hand grab her arm, holdin her back. It was her mother.

"Let it go, child. There's nothing ya can do," Lailah whispered into her ear.

Angela broke into a fit of crying, falling to her knees. She felt her mother's hands helping her back to her feet.

"Stand up, child. Ya must watch or you'll be next."

"I can't watch," Angela cried, turning her head away.

Lailah took hold of her daughter's chin, gently guided her gaze forward.

"Do it for your father," Lailah said. "It would kill him if anything bad happened to ya, and he was the cause. Cry all ya want, but ya gotta watch."

Mother and child stood holding each other tightly, watching.

The large overseer tossed off his hat. He brought his hand holding the bullwhip far behind him. He let it fly. There was a whistle in the air, and then a crack like thunder as the sharp point of leather tore into the flesh of Micah's back. A long red line appeared like lava flowing from a volcano. Micah shouted in pain, his body ached, and then went limp.

One dozen lashes in all. They cut Micah from the wheel. He fell to the ground like a rag doll.

"I don't like doin' this," Bunter shouted. "I do it for the good of all of ya. Let this be a lesson to ya."

The crowd was quiet, walking away with their heads bowed in hopelessness. Some of the men rushed forward, taking the limp Micah up and carrying him to his home.

Lailah had them place Micah face down on the bed. With a bowl of hot water and a clean towel, she cleaned his wounds. The pain woke him. He howled in agony.

This cruelty was made more so, by the fact that Micah was a good worker. The powers that be liked to have a lashing every now and then. It kept the slaves in line. Also, most cruel was that though he was whipped to such a point, Micah would have to be ready for work the next morning. Making his daily quota or he'd receive another lashing, even if it killed him.

Angela sat on the edge of the bed opposite her mother. Her mind raced with thoughts of revenge, even though she knew they were useless.

The anger she felt towards *them* was never so great. The seed of hate that was buried in her heart for so long now blossomed into full bloom, watered and nourished by the blood of her father.

Three

In the Beginning

Late one night after supper, Lailah looked across the table to Micah. "It's time we dug up the '*you-know-what*'. I think she's old enough, now."

Without a word, Micah rose from the table, leaving the shack. They could hear him taking out the shovel from under the porch.

Lailah turned, looking to Angela. "I've wanted to do this for a long time. But I was afraid if I showed ya when ya were younger, ya might not understand how important this is, and said something to somebody else on the plantation."

"What is it, Mama?" Angela asked, sounding worried. A worry brought on by the serious tone of her mother.

Just then, they heard Micah toss the shovel back under the porch. A moment later, he entered carrying a metal tin container. He placed it on the table before them.

Rust covered the container. The writing on the lid was no longer clear, worn away.

Lailah reached across the table, placing her hand on her daughter's. "We've kept this tin buried out back since the day ya came to us. Ya must promise to tell no one about this, not even your closest friend."

There was a moment of silence till Angela realized her mother waited for her reply. "Yes, Mama, I promise."

Micah stood a few feet away, silently watching. Lailah let go of Angela's hand. She moved the container closer to her. Using her nails, she pried the metal lid from off the container. Within was a rectangular object wrapped in old rags that were as brown from age as the outside tin. Lailah lifted the object out, placing it on the table. She pealed away the rags. It was a book! It was black leather-bound with thin pages.

Lailah placed her hand on the book. "This, my child, is a Bible. We believe it is the word of God. Havin' it has been our secret for years. Now, we want to share it with ya." Lailah brushed the dust from off the cover. "There are two things ya must always remember. On this here plantation, it is forbidden for a slave to have a Bible, and it is forbidden to know how to read."

"Ya know how to read, Mama?"

"Yes, I do. When I was about your age, I lived on a different plantation. A white lady taught me, even though she weren't supposed to. She was old and sickly, so much so she couldn't read anymore. She spent most of her time in bed. She needed someone to read to her. So, she taught me to read. Now, I'm going to teach ya."

"Do ya know how to read, Papa?"

"No, child, just your mama, but I likes to hear her read it."

Lailah's voice became solemn. "This is very important to remember, Angela. On this here plantation, the penalty for knowin' and teachin' readin' is death. It's the same for havin' a Bible. They kill ya for it."

"Then we should burn it, before they find out," Angela pleaded.

"No, child, it's that important. You'll see. Now, move in closer to me and let me show ya." Lailah opened the book, pointing to one of the pages. "All these groups of signs are words. Words are made of letters. Look here, the first letter is *I*; the letter next to it is an *N*. These two letters, together, make up the word, *In*. These first few words are very important."

"What do they say, Mama?"

"They says, *In the beginning...*"

****

Every night after supper, Lailah spent time with Angela, teaching her to read and learning her Bible. Micah sat off to the side, listening, smiling, and proud of both of them.

After a year, Angela was able to read fairly much on her own. As she read aloud, Lailah and Micah would sit back, listening. Lailah corrected her whenever needed.

Now, there was a new problem. As Angela's reading improved, her comprehension increased. Now, she truly was reading the Bible. This left her with more questions than answers. Lailah answered when she could. Surprisingly, it was Micah who held a good grasp of what was being read.

"How come ya know so much, Papa?" Angela asked, one night.

"I didn't always live here at Abernathy. Like your mama, when I was a boy, I lived on another plantation. They weren't so harsh like they is here at Abernathy. They let us do lots of things we can't do here. For instance, we were allowed to go to church on Sunday. A black church, of course, but it was a for-real church. My mother, your granny, was a strong believer; making sure all us children got religion."

"My granny...? Who she be? Do I got aunts and uncles?"

"Your granny is long gone. When she died, they sold my brother and sister and me. All gone to different places, I ain't never seen 'em, again." Micah went silent for a moment, lost in memory, and then he spoke, "Is there any other question ya got, child?"

"I got a whole plenty, Papa," Angela said as she thumbed through the Bible. Halfway through she stopped, pointing at one of the pages. She ran her finger over the words as she read them. "*But, I say unto you, love your enemies, bless them that curse you, do good unto them that hate you, and pray for them which despitefully use you, and persecute you.*"

Micah and Lailah looked across to each other, knowing what Angela's question would be, before she spoke it.

"That be from the book of Matthew," Lailah said, "What be the problem, child?"

Angela took a long moment of thought before saying a word. "I don't believe this. How can ya love pain and sorrow?" She looks to her father. "When they whipped ya to near death, did ya love 'em?"

"I can't say that I did, at that moment. Once it was over, I forgave 'em."

"Forgave 'em…!" Angela cried. "When I was little, I didn't see what the world was like. Now, I know. They treat us like animals. We work hard day and night for 'em with no pay. We can't go where we want; we can't do what we want. Our lives ain't even our own, and ya forgive 'em?"

Micah took a seat next to Angela, reached out, taking hold of her hand. "I didn't say I think they're right or what they do is good. It ain't, but one day it ain't gonna be this way. I hate what they do, but I forgive 'em all the same. Ya can't carry that kind-a burden in your heart, forever. Hating somebody is like drinkin' poison everyday and expecting it to hurt 'em. But it don't; it hurts ya, instead. If ya forgive 'em then the Lord will take all of that out of your heart. I guess that's when ya be able to love 'em. Let the Lord do his job, Angela."

Tears welled up in Angela's eyes. She pulled her hand away from Micah's.

"It's not true!" she shouted. "I don't believe it! I hate 'em, every one of 'em, and I always will." She got up from her seat, rushing to the door. "One day I'm gonna run away from here to where they never can find me, where I'll never have to look at another white face again. And if any of 'em try to stop me, I'll kill 'em!" Crying hysterically, she ran out the door.

Lailah reached across the table, placing her hand on Micah's.

"Ya said your piece, Darlin'. Ya planted a seed. Let the Lord take it from here. She's a good child. She'll be just fine."

"I hope you're right, Lailah. I pray to God you're right."

Four

Goin' Rabbit

At the age of fifteen, it became clear to all Angela was to be a rare beauty. Her face was oval with high cheek bones. Her lips like two rosebuds pressed together. Eyes like two deep green wells that looked not only into her soul but that of the one looking into them. Her skin was a rich brown, smooth and flawless. Even at such a young age, the feminine lines of her body were already obvious and attractive. A striking beauty, one could only wonder what she will look like in a few years.

Many young men were under her spell, bedazzled by her charms. But she would have none of them. That is until Kwame. One of the few born on the Abernathy Plantation to be given an African name, in fact, he was the last. After Kwame, the use of such names became forbidden. Another uprooting, forcing the ways of the past to remain there, forgotten.

If you were to ask a young man what first attracted him to a certain young woman, he could give a list as long as your arm. Most strange is that every young man's list would be amazingly similar. Oddly enough, no one can say what attracts a woman to a man. What Angela saw in Kwame only she knew.

He was not an unattractive young man, though not the most attractive. Nor was he the strongest or the smartest. He was tall and slender with little muscle. Like his parents, his skin was midnight dark and beautiful. His hair was so unmanageable, his mother kept it cut short, cropped close to the scalp. Always thankful he was born a male and not a female. His smile was contagious to all who saw it. At sixteen years old, his manner was calm and thoughtful. Most notable about Kwame was that he was in love with Angela. He followed her around like a puppy; always trying to please her. Thankfully, for his sake, she felt the same, responding in kind. Both the parents of Angela and Kwame secretly foresaw a *Jumping the Broom* for the two young lovers in their future.

With such a heavy workload placed on the slaves of the Abernathy Plantation, there was time for little else but work. Time spent between Angela and Kwame was seldom and precious. Often the two would sneak off passed the field behind Ravenna and Azrael's shack to the edge of the forest. As long as they remained in view at the forest's edge, none of the overseers would bother them. Fraternizing was encouraged. Romance meant babies; babies meant more slaves adding to the wealth of Aamon Abernathy.

The two lovers never spoke about *Jumping the Broom*, it went without saying. They did talk about building a shack of their own, living together, and having children. Between all the conversations there was lots of kissing and hugging. Kwame would gladly have gone further. Angela held back. Thoughts of her mother warning her to wait, kept those feelings at bay. As well, always being under the watchful eyes of the overseers made her uncomfortable. Though it met with the overseers' approval, she could not bring herself to ignore them. This pushed the couple to thinking about jumping the broom, and soon. In their own home, Angela would have her parents' approval. They could be alone, and not under the overseers' gaze. They would be a married couple to live and love as they pleased.

This thought affected Angel's thinking. Seeing things in a new light, one that Kwame never fathomed. One late evening after supper, as the two lay in each other's arms, hidden in the tall grass on the edge of the forest, Angela let her thoughts be known.

"It will be so wonderful when we have a place of our own," Angela cooed, her head resting on Kwame's chest.

"Hmmm…" Kwame responded, his eyes closed, his mind drifting with the image of them together forever.

"We should do it soon, jump the broom, that is," she said.

"My daddy says when we do, he's gonna give us some of his chickens to start us off."

Angela giggled. "Ya know what would be better than havin' a place of our own?"

"What's that, darlin'?"

"…havin' a life of our own."

Kwame sat up, holding Angela's shoulders, looking into her eyes. "What do ya mean?"

"I mean our lives are not our own, here."

"But what can ya do?"

Not that anyone was listening; she lowered her voice to a whisper. "We can run away."

"To where…?"

"Up north, some places up north don't even have slavery. That's where we'll go."

"But how?" he asked.

"What a silly questioned. We just leave. It won't be easy, but we can do it."

Kwame thought it over for a moment, and then smiled. "We can sneak off right after we jump the broom."

"No…" Angela came back, sounding strong and determined. "We leave as soon as possible. We don't have to jump the broom. When we get to someplace safe, we can marry…a proper wedding ceremony. What do ya think?"

"I think I love ya, Angela," he said, smiling.

"I love ya, too."

They fell into each others arms, kissing long and deep.

When they broke free from each other, Kwame announced, "We mustn't tell this to anyone, not even our parents.

"You're right," Angela said, knowing he was right. Also knowing how difficult it would be not confiding in her parents; and how hard it will be on them once they were gone.

They stood, kissed once more, and then started from the forest's edge, crossing the field, holding hands and smiling. They kissed one last time before they went to their homes, every so often looking back as they walked away from each other.

They were now full of hopes and dreams, perhaps for the first time in their lives. But the hopes and dreams of those as young as they, as good as they may seem, founded on strong emotion are without forethought and understanding. They held no idea what they were in for.

****

All day long all slaves moved under the watchful eyes of the overseers. There wasn't a square foot of the property where they could move freely. To try to escape from Abernathy Plantation in the daytime would never work. The only possibility would be a night attempt. Curley knew that, so he planned his escape for the next night when there would be no moon. It would be soon, the end of the month.

Compared to the other slaves, Curley's life was far better. He had a skill. He was one of two carpenters, which made him an important figure on the plantation. For this reason, he was treated well. They gave him a shack of his own, more and better food rations, and freedom to come and go as he pleased, within reason. Still, the life of a slave was a harsh and sad one. Curley wanted out at any cost. Now a middle-aged, single man, Curley believed even death would be better.

No one knew or understood why Curley never took a woman. As men go on the plantation, Curley was a prize compared to some. A fair looking man, boney in structure, his hands deeply scared from his work. He maintained an unkempt, scruffy look; this was common among most of the single men on the plantation. In the hands of the right woman, the problem would easily be solved. Still, Curley was content to remain alone.

Curley's plan of escape was not haphazard. He prepared for weeks. With what cloth he could get his hands on he sewed a backpack, proceeding over the next few weeks to fill it with lightweight, nonperishable foodstuffs. From what information he could learn from talking to others, he drew a map of the area. The last day of work before his flight, he snuck metal tools back to his shack, putting them in his backpack. The items were sharp, taking the place of a good knife and saw. Lastly, he bribed one of the kitchen help at the main house for a jar of bacon fat – he had plans for that, also.

He told no one of his plans, not even a hint. If he succeeded, fine. If not, no one would be to blame but himself; only he would suffer.

He lay in bed waiting for the hour to pass midnight. His one-room shack was pitch-black dark. This meant there was no moon. It would make the going difficult, but the hunt of his pursuers difficult as well. Hopefully, the darkness would even the odds.

At what he felt was just the right time; Curley left the shack with his pack on his back. Moving from shadow to shadow, he made it to the edge of the forest. He ran as fast as he could in the dark. A mile into the forest, he stopped, opening the jar, he smeared bacon fat on some of the trees that pointed away from the direction he was moving. Remaining careful, he stopped every quarter mile, smearing bacon fat on trees along the way. When all the fat was gone, he tossed the open jar up into a large pine tree.

"That should confuse the hell out of 'em and their dogs," he laughed to himself.

Still, to be on the safe side, he used an old tracker's trick. When he got to a stream, no more than knee-high deep, he took off his shoes, waded in, walking south for a mile or so.

It could have been no more than three in the morning when he stopped to rest. Not for long, just long enough to catch his breath. Sunrise wouldn't be for hours. They wouldn't know he was gone until an hour later when he didn't show for work. All in all, that gave him a six-hour lead over them. With that, the beacon fat and wading in the stream, Curley felt his chances were good.

****

At sunrise, every slave reported to their assigned areas for work. When Curley didn't show for work on time, they paid it little mind. If he was late, they'd punish him, nothing severe, perhaps take away one of his many privileges. Not that Curley was beyond physical punishment. It was just that his skills were important to the plantation. They needed him working at his top form.

When it was clear Curley was more than late, Carl Bunter, the head overseer, had one of his men run to Curley's shack. A few minutes later, the man returned.

"He ain't there, Boss."

"Ask around; see if anybody's seen him."

After the passing of another half hour, plus the missing carpenter tools, it was clear Curley was a runaway. Bunter took what men he could spare. They took to the hunt on horseback along with a dozen vicious dogs trained for just such a purpose.

The slaves in the fields silently watched as the group of overseers rode off. They secretly watched till the billow of dust the group kicked up vanished over the horizon.

****

The entire day, there was no word of Curley or his pursuers. At sunset, when all the slaves walked back to their homes, they talked among themselves. It was all speculation, none of it based on facts. One truth was certain, if the overseers didn't capture Curley, others would try to escape. There was an air of desperation hanging over the plantation for both sides: the slaves and the overseers.

The sun sunk over the western horizon, its golden rays still shooting to the sky. Darkness crept in, slowly depriving the world of its colors, yet enough light to see by. Just after supper, at the main house as well as the slave quarters, the dinner bell rang, breaking the silence.

All the slaves walked to the main house, knowing what they would find. They'd captured Curley. Now, they went to witness his hanging.

Instead, they found the overseers standing by their mounts. Curley's limp, dead body tied over the back of one the horses.

Bunter took hold of Curley's hair, raising his head for all to see his face. It had been clawed bloody. They barely recognized it as the face of Curley.

"Ya see this!" Bunter shouted. "This is the face of a runaway. It'll be your face if ya thinkin' wrong, like Curley here." He released his grip; Curley's head fell back down. Two overseers cut Curley loose, taking his body from off the mount. Bunter started in again, "We got horses! We got dogs! What da ya got? Even if ya did get away, which would never happen in a million years, where would ya go? Ain't nobody goin' to stick out their neck for some darkie. So, if you're feelin' rabbit, just get it out of ya head!"

The overseers dragged Curley's body to the large tree in front of the main house, known to all as the *Hangin' Tree.*

Bunter walked closer to the tree, hollering in a commanding voice. "The dogs got to Curley before we got to him. Or he'd be alive right now, and we'd be hangin' him. Now, I don't hold it against the dogs. They were just doin' their job. I'll be damned if any dog is gonna do us out of a good hangin'."

Bunter gave the overseers the go-ahead. They tossed the heavy rope over the largest limb on the tree. They placed the noose around Curley's neck. They walked to the other end of the rope, taking hold of it.

Bunter bellowed his next remarks. "Just because Curley's dead, don't make no difference. It's like any other hangin', if ya turn not ta look, ya in deep trouble." He nodded the go-ahead to the overseers. They pulled on the end of the rope, sending Curley high up to the branch.

"Take a good look," Bunter shouted. "Let it burn into your mind. If ya go rabbit, ya gonna be a dead one."

Bunter walked off, as the overseers tied the rope's end to the trunk of the tree. When they felt it was safe to turn and walk away, all the slaves slowly and silently made their way back home.

Curley's body hung there for days. It was a hard sight to see. Black birds feasted on his body till nearly only bones and tattered clothing remained. If the wind blew just right, you could smell the rot. On the fifth day, they cut Curley down. They didn't even have the decency to bury him. That night they lit a large bonfire. When the flames were high, they threw Curley's body into the pyre. Aamon Abernathy had one of the house slaves bring out a bottle of the finest whiskey from his private stock. The overseers drank, sang, telling jokes late into the night sitting around the fire.

****

It was the usual rendezvous for Angela and Kwame at the edge of the forest, passed the field behind Ravenna's home. Angela ran into Kwame's arms and kissed him. She backed away slightly, looking at him. There was something wrong. It was a naked kiss, without feeling.

"What's wrong?" she asked softly.

Kwame turned his head, looking at the ground, ashamed to speak with her face-to-face. "I'm not goin'."

"What do ya mean, 'You're not goin'?"

"I'm too afraid," he said, finally turning to face her. "Ya saw what they did to Curley. We ain't got a chance in hell. I love ya, Angela. I want to live the rest of our lives together. What good is it if we die, now? I know it ain't perfect, but we could have a good life here...a long life."

"A long life!" she sobbed. "Ya call this a life? Well, I don't. I'm askin' ya one last time, Kwame. Are ya comin' with me or not?"

Again he turned from her, looking to the ground. "I ain't," he said in a whisper.

Running off in tears, over her shoulder she heard him say, "I'm sorry, Angela."

She ran across the open field, past Ravenna's shack, into the small community of slaves. She could hardly see through the tears. At her home, she pushed the door open. She hoped her parents weren't home, not wanting them to see her in such a state. Both of them were home. They turned to see her standing in the doorway, crying.

"Why, Sweetheart, what's the matter?" Lailah asked.

Angela couldn't speak; all she could do was cry. She ran to her bed, throwing herself facedown. She sobbed into her pillow violently. Her body shook from head to toe. Her chest and back heaved up and down as she struggled to take in air. She felt someone sit on the edge of the bed, placing their hand gently on her back. To her surprise it was Micah.

"What's the matter, Darlin'?"

It took a moment to gain composure. "It's over between Kwame and me."

"Ah, Darlin', couples have their bad days, too. Me and your momma have had our scraps, too. But it always works out in time. The best part is makin' up."

"No, this is different. It ain't never gonna be right, again."

"Do ya want to talk about it?"

"I can't."

"Well, if ya ever do, your mamma and me are always here."

Angela sat up quickly, threw her arms around Micah's neck, crying into his chest. She felt her mother's hand gently pushing her hair away from her eyes.

"There, there, never ya mind, honey, never ya mind."

Five

The Main House

Aamon Abernathy took pleasure in spoiling his two daughters, Lilith and Emily. He knew it would make them demanding, shallow creatures like their mother. But he saw no harm in it. He'd use a different approach, if he'd had a son. A man cannot afford to be frivolous. If he had a boy, he'd make it hard on him so he'd become hard, just like his father did for him. He didn't worry about spoiling his daughters. He'd marry them off someday. Then the men they marry could spoil them. If a man couldn't spoil his daughter, they weren't worthy of marrying her, and he would never give his consent to the pairing.

He also spoiled his wife, but for a different reason. Through his wife he could shine. At church and at gatherings, if his wife entered a room like a peacock, dressed in the most expensive fineries, the more envious heads turned. It was a feather in his cap. It showed him as a man of wealth and power. In short, it made him feel superior. Also, it was good for commerce. Every man of substance in the county wanted to do business with a man who could afford such a lifestyle.

Another way of showing off to the world his affluence was to make his wife a woman of leisure. Amy played a minimal part in the raising of her children. As early as infancy, they were placed in the care of one of the older slave women who worked in the main house. A kind and caring *Mammy* was common in the south, a true sign of material comfort among the privileged class.

Now, Lilith and Emily turned the corner of childhood, entering the world of womanhood. The mammy would remain, but other hands were needed, a maidservant to see after their every need. The choice for this position was an easy one for Aamon. He picked Angela out of all the other young woman of the plantation. The choice was easy not because of any particular skills Angela possessed. Aamon had an ulterior motive.

At first, the thought of the new position upset Angela. She did not want to leave home and her parents for she'd have to move into the main house to be at Lilith and Emily's disposal at all hours of the day and night. Her parents assured her it would be a good move. She could visit them whenever possible. They also reminded her that she would someday need to move out and go it on her own, anyway. They had hoped it would be as the partner of a good man. They had hoped it would have been Kwame. But it was not to be. Either way, a time to leave home was sure to come, so why not now? They also believed that working and living in the main house would be an easier life for their daughter. After all, she would no longer have to sweat in the fields, the food would be better; it would be good, clean living. That is at least what they believed.

So, reluctantly, Angela gathered what few bits and pieces she owned, putting them in an old tied up rag, knotting the four ends together. The next morning she kissed her parents good-bye, vowing to see them again as soon as possible, and headed to the main house.

****

Never had Angela been close enough to the main house to even look in through the windows. She had no idea what to expect. Standing on the front porch, she knocked on the front door. A moment later, the door opened. An elderly black man stood before her, looking her up and down. He was dressed in black pants and waistcoat, a white, lace ruffled shirt with a black ribbon tie. His hair was white with a large bald spot at the top of his head. There were so many wrinkles in his face he looked like a dusty field that had been newly plowed.

"What the hell are ya doin' here, girl?" he grumbled at her.

"I'm supposed to report here for work."

"Don't ya know no colored folk can come in the front door? Who ya think ya is? Be glad the lady of the house don't see ya. All colored folk gotta come in from the back at the kitchen. Now, get yourself around back before ya get us both in hot water."

He slammed the door in her face.

Angela got off the porch as fast as she could and ran around back. The door to the kitchen was open. Wonderful smells hit her in the face. Entering the kitchen, there were three black women busy preparing food.

"Ya the new girl?" asked one of the women.

"Yes, I am."

"Good, cut up those onion," the woman said, pointing to a bucket of onions on the floor and handing Angela a knife.

Angela put her stuff in the corner, picked up the bucket of onions, placing it on the table in the middle of the room.

"I want 'em in slices, not chopped," the woman ordered. "And make 'em thin or they takes too long ta cook."

Just as Angela took up the first onion, the kitchen door leading into the house flung open. Aamon Abernathy, the master of the house, entered.

"Put that down," he demanded, pointing at Angela, and then at the knife and onion she held. Angela dropped them as if they were hot coals.

"Agnes!" he called to the woman who'd ordered Angela about.

"Yes, sir," said Agnes, softly, holding a dish towel.

"This new girl is not going to work in the kitchen. She's to be my daughters' servant. I don't want her cooking, cleaning, or doing any labor other than what my daughters tell her to do. And I certainly don't want you ordering her about. She'll answer only to the family. Do you understand?"

"Yes, sir, I does."

"Good." He looked again at Angela. "Come with me."

Angela grabbed her things and followed Aamon out of the kitchen.

Walking through the main house, Angela couldn't help looking about. She had imagined it would be grand, but it surpassed even what she believed heaven might look like.

Aamon brought her to the staircase leading up to the second floor. The underside of the stairs was covered in dark wood paneling. He reached out for a small knob, hardly noticeable. There was a door with a seam so fine you would not have known it was there. Opening the door, Aamon pointed into the small room.

"This is where you'll be staying."

Angela peeked inside, it was tiny. Crammed inside was a single bed, next to it was a nightstand with a lantern and a few matches on it.

"Each night, once you are dismissed, you will sleep here. There's a chamber pot under the bed, so there is no need to be seen till morning." He pointed to her belongings. "You can leave your things here."

Angela placed her things on the bed. Aamon closed the door.

"Come with me," he said, leading her to the foot of the stairs.

At this point, Angela became aware of something strange. When he steered her to the stairs, she felt the palm of his hand pressed against her back, guiding her upward. This confused and frightened her. It was well known blacks were forbidden to touch whites, but it was understood and considered bad taste for a white to touch a black – except to punish. Had he just simply forgotten himself? Was he showing kindness? She dare not consider any other reasons.

At the top of the stairs they veered left to a large door; he knocked.

"Yes?" a female voice seeped through the wood.

"It's your father."

A moment later, the door opened. Aamon entered, followed by Angela.

Two young white women stood in the center of the large room. They were very pretty and dressed in the height of fashion. Clearly, they were sisters; they were so identical. Though both were blonde, one's hair was sandy, a bit darker than the other whose hair was like spun gold.

The room was bright and clean with two beds, each on opposite walls. Along one wall was a built-in closet. The doors were open; you could see dozens of dresses in various colors. There were two dressing tables with countless bottles on top; each table had an oval mirror. The air was filled with the scent of fresh cut flowers.

"This is your new handmaiden that I promised you," Aamon said, pointing to Angela.

"Thank you, father," they both said, almost in unison.

Angela couldn't help but notice the distant coldness between father and his daughters. It was that obvious.

Aamon stood, putting his weight down on one foot, then the other. He moved clumsily, as if being uncomfortable within such strange, feminine surroundings.

"Well, there you have it. I leave you both to it."

Without a word on his or his daughters' part, he left, closing the door behind him.

For the longest time, the three women stood silently, this made Angela uncomfortable. She could feel their eyes on her, judging her.

"What is your name, girl?" asked the golden blonde sister.

"Angela."

"My name is Lilith and this is my sister, Emily. But you will address us as *Madam*."

A worried look washed over Emily's face. "Oh, no, mother is the madam of the house. If she hears this girl calls us *Madam*, she's sure to be cross."

Lilith thought this over for a moment. "Very well, you are to address us as Madam, but in the presence of our mother you will address us as *Miss*. Do you understand?"

They waited for Angela to respond correctly, and she did. "Yes…madam."

It became instantly clear which sister was the strongest and in charge. It was Lilith. The young woman walked up to Angela.

"Your clothes are dreadful; they'll have to go." Lilith moved just inches from Angela. "And you smell, too. Well, that will all have to change." She walked to the far wall. There was a long piece of red velvet dangling against the wall. Lilith gave it a tug.

A few minutes later there was a knock at the door. In walked a short, stout, older black woman wearing a full white apron over her cotton dress.

"Abby, this is the new girl," Lilith said, pointing at Angela. "I want you to get her washed up and looking presentable. Those clothes she's wearing, burn them." She turned to Angela. "This is Abby. Go with her and do what she tells you." Lilith stepped back, taking one last look at Angela. "From the looks of it, it's going to take all day. Report back here first thing in the morning, seven o'clock."

"Yes, madam," Angela said, still sounding unsure of herself.

"Come on, girl," Abby said, guiding Angela out of the room and closing the door behind them.

They heard Lilith shouting at them through the door," Knock...don't forget to knock. You always knock before entering."

****

Years of service left Abbey indifferent. She wasn't cruel nor was she friendly, just matter-of-factly. She took Angela to the back of the house. There was a grassy area just outside the kitchen door, after that, a vegetable garden, and beyond that a large chicken coop surrounded by a wire fence.

Always one step ahead, Abbey had placed a large tub in the grassy area. It was filled with water; there was soap and a towel.

"All right, take off your clothes," Abbey said, testing the water temperature with her hand. "Hurry, while the water's still hot."

Angela stood frozen, staring at the tub. "I can't take off my clothes, not out here in the open."

Abbey rolled her eyes. "Girl, ya ain't got nothin' we ain't already seen before. Ain't nobody gonna see ya except the girls in the kitchen, and they couldn't care less. Now, get into the water while it's still hot."

Angela turned her back to Abbey and began to undress. Abbey rolled her eyes, again. She handed her clothes to Abbey. She tested the water with her toes.

"It needs to be hot if ya wants to get really clean. Now, get in!"

Slowly, Angela worked her way down into the water, her back to the house. Abbey inspected Angela's clothing.

"What'cha gonna do with my clothes?" she asked Abbey.

"I does what the madam says. Madam say burn 'em, I burns 'em. I'll be back with new clothes. Ya scrub good, and use the soap!"

Angela did the best she could in such a small tub. She'd just finished soaking her hair when a strange feeling came over her. She had a strong feeling she was being watched. She turned to look at the house; no one was there. A moment later, the feeling came over her, again. She turned to look. Still, no one was there. Just when she began to feel secure, she saw something move in one of the top floor windows.

He didn't move away or try to hide. Aamon Abernathy stood at a window, looking down, watching her every move. His stare was cold and calculated, like a wolf on the hunt.

She turned her back to him. A minute later, she turned to look. He was still there. Again, she sat forward, continuing to wash herself. Her mind was racing about what to do, but she could think of nothing. Finally, she turned to take another look; he was gone.

Just then, Abby returned with a dress that was far more elegant than anything she ever wore. Best of all, there were undergarments. When she put them on, she couldn't stop smiling.

"We gonna be spending the rest of the day doin' the madams' laundry. I show ya how to do it this once. But from now on, it'll be your job to do by yourself, every week. Now, follow me."

Doing laundry wasn't hard work, not compared to picking cotton in the fields. Still, it did take all day. By suppertime, Angela felt tired. She ate with the others in the kitchen at a big long table at one end of the room, under a window. The last rays of daylight shown on them.

There were the women who worked in the kitchen, the young men who did the gardening and heavy labor around the house, Mrs. Abernathy's handmaiden, Mr. Abernathy's valet, and of course, Abby.

Angela was so hungry she didn't notice the lovesick young man at the table watching her every move. Other than him, no one seemed at all interested as to whom she was.

Her parents were right. The food was far superior to what they ate in the slave quarters. It was leftovers from that night's dinner. The same food the Abernathy's ate. When she finished, her full belly made her sleepy and ready for bed. She excused herself and went to her little cubbyhole under the stairs.

She undressed, leaving her clothes at the foot of the bed. Once under the covers, looking up at the bottom part of the stairs just a few inches from her face, she became uncomfortable. The small room reminded her of a coffin. She blew out the lamp. Rather than staring up at the black wooden planks, she welcomed the dark.

Just as she shut her eyes, the door opened. Little light came into her space, just enough to see the silhouette of a man. She recognized the voice immediately.

"Are you all right?" Aamon asked.

"Ah-ha," Angela whispered shyly, feeling very uncomfortable.

"Very well…goodnight, Angela."

"Goodnight, sir."

With that he closed the door, sending her back into darkness.

It was all too strange, the master of the house worried about her comfort, and calling her by her name, instead of *girl*. Again she thought; had he forgotten himself, was he just being kind. No, not so. The reason he acted in such a manner was the reason she had dared not to consider. Now, it was her main concern.

Six

Scared

Angela worried if she would wake in the morning on time. There was no need to worry. The sounds of other house slaves preparing for the day woke her. Her little cubbyhole under the stairs was still pitch-black. She could not shake off the feeling she was in her coffin. She dressed in the dark. When she walked out, she went to a wall mirror to make sure she was presentable. Abby appeared as if from nowhere.

"Ya gonna have to learn to sleep less. Now, listen up. The madams will want tea while they dress for the day. Go into the kitchen. I laid out a tray with all you'll need. Just put some hot water in the pot. Take the tray up to the madams. And don't forget to knock before ya enter. Ya got that. Now, get movin'."

The atmosphere in the kitchen was chaotic. The young men were out back chopping small cut logs down to smaller pieces, bringing them into the kitchen, and stoking the wood burning stoves. The women were moving about preparing breakfast. Angela caught sight of the tray Abbey laid out for her. It and everything on it was silver except the two cups and saucers and teapot of fine China.

Walking across the room to the tray, Angela got pushed around by the others. "Out of the way!" they shouted. They hollered at her when she took the water kettle off the stove, when she filled the teapot with hot water, put the kettle back, and carried the tray out of the room. "Out of the way!" they barked, pushing her this way and that. When she left the kitchen she let out a sigh of relief. If that was the way it would be every morning, she needed to come up with a different approach.

In her mind, Angela believed it would be easy to carry the tray through the house, up the stairs to her mistress' room. But it wasn't. She moved slowly, carrying the tray before her. The cups and saucers rattled as she moved. There was a small container of cream and one of sugar, the contents sloshed and spilled. It was worse going up the stairs. She feared she wouldn't make it without dropping the entire tray. When she got to Lilith and Emily's door, she was lost for what to do. How could she knock with both her hands busy? She gently kicked the door with her foot.

"Yes, who is it?" a voice came from within.

"It's Angela, Madam. I've got your tea."

"Come in."

This presented another problem. How was she to open the door? She couldn't ask the sisters to open the door. This would not be acceptable, surely making them angry. Very carefully, Angela placed her arm underneath the tray, supporting it with her forearm. With her free hand, she slowly opened the door.

Inside was mayhem. Dozens of dresses were sprawled atop both beds. The sisters took turns holding a dress up in front of them, each modeling for the other.

"What do you think of this one?"

Seeing a near-empty table near the window, Angela moved across the room, placing the tray on the table.

Emily held a dress to the front of Angela. "Here, hold this up. I want to see how it looks."

Before Angela could take hold of the dress, Lilith snatched it from her. "Are you out of your mind?" she scolded her sister. She then looked to Angela. "Girl, I want you to go downstairs to the dining room and tell our parents we're running a bit behind but we'll be down for breakfast in a minute." Angela started for the door. "Run, you stupid girl, run," Lilith shouted. Angela raced out of the room and down the stairs.

Mr. and Mrs. Abernathy were seated in the dining room when Angela came rushing in.

Amy Abernathy, holding a cup of tea, looked at her sternly. "What is it, girl?"

"The madams are going to be late, but they will be down soon."

Amy put down her teacup. "What did you just say?"

It was then Angela remembered one important demand Lilith made: to call them madam, but never to their mother. Angela thought fast.

"Your daughters will be down soon."

"That's not what you said, girl. I want you to repeat to me what you first said," Amy demanded.

Angela was so afraid she couldn't speak.

"Never mind, go up and tell those two to hurry right down."

In a fluster, Angela left the room. Just as she got to the stairs, Lilith and Emily were coming down. Emily passed Angela without a word or a look.

"Get upstairs; I want all those dresses hung back in the closet…now!" Lilith ordered without slowing down for a second. Angela ran up the stairs, as the two sisters entered the dining room.

"Good morning, mother. Good morning father," they said as one, taking their seats.

Aamon busied himself with buttering his toast and cutting his eggs. He knew what was coming next, and he wanted nothing to do with it.

Amy folded her hands on the table in front of her. "Well, so nice of you two *Madams* to join us."

Instantly, both sisters knew what she was talking about. Emily lowered her head in shame; Lilith's face grimaced in anger.

"I'm not going to say a word on the subject," their mother continued, "because I don't expect it will ever happen again. Will it?"

Both sisters remained silent.

"Will it?" Amy said loudly, this time expecting an answer.

"No," they said, softly.

"No…who?" insisted their mother.

"No, Madam…"

"That's better."

No one spoke for the rest of the meal.

****

Upstairs in the sisters' room, Angela franticly put away all the dresses lying on their beds into their closet. She wasn't sure where what dress went where, which worried her. She could only hang them and hope for the best.

Angela was nearly finished when the sisters returned. Surprisingly, they ignored her. She was expecting them to be angry about the *madam* reference, or at least criticize the way she put the dresses away. But, they said nothing. Instead, they ordered her to strip the beds and take the sheets to be cleaned. As well they wanted six pairs of white gloves to be cleaned and starched. They also gave her a half dozen garments that needed buttons sown on properly, as they were coming loose, also three pairs of stockings that needed darning. All in all, it was a full day of work. As she left the room with her arms full, she felt lucky nothing was said.

Lilith and Emily busied themselves the entire day in the library reading and doing needlework. In the afternoon, they went with their parents shopping in the nearest town.

Angela worked hard; by the end of the day she'd completed all her assignments. She brought the items up to the sister's room. It was well after dinner, the two were already in their nightgowns.

"Put them on the bed," Lilith told Angela who stood in the middle of the room with her arms full. "Come here, girl," Lilith ordered after Angela lay the items down.

Angela walked to her, not knowing what to expect.

"Just stand there," Lilith ordered. She looked to her sister, "Emily…?"

40

Emily cringed for a moment. "I don't want to. Please, Lilith, don't make me."

Lilith didn't say a word. She gave her sister a cold icy stare. Even when they were much younger, Emily never had the ability to say no to her. Now, years later, Emily was little more than her sister's obedient servant, as well as her unwilling partner in crime.

"Hold her arm out," Lilith demanded.

"Lilith, please, don't make me," Emily pleaded again to deaf ears. She knew there was nothing she could do or say, only do as she was told. She took hold of Angela's right hand by her wrist, holding her palm down, stretching her arm out in front of her.

Lilith went to a bedside table on which sat a lit candle. She took it up, bringing it to where Emily and Angela stood.

"If you scream out, I'll only do it longer. Emily, hold her tight."

Lilith held the flame two feet under Angela's palm. At that distance there was not pain, but Angela could feel the heat. Lilith slowly moved the candle higher. The heat built with each inch she came closer.

"If you scream, I do it longer," Lilith repeated as Angela began to feel intense heat. She began to try to break away. "Hold her," Lilith commanded. Now, Emily was using both her hands, holding Angela's wrist as tight as she could.

The pain became unbearable for Angela. Tears poured from her eyes. She bit down hard on her quivering lips, trying not to scream. Finally, she went limp, close to a faint. Lilith pulled the flame away, placing the candle once more on the nightstand. Emily let go of Angela's wrist. The poor girl fell to her knees.

"Get up and get out," Lilith said in a bitter tone. "Let this be a lesson to you."

In a haze of great pain, Angela rose to her feet and shuffled slowly out of the room. Somehow, she made it down the stairs and to her little cubbyhole under the stairs. She fell on her bed, weeping in the dark.

The door opened. Angela saw the outline of someone holding a lantern. When the lantern was lifted, she saw that it was Abby. In one of her hands she held a cup of butter and a few strips of cloth. The woman took hold of Angela's hand, gently coating the burned skin with butter. Angela's moan came deep from her chest and throat. Then Abbey wrapped the strips of cloth around Angela's hand. Abbey held the lantern close to see if the bandage was secure. In that moment, Angela got a good look at the palm of Abbey's right hand. The skin was scared from burn marks.

"There, that's the best I can do," Abbey said. "It's gonna hurt like hell for a week or so. But it won't hurt forever. I should know. Try to get some sleep. I'll come back early in the morning to change the bandage."

Angela wanted to say thank you, but she could only moan. Abbey left, shutting the door. Once again, Angela was left in the dark. She cried herself to sleep.

****

It was two weeks later when Angela was able to take off her bandage. The Abernathy family was invited to a party at a neighboring plantation that day. After completing her daily chores, Angela received permission to visit her parents, for dinner only.

Her father waited outside their shack to greet her. Angela ran into his arms.

"I'm so happy to see ya," he said, holding her close. "Ya momma would be here too, but she's inside cookin'. She wanted everything to be perfect for ya. Come on, let's go inside."

Lailah faced the oven, stirring. When she heard the door open, she spun around. The two women stood silently for a moment, just looking at each other.

"Angela!" Lailah cried, holding her arms out. Angela rushed into them. "Let me look at ya," Lailah said, standing a few feet back. "Ya gettin' more beautiful every day. Those clothes are..." Lailah was lost for words.

"I've two pair of everything," Angela announced with excitement.

"Come, sit down. I've made all your favorites. Ya can tell us all about it."

Seated at the table together, Lailah and Micah lowered their heads and placed their folded hands in front of them on the table, ready to say Grace. None of the house slaves ever said Grace. Not being a religious person like her parents, she never missed it. Rather than question it, Angela went along.

Micah did the honors, "Dear Lord, we thank ya for all your provisions, and for watchin' over our sweet Angela. Keep her strong and well. We thank ya and praise ya. Amen!"

"Amen!" Lailah echoed.

Not wanting to cause a stir, Angela let out a shy and weak, "Amen."

Angela enjoyed eating everything her mother made. The flavors she'd always loved brought back sweet memories. After eating so well at the main house, she could tell the difference. The slaves made do with what was available to them. It was just enough to keep them alive and able to work.

Angela told them everything, up to a certain point. She told them about how well she ate each day, eating the same meals the Abernathy family ate. She told them of her work, and how easy it was. She spoke of having her own bedroom, omitting the size and location of the room. As well, she said little about the sisters she worked directly for. She told them how beautiful they were and how grand they lived, never mentioning their cruel ways, nor the harshness of their mother. Most importantly, she said nothing about Aamon Abernathy, other than his physical features. She could not bring herself to tell them of her fear of him. How he'd stare at her whenever they came in contact with each other. How she feared that someday, when he knew no one would find out, he'd try something.

All through dinner, Angela did her best to hide the palm of her right hand from her parents. But feeling so at ease in an unconscious moment; she placed her hand, palm up, on the table.

Lailah reached out, grabbing Angela's hand. "What is this?" she shouted, examining the wound, and then showing it to her husband.

"My God…" said Micah.

"It's nothin'," Angela said, pulling her hand back. "It was an accident." Her mind raced, thinking up a convenient lie. "I accidentally placed my hand on the stove in the kitchen."

"That must have hurt bad," Lailah replied.

"It did, for a long time," Angela said, clearly trying to make light of it and move to the next subject.

Micah thought it a time to give some fatherly advice. "Well, ya need to be more careful. Promise me, ya be more careful."

"I will, Papa."

An hour later, they sat at the table by candlelight. "I need to leave. I need to get back," Angela said sadly.

Her parents walked her outside. They all hugged together as a family.

"Dear Lord, watch over our child," Micah whispered as he held her.

Reluctantly, Angela pulled away, starting back to the main house. She looked back one last time to see her parents still standing in front of their miserable shack. She began to cry. It would be far better to live in that miserable shack with the ones she loved, than have to return to the fineness of the main house. Back she went to her coffin of a room, the abuse of the sisters and their mother, and worst of all the haughty and lustful eyes of Aamon Abernathy.

Seven

Ashes and Bones

Life moved slowly for Angela. Each day was the same. Even when she did her best, she lived in fear of punishment. The sisters were never pleased. Besides, physical abuse, they constantly belittled her. All this continued, till she became numb. She got to a point where nothing they could do or say fazed her. The hand slaps, the belt whippings, and foul names became part of her life. She accepted them and kept moving, never thinking of an alternative life. She feared such a thought would drive her mad.

Her dealings with Amy Abernathy were seldom, which was a blessing. She could be far worse than her daughters. Being Lilith and Emily's servant, Amy gave her little attention. She was too busy making the rest of the house staff miserable.

Angela's dealings with Aamon became disturbing. He'd stare at her as if he was reading a book, no longer deferring his shameless gaze. She couldn't imagine what evil thoughts nested in his mind waiting to hatch. Whenever he was close to her, making sure no one else was watching, he'd reach out to her, touching her in ways even a husband wouldn't consider touching his wife. This disturbed her to tears, what could she do, what could she say, and to whom? Any action against his action on her part meant sever punishment, even to the point of death.

The only saving grace was Amy Abernathy hardly ever walked out of the main house; never mind ever being off the plantation. What few times she did was always in the company of her husband. Angela knew that if she were ever alone in the main house with him, and the madam not at home, things would go bad.

So, Angela put her head down and drudged through life. One thing and one thing only gave her any joy, her monthly visits to see her parents. Once each month, the sisters would have one of the slaves drive them by carriage to a neighboring plantation. There were two siblings, a brother and sister about their same age. Lilith and Emily would spend a good portion of the afternoon visiting them. They were always welcomed to supper by their host, and would not return home until late. During these visits, Angela received permission to have supper with her parents, providing she returned to the main house before the sisters, in case she was needed to serve them.

It was on one such day, when the workday finished and all the field slaves were in their shacks preparing supper, Angela walked the dirt path to her parent's home. A few yards up the path, Angela saw the outline of a woman standing alone, as if waiting for her. As she drew closer, to her surprise, it was the widow Ravenna.

Angela knew little about Ravenna. She'd been there all her life, working and living with the other slaves, yet living apart. When Angela was a girl, she feared Ravenna. The stories folks told about Ravenna scared her. Though many adults never admitted it, they too were afraid of her. Her ways were strange, her manners coarse, and her attitude and speech always cruel. Some said she was a witch. She never allowed anyone close enough to know her, which clearly was the way she wanted it. Her husband, Azrael, passed three years earlier of consumption. Ravenna lived alone; again, it was the way she wanted it to be.

"Hello, Angela," Ravenna said when they were but a few feet from each other.

Though it took Angela by surprise that Ravenna knew her name, it shouldn't have. There were no reasons she wouldn't know. It was just that they never spoke.

"Hello," Angela said back. Then she thought it rude to not acknowledge her by name, so she repeated herself. "Hello, Ravenna."

"Goin' to visit Lailah and Micah, aye?"

"Yes, I'm gonna see my parents."

"Your parents, aye…?" Ravenna cackled. "That's right, they was the ones who raised ya, didn't they?" Ravenna moved in closer, her crooked smile beaming at Angela. "They never told ya who your parents were, did they?"

Angela remained silent, stepping back, but Ravenna stepped forward, making up the difference.

"What is it they told ya who be your parents? What if I told ya I was you mother and my husband, Azrael, was your father?"

"I don't believe ya," Angela answered back.

"No, why should ya. But ya'd believe Lailah and Micah…wouldn't ya, now? Why don't ya ask them?"

"Why are ya telling me this?" Angela asked.

Ravenna gave off a low chuckle coming from deep in her throat. "I guess I can tell ya. It won't make no difference, no how. I does it for hate."

Angela shot her a look. "I don't understand."

"Of course ya don't. Ya is like all the others, ya hate, ya love. But me, I loves to hate…all of ya. I hated ya from your first breath. I hated Lailah and Micah for raisin' ya. My husband's been dead for years, and I ain't got much time myself. I just figured it be time for the truth, for no other reason than hate." Ravenna backed off, turned and started to walk off. "Ya has a good evening, child," She laughed over her shoulder.

Angela stood silently till Ravenna was gone. Her mind whirled. She had no idea what to make of it all, but she was determined to find out.

****

Angela knocked on the door. A moment later, Micah opened it, looking confused. There was no reason for Angela to knock; she could have just walked in as usual, the way they expected.

"Why, Honey, it's so good to see ya. Come in…come in."

Micah reached out, taking her in his arms. He could not help but notice Angela's distance and coldness, as she stiffened up.

Lailah smiled at her. Carrying two bowls, she placed them on the table. "Let's all sit while it's still hot."

"I'm not hungry," Angela announced.

Both her parents looked at her in a questioning manner.

"There's something we need to talk about."

"Talk about what, child?" Lailah asked, worry covering her face.

"Who are my real parents?" Angela demanded to know.

Neither Lailah nor Micah answered.

"I just spoke with Ravenna. She tells me she's my real mother. Is that true?"

Lailah and Micah stood silent for what seemed like a long time, then Micah spoke, "Yes, she be your real mother." Lailah shot Micah a look that said, 'why did ya do that?' Micah gently gave her a look that said, 'what else could I do?'

Micah continued his story. "Your parents didn't want ya. I found Azrael, your real father, fixin' to bury ya out in the field. I begged him to spare your life, and give ya to me for us to raise up"

"Ya never told me!" Angela was in tears, now.

"It was the only way," Lailah said. There was a strong pleading in her voice.

"Ya lied to me! All these years, ya lied to me!"

"Ya don't understand, Darlin'," Micah said, almost in tears himself.

Angela opened the door, running out. "I never want to see either one of ya, again!" she shouted.

She ran up the pathway too fast for Micah to catch up with her. She could hear him far behind, shouting to her. She was filled with emotion. It was all emotion and not logic. She could not think of any good reason she said what she did. She only felt the anger.

The world was a blur of tears, but somehow Angela made it to the main house. In her room, she sat on her bed, in the dark, crying.

****

Months went by and life went on. Angela worked hard everyday, not to do her best but to avoid punishment. She could not avoid Aamon Abernathy's advances. Many were the times; he cornered her in the hallway, his hands all over her. He tried on numerous occasions to corner her late at night in her room under the stairs, but the shouts from his wife to hurry to bed saved her each time. She feared the day, his wife was not home, for she knew someday it would be so.

Despite her prophecy, Ravenna did not die. The recluse never looked well, but belief among the slaves was she would outlive them all. As for Angela, she'd feel no remorse if Ravenna died. Nor would she feel deprived for never getting to know her real mother.

Not once since the night Angela walked out of her parents' home in anger did she visit again. A part of her knew it was foolish to be cold and distant to her parents. She loved them. But foolish, youthful pride and the feeling of betrayal got her thinking wrong. Time is the great healer, and it also is the great teacher.

****

After a full day's work, Angela sat in the kitchen eating with the other house slaves. Seated with all the women was Tom-Tom, Aamon Abernathy's manservant. He was an old man, nearly ancient by his looks. He was tall and slender like a rubber tree. His white hair sat on his head like snow on a hill of dark sandstone. Rumor was he was born in Africa, stolen from his tribe while still an infant, and sold into slavery. After being shipped to the Americas, he was purchased by Aamon's grandfather, serving three generations of Abernathys. As for his name, Tom-Tom, no one knew how or when he acquired the name. When asked about it, he always refused to speak on the subject. Being the quiet type, he seldom spoke. But when he did speak, everyone stopped to listen. He would take a wagon into town, some twenty miles away, once a month, to fetch things from a list the Abernathy family gave him. Any news of the outside came from Tom-Tom. He was their only connection with life other than on the plantation. So, they listened intensely to his every word.

"I hear tell there's gonna be war. That what all the white folks are talkin' about in town, the last I was there."

"What'cha talkin' bout, old man?" laughed Agnes. "The only war I knows about it be the Revolution War, and that was a hundred years ago."

"Well, this here's gonna be a new one," insisted Tom-Tom.

"Who be doin' the fightin?" asked one of the women.

"The North and the South," Tom-Tom replied.

"Ya mean, they gonna be fightin' the Mexicans?"

"No...not that far south. Then the old man said something that confused them all. "We is the South."

"What'cha means, 'We is the south'?"

Tom-Tom rolled his eyes. "This here's a big dang country. There's a northern part and a southern part."

"And there's an east and west," Agnes added.

"That be true, but they doesn't' see it that way. They only sees north and south. Well, the southern part got plantations and slaves. The northern part says that be wrong. So, they goin' to fight a war to see who's right. They already be killin' each other."

"So, what happen if they fight and the South wins?" asked another woman.

"If the South wins, then nothin' changes. In fact, it probably get worse. Ya knows how southern white men get about being right. They likes to shove it in ya face."

"But if the North wins, then we'd be free," Angela thought out loud.

Agnes turned and laughed so hard her large belly shook up and down, rubbing against the edge of the table. "Child, don't talk crazy. We slaves been here since the first white man got here with us in tow. Your great, great grandchildren, are gonna be sittin' in that same chair ya sittin' in now. They'll be in this here kitchen, servin' breakfast, lunch, and supper to Aamon's great, great, grandchildren. So, don't talk crazy, child."

With that, the mood turned cold and sour. No one felt like talking or hearing anymore. They ate in silence.

Just then, as they were finishing their supper, the outside dinner bell sounded. Each person at the table woofed down one last bite, then rose and walked out of the main house. Daring not to dally, knowing it was to be a whipping or a hanging. To be late or miss the event would mean certain server punishment, even to being whipped or hung yourself.

Stepping outside, they immediately knew it was a hanging. A thick rope was thrown over the large limb of the hanging tree. A hangman's noose hung in midair, ready and waiting.

All the field slaves were gathered. Bunter stood on top of a buck wagon, giving his usual speech of hell and damnation on any and all transgressors. Angela caught only the first few words of his speech. It was something about the penalty for raising your hands against one of the overseers. Just then she caught sight of whom they were going to hang, and the world faded into the mist. It was Micah, her father.

She no longer heard Bunter, nor saw the crowd, or even the sky. All she saw was the dangling noose and Micah's fear filled eyes fixed on it. She wished she was closer for him to see her, but he was too far away, and there were too many people between them, blocking his view.

Two overseers guided the horse under the noose. It took five overseers to clumsily toss the hand bound Micah into the saddle. They made sure his feet weren't in the stirrups. Another overseer on horseback reached out, placing the noose around Micah's neck.

Angela looked frantically about, as if looking for a miracle. Her eyes caught the vision of her mother across from her. Those around her were holding the poor grieving woman up.

Angela felt a strong urge to run out into the open to her father and cut him down. She took one step forward, when she felt someone grab her by the arm. She turned to see who it was, it was Abby.

"Don't do it, child," she whispered softly to Angela.

Before anyone could take another breath, an overseer lashed the hind of the horse; it dashed forward leaving Micah dangling in midair. He kicked, his legs going in all directions, as if doing a morose dance. He bobbed up and down, each time putting more pressure around his neck. Suddenly, he went limp, hanging motionless. As if after a great storm, the world went silent. Angela looked across to her mother. She went limp, fainting. The men around her lifted her up and then started carrying her home.

So many emotions raced through Angela. She could take no more. She turned, pushed the others aside, and entered the main house. She didn't care who saw her. If the penalty was death, then so be it.

****

Late that night when Angela felt sure everyone was asleep, she left her room under the stairs. In the kitchen, she took one of the sharpest knives. As quietly as she could, she went out the backdoor, making her way to the hanging tree.

They always left the body hanging for three to four days, to put the fear into the field and house slaves. Without saying, it worked.

Standing under the tree, the silver light of the moon allowed her to see the body of her father clearly, shining like a ghost in the night. With the knife, she cut him down. His body hit the ground with a thud. She gently took the noose from around his neck. With all her strength, holding him by his arms, she dragged his body out into one of the newly plowed fields. Returning to the house, she filled a wheel barrel with logs they kept by the kitchen door and a can of kerosene. Back in the field, she placed the logs around Micah's body, and then poured the kerosene over the logs and her father. Striking a match, she tossed it atop of the pyre. There was no time for words or tears. In seconds, flames were flaring to the sky. She ran back to the house, back into her cubbyhole.

The fire was too far from the house for its flames and its roar to wake anyone.

In the morning, the fire was out. All that remained were ashes and bone. When Bunter saw the cut rope under the hanging tree, he summoned all his overseers. One of them ran to him, telling what they found in the newly plowed field.

Bunter was beside himself with anger. He demanded answers. He wanted a full investigation. He vowed the culprit would suffer long and hard before they were put to death.

Normally, Angela would have been the first person to question. But everyone knew she'd no longer been on speaking terms with her father. She hadn't visited her parents for months. Surely, she was not the one. That left only one person to suspect – Lailah.

Eight

Into the Sea

Just two days after the hanging, life returned to normal on the plantation. The investigation of the cremation stopped. This surprised Angela. She suspected they would at least question her mother. The thought of this weighted heavy on Angela, it only came to her after she cremated her father. She never wished evil on her mother, and it concerned her deeply. Angela was confused, that is until…

Angela and Abbey were sitting on the back porch, mending gloves and socks for the sisters. At first, Abbey sat quietly working. Then her mood changed and her voice was low and sorrowful.

"I'm sorry about what happened to your father."

Not particularly wanting to talk about it, Angela just nodded in recognition.

Abby continued, "I've been working here all my life, here at the main house. I gets to hear things none of the others gets to hear. Just yesterday, I hears something I think ya needs to know."

Angel waited as Abby took a reflective moment to put her words together.

"I just come right out and say it. Your momma, Lailah, is dyin'. The shock of what happened was too much for her. She's been laid up since they took her home that day. They say she ain't got long."

Angela looked up from her work at Abbey. "I need to see her."

"I knows, child. I don't know how. I'll help ya anyways that I can."

The two remained silent, thinking.

****

Early that afternoon, Abby and Angela were called up to the sisters' room. Lilith showed them baskets of dirty clothes that needed cleaning. Normally, this would be a cause for both women to groan inwardly, only inwardly, because any showing of disapproval of either of the sisters' wishes was considered disobedience. To do so meant punishment. Abby and Angela knew this all too well; both carried the scars on their hands.

When they got all the clothing to the back of the main house, they started a fire on which they'd boil the clothes in hot water and lye.

Once the water was boiling, Abby turned to Angela, "I can take it from here. Ya go sees your momma."

"But there's so much to do," Angela said.

"I knows, but it won't be the first time I had to work hard, and I don't think it'd be the last. Ya go on; I take care of all this."

"I'll be back as soon as I can," Angela said as she ran off.

Angela raced all the way to her parents' shack. When she got to the front door, she hesitated. Finally, she took in a long deep breath, exhaled it slowly, and then entered.

Her eyes immediately focused on the bed across the room. On it sat Loretta, the oldest slave on the plantation. No one knew how old she really was; not even Loretta knew. Because of her age, she was not required to work the fields, though she was expected to look after expected mothers and the sick. No one went without serving the plantation.

Sitting straight and tall on the edge of the bed, her hands folded in her lap, her youthful eyes framed in a sea of wrinkles, she spoke softly. "She's gone, child," was all she said, and all she needed to say.

"But…how?" Angela asked.

Loretta spoke the cold truth, "I've seen it before. She died of a broken heart."

Angela moved in closer to see her mother's lifeless body atop of the bed. Her hair spread upon the pillow like the roots of a tree. Her solemn face finally washed in calm.

"She looks so at peace," Angela remarked.

"It was peaceful, once she settled into it," replied Loretta. "Probably the first peace the poor woman's ever known." Loretta pulled back the bedcovers to reveal she'd died holding her beloved Bible. "She was at peace with the Lord, so there was no fear in the room," Loretta added. "In my life, I've been at the bedside of many of the dyin'. I can feel when the end is comin'. Sometimes it ain't so pretty, there's cryin', and wailin', and gnashin' of teeth. Other times, I can feel the Spirit come down and take them by the hand. Your mamma's passin' was a joyous occasion, have no worry about that."

Angela moved to the head of the bed, placing her hand on her mother's forehead. Warmth was still there.

Loretta rose from off the bed, starting for the door. "Her last words were of you and Micah. How she loved ya both all her life, how she'd keep on lovin' ya even in heaven, where I suspect she and Micah are now." Loretta opened the door, stepping out she spoke once more as she closed the door, "Well, I best be goin'. I'll leave ya two alone. I suspects ya both got lots to talk about."

The moment the door closed, Angela fell down upon her mother, her face buried in her hair. She could still smell the scent of her.

"Oh, mother, please forgive me," she cried. "I should never have acted that way. I love ya and papa. Please forgive me, Momma," she moaned, her face pressed against her mother's cheek. Tears ran from her eyes like a river runs into the sea – her mother the sea.

****

When Angela returned to the main house, all was quiet. She snuck in through the front door. She knew it was forbidden for her to do so, which is why she did it. They would not be looking for a slave to enter through the front door. Thus she hoped to go undetected. Thankfully, this time she was right.

As quietly as she could, she moved through the house. She opened the door to her tiny room, placing her forbidden treasure under the bed.

She found Abby in the back of the house, finishing the sisters' laundry. She'd strung the clothes across clotheslines. The fine materials flapped in the cool wind like flags. Now they were dry; Abby was about to take them down.

"How did it go?" Abby asked.

Angela's eyes began to well up, again.

"That bad, aye?" Abby concluded.

Angela just nodded.

"Ya lucked out," Abby told Angela as she approached. "None of 'em missed ya bein' here, and I got all the wash done. Here, help me take 'em down and fold 'em."

The two women busied themselves, folding the dresses and petticoats, placing them neatly in wicker baskets. They spoke not a word, hurrying to get the job finished. There were so many baskets of clothing; it took them three trips to get it all up to the sisters' room.

Slowly and carefully, Lilith and Emily inspected every piece. To Abby and Angela's surprise, there were no complaints. This seldom happened. The sisters, especially Lilith, seemingly enjoy complaining, just like their mother. But they spent most of the day riding their horses with visiting friends. Now, they were too tired to make a fuss about anything.

After being excused, Abby and Angela went to the kitchen for supper. As they ate with the others, no one said a word about not seeing Angela around all day. Perhaps, Abby and Angela got away with a foolproof plan or the others thought it best not to say a word. Either way, it would seem they got away with it. Abby smiled across the table at Angela.

****

The sun was nearly set, when Angela retired to her room under the stairs. Closing the door, she did something she never liked doing. She reached for the lamp sitting on the nightstand and lit it. The small flame illuminated the tiny room. That feeling of being inside a coffin returned. She undressed, placing her clothes neatly across the foot of the bed.

Once in bed and under the covers, she leaned over the edge of the bed, feeling around for her forbidden treasure. Taking it in hand, she sat up in bed, randomly opening to the middle of the book.

She'd taken her mother's Bible; knowing full well it might be at the cost of her life. It meant so much to her mother. She wanted to know why. Perhaps, if she understood the book better, she might know her mother better.

Nine

If I Don't Go Mad

As sure as the sun rises and then sets, as one day follows another, some things are a given. This is the surety Angela lived with when it came to Aamon Abernathy. His eyes and hands grew bolder with the passing of time. It would only be a question of time before he struck, pouncing on her as a lion on a lamb.

This is the deepest cruelty of slavery. Lives are broken, flesh is tortured; these are sins that make even God cry. To torment the spirit of another sends an echo across creation that may never be forgiven.

After dressing, Angela went upstairs to the sisters' room. As always she knocked, waiting for permission to enter. There was no answer. She could hear the sisters jabbering away. So, she knocked again. Once more, she knocked, only this time with more force.

"Come in!" shouted Emily.

As she entered, Lilith shot her a cold look. "There's no need to hammer on the door. Don't do it again."

"Yes…madam."

They were never satisfied. Angela was used to the complaining by now. She paid little attention to the warnings. She knew she never could win. So, why bother?

The room was in disarray. It was worse that Angela ever saw. Both beds were completely covered with dresses and undergarments. All the chairs were covered with hats. Gloves and bows masked the tops of the dressers. Shoes plagued the floor till only inches of carpet shown through. The closet, usually filled to capacity, now, was an empty shell with a few ribbons on the floor.

"The family is not having breakfast downstairs this morning," Emily announced. "We want you to go down to the kitchen and bring us up our breakfast."

"Yes…madam," Angela said, making for the door.

"And hurry!" Lilith shouted. "I don't want to eat cold eggs."

"Yes…madam," Angela said, running out of the bedroom and down the stairs.

Angela flew into the kitchen. "The sisters want…"

"I know all about," said Agnes. "Come here, girl, I'll show ya."

It was difficult to tell how old Agnes was. She was no spring chicken, but there wasn't a gray hair on her head and her skin was flawlessly smooth. She'd been head cook for the

Abernathy family since Aamon was a baby. She was a short but wide woman, nearly as wide as the stove she stood in front of everyday for the past thirty- eight years.

Angela walked over, standing by her. Agnes pointed out all the finer details. "This here is the best tray in the house," she said, placing the silver tray on the table. She placed two plates of fine china on the tray. Next to each plate was a napkin on which were utensils. Bringing back a skillet from off the stove, she put a fried egg on each plate, two pieces of bacon, and a slice of toasted bread. To one side of the tray she placed a small plate of butter and a butter knife. "The sisters do loves their butter," she said turning once more to the stove. "Come, look see, girl, I'll show ya hows to do it."

Angela moved in closer. She felt tiny standing next to this massive woman.

"Ya put some hot water in the teapot and swirl it around to gets it nice and hot. Then ya throw the water out. Then ya put five heapin' spoonfuls of ground tea leaves in the pot, and then fill the pot up with more hot water." She put the teapot in the center of the tray.

She was just about to put the lid on the teapot when she stopped. "Oh, I nearly forgot. There's one more ingredient. It's my special secret ingredient."

Agnes bent over the teapot, made a groveling sound from her chest and throat, and spit into the teapot. Then she placed the lid atop.

"There, now it's ready," Agnes announced with pride.

Angela couldn't do anything but stand, staring at Agnes in amazement.

"Don't ya worry, child, "whispered Agnes, looking left to right, to give it more drama. "If ya don't say anythin', I won't. Now, take this tray upstairs before the eggs get cold, and the sisters pitch a fit."

Angela rushed the tray upstairs. The room was in such disarray, it was hard to find a clear spot to place the tray down. She carefully pushed a dress to one side, placing the tray at the foot of one of the beds.

"These eggs are cold," complained Emily. Angela expected that. Even if the eggs burned her, she would complain. The sisters lived to complain.

They finally decided what they'd wear for the day, beginning to dress.

"What are you staring at, girl?" Lilith growled at Angela. She stood with her mouth open, gapping at the sisters as they drank their tea, cup after cup, the tea with Agnes' special secret ingredient.

While hanging the clothes back in the closet, Angela heard bits and pieces of their conversation. From it, she learned that the sisters and their mother received an invitation from a nearby plantation family. Other neighboring ladies were also invited. The invitation was extended to women only. It would be a day of showing off their new clothes, gossip, eating, and more gossip.

The day had finally come. The day Angela feared since coming to the main house. The Abernathy women would be gone for the entire day, leaving Aamon to himself. Angela could see no way there would not be a war of wills between her and her master. It was sure to be a sorrowful day. She just knew it.

Angela watched from the upstairs window. Aamon stood in front of the house watching the family carriage driven by one of the overseers carrying the madam and his two daughters in the back. He waved them off; they waved back. Aamon gave an order to one of the slaves, and then entered the house. Angela couldn't hear what was said.

She watched with relief as the wagon drove off the property. It would be a day without the sisters. Only now she would have to contend with Aamon.

She was just about to walk away from the window when to her surprise she saw Aamon come back out of the house. The slave he ordered came back with the master's horse, saddled and ready.

Aamon placed something in the saddlebag. Angela strained to see what it was – it was a bottle of whiskey. The good news was Aamon was going riding, hopefully till his wife came back. The bad news was he'd be drinking.

****

Angela stayed busy throughout the day, doing her usual chores and helping in the kitchen. It seemed that she might get through the day without confronting Aamon. Then midafternoon, the sound of a galloping horse could be heard coming from outside and echoing through the main house. Angela kept to the kitchen with the other woman. She assumed safety in numbers to be the rule. She was wrong.

The slave who helped Aamon off his horse knew the full story. There was no use of looking in the saddlebag. Surely, the whiskey bottle was empty. Aamon nearly fell when getting off the horse. His breath smelled like a still. He slurred his words, staggering to the front door.

Like a mule kicking down a stall, Aamon kicked open the kitchen door. Everyone stopped what they were doing, turning to see Aamon at the door, breathing like a wild animal. They stood silent and motionless, their eyes wide with fear.

Aamon looked about till he found what he was looking for. "…You!" he shouted, pointing at Angela. "I want you! Come with me!"

Angela didn't move, nor did anyone else.

Aamon wheeled the riding crop he held in his hand, pointing it at Angela. "Now…I want you, now!"

Fearfully and slowly, Angela stepped forward and followed Aamon out of the kitchen. When the door closed, everyone breathed a sigh of relief. They could not help feeling sorry for Angela. Abby wept, Agnes prayed.

Angela followed Aamon down the hall to the library. When they were both in, he slammed the door shut.

Aamon used his riding crop like a third arm. With it, he poised Angela in front of an easy chair. "Stand there, girl," he said as he sat down. "Now, turn around; let's have a look at you."

Angela wasn't sure what he wanted. She stood dumbfounded.

Aamon held his riding crop facing the floor, spinning it to indicate what he meant. "Go ahead, turn around slowly."

She did as she was told, slowly turning to the right. She felt uncomfortable, his roaming eyes all over her.

"That's enough," he said, when she'd made a full turn. Using his riding crop, Aamon reached down, playing with the hem of her dress. Then he lifted the hem revealing her legs. He didn't lift it high, but it was as uncomfortable as a snake crawling under her skirt.

"Would you like some brandy?" Aamon asked, smiling up at her.

Not knowing what he was asking, Angela remained silent.

When he realized her confusion he laughed. To his right was a small table; on it was a silver tray holding four long stem glasses and a decanter filled with a deep cherry colored liquid. He poured them each a glass, handing one to Angela. She lifted it to her nose, taking a whiff.

"Don't smell it," Aamon laughed. "Drink it."

Angela took the tiniest of sips. Her face scrunched from the flavor.

"No…no, take a big drink," he said.

This time she took a mouthful and swallowed. The inside of her mouth was on fire, which was nothing compared to the burning sensation it caused in her throat as it went down. Before it hit her stomach, she choked. Some of the liquid came back up into her nose, which burned all the more.

Aamon laughed at her. Then his laugh faded and his face grew stern. "Drink it! Drink it all!"

Fearing for her safety, Angels closed her eyes, held her breath, and drank it down. Immediately, she began choking.

Aamon stood up. Taking her glass, he poured her another drink. "Here, drink it down."

She could only stare at the glass, unable to bring herself to drink.

"I said drink it!" he shouted, slapping her across the face with the back of his hand. The blow shook her violently. She spilled the entire drink. He filled the glass, again. "Now, drink it!"

She did what she was told. He immediately filled another glassful. "...Drink!" Anything was better than another slap to the face. She quickly drank it all down. To her surprise, he filled the glass. "Again!" he commanded. Once more she forced the liquid down in two gulps.

Angela was beginning to feel strange. Something wasn't right. *This is what it feels like to be drunk*, she thought.

Again, he filled her glass. "One more," he demanded.

The words *one more*, hopefully meaning the last, allowed her to go past what she was feeling and swallow it down.

The room was spinning around Angela. She experienced a feeling of being detached from the situation. Still, she was aware of Aamon's hand groping her. It was as if he had multiple arms; his hands seemed to be everywhere at once. She tried to fight him, but between his more powerful strength and the oncoming dizziness from the liquor, it was a useless fight.

Holding her in his arms, he tilted her backwards. Her head flew back. Aamon placed his mouth on her neck. Holding her up with one arm, he freed his other hand, pulling at the top of her dress. The sound of cloth ripping filled the air, as first her shoulders were made bare. She knew he would not stop there, in her panic, she screamed, "Help!"

At that very moment, the doors to the library crashed open. Amy Abernathy flew into the room.

"What the hell is going on?" she screeched.

Immediately, without a second thought, Aamon threw Angela to the floor and began whipping her on her shoulders with his riding crop.

Amy rushed forward. Again, she bellowed at the top of her lungs, "What the hell is going on?"

Aamon looked up at her in surprise, as if he wasn't aware of her till then. He bent down, picking up the brandy glass Angela dropped. He held it up to his wife.

"I caught this wench getting into my good brandy. I was just whipping her *what-for*." Then he looked back down on the half-naked, sobbing Angela. "I should have her taken outside and hung," he concluded.

His wife noticed the other half-filled glass of brandy sitting on the small table next to the chair. Then and there, she understood what really happened. She could confront him, but she knew he'd deny it, and they would argue about it all nightlong. No, she'd bide her time, and get both of them in her own time and way – the master and the slave girl.

"Don't kill her," Amy said softly. "There are worse things than hanging."

"And who better to carry them out than you, my love," Aamon said with pride. "Go upstairs, I'll be right up."

Amy said not a word and left.

Aamon kicked Angela hard – twice.

"Get up, girl, and go to your room!" Angela didn't move; she remained on the floor crying. "I said, 'get up'!" he hollered, kicking her, again.

Slowly, in tears, with one hand holding her dress close covering her nakedness. Somehow, she made it to her room under the stairs. In pain and shame, she fell face down on her bed.

****

A sharp shooting pain woke Angela. She felt the touch of cool hands on her back. Turning, she saw Abbey sitting on the edge of the bed, applying butter to the welts on her back, just as she did when her hand was scorched by the sisters.

"I'm not gonna make it, Abby. If it's not Aamon or his wife it's the sisters. One day, one of them will go too far, and that day will be my last, if I don't go mad first. I have to run away."

"Where would ya go?" asked Abby.

"I don't know. Let me get out of here first, and then I'll worry about that."

"But…how? Ya saw what happened to Curley."

"I did, and I've learned from his mistakes. I've a plan that I think might work. But I'll need some help."

"I'll help ya anyways I can," Abby offered.

"That's very kind of ya, Abby, but you're not the one I was thinkin' about. The one person on this plantation who can help me is…Ravenna."

Ten

The Potion

It was one of those rare days when the entire Abernathy family left the plantation for the day and a night. They'd not be home till the next day. There was a time on such days Angela visited her parents, but those days were gone. Now, it was no different from any other time, though one particular day did stand out. Angela had a purpose to visit the shacks of her childhood.

Angela felt as if her feet were nailed to the wooden planks on the porch in front of Ravenna's shack. It took all her courage to step forward and knock on the door.

"Go away!" Ravenna shouted through the door.

"It's me, Angela," said Angela, hoping it would make a difference. It did not.

"Burn in the lake of fire, ya brat, now, go away!"

"I'm not goin' away till ya talk to me." Angela waited, there was no answer. "I'll keep knockin' until ya open up."

The door flung open. Ravenna stood in the doorway, eyeing Angela – an evil eye. Ravenna was never a pretty woman, even when she was young. Age and a lifetime of being spiteful and cruel now showed on her face. Children ran at just the sight of her. Adults would turn, walking the other way when they saw her coming, rather than have to deal with her.

"What do ya want?" she hissed.

Angela took a small pouch from her pocket, handing it to Ravenna.

"What's this?"

"Tobacco, I heard ya like to smoke." It was tobacco Angela robbed from Aamon's study. "I just want to talk to ya for a few minutes."

Ravenna thought it over for a moment. She put the pouch in her apron pocket. "Very well, come in," Ravenna said, stepping back into the shack. "Close the door behind ya."

It was darker than night inside the one-room shack. Any light from the outside world she'd blocked out with rags. The only light was from a lamp on a table in the center of the room. There was a single bed to one side. Ravenna stashed away the pouch of tobacco in the drawer of her nightstand.

"So, what do ya want? If you're here to start a mother and daughter relationship, ya can go to blazes."

"That's not why I'm here," Angela replied. "Some folks say you're a witch. Is it true? Are ya a witch?"

Ravenna laughed, "Maybe I am, and maybe I ain't. What's it to ya?"

"I need a potion. Witches work with potions, don't they? Well, I need one."

Ravenna shook her head, laughing, "What, a lover potion? Well, I don't do them. I don't believe in 'em. Love, I mean."

"I need a potion to knock somebody out."

Ravenna smiled, as if the conversation was going in a direction she enjoyed. "Ya wants to kill them?"

"No, I just want to put them out for a spell."

The smile left Ravenna's face. She was clearly disappointed.

"Why should I help ya?" the old woman asked.

Angela decided to tell the truth. "I plan to go rabbit from this here place. I want a potion to knock out all the overseers and the dogs, too. By the time they wake up, I'll be long gone. Ya don't have to help me, but if ya did it would certainly hurt Aamon Abernathy's pride and degrade his overseers." To Angela, this seemed like a lame excuse, but she understood how Ravenna thought. She hoped such reasoning would appeal to her – and it did.

Ravenna laughed loud and hard. "I'd love to see Abernathy's face. Yeah, I'll help ya."

One wall held nothing but shelves. On them were jars of various sizes. Ravenna took one down, placing it on the table. She put a rag down next to the jar, proceeding to fill it with the contents of the jar. She held some of it up to Angela.

"Ya see this, girl? Ya see these little blue flowers?"

"I recognize 'em. I've seen 'em in the field by the forest," Angela said.

"Ya recognize this here mushroom?" Ravenna said, holding one mushroom to Angela's face.

"I do, but I thought they were poison?"

"They can be, if you're not careful." Ravenna tied the ends of the rag holding the contents of flowers and mushrooms. "Take this; boil it all in a big pot of hot water to make a tea. Ya give a cup to each man and half that amount for each dog. They'll sleep like babies."

"But how do I get them to drink it?"

"Ya are a stupid girl, ain't ya? Ya put it in their food. It ain't got no smell or taste. They won't even notice."

Angela took up the rag. Holding it to her breast, she walked toward the door.

"Now, this ain't gonna hurt them or anything?"

"They'll wake with the worst head pain of their lives, that's all."

"Thank ya," Angela said before opening the door.

"Don't thank me, just do it!" Ravenna said, sounding happy or at least as happy as a woman such as she could be.

Closing the door and stepping off the porch, Angela heard the old woman laughing, though it was more of a cackle – like you'd expect from a witch. As Angela made her way back to the main house, she wondered if she did the right thing.

****

It was still early in the day when Angela returned to the main house. The kitchen staff already cooked, served, and cleaned up lunch, which was today only for the overseers and the staff. The kitchen would be empty for the next few hours until the staff returned to prepare supper. This would give Angela more than enough time to prepare her concoction.

She brought a full pot of water to a boil. After brewing the mixture for a few minutes, the water was a deep murky brown. She forgot to ask Ravenna how long to brew the tea. But from the color, she assumed it ready. There was no way to taste and test it. She could only cross her fingers and hope for the best..

She strained the liquid into a large jug. Since the Abernathy family would not be home till the next day. There would be no meal prepared for them. Besides, she only needed the dogs and the overseers out of the way. By the cut ingredients lying on the table, she knew they'd be preparing stew. The trick was to only get the mixture in the food of the overseers but not the staff. Angela had a plan.

She hid the jug in with a large pile of potatoes. When the staff returned to the kitchen, Angela offered to help with supper. In no time, a thick stew was prepared. Nonchalantly, Angela took up the hidden jug, quickly pouring half the mixture into the stew. The others were so busy, cleaning up and cutting bread, she went unnoticed. She retuned the jug into hiding.

Abby was there helping as well. She took a spoonful of the stew and was just about to taste it when Angela slapped the spoon out of her hand.

Abby shot her a look of anger mixed with confusion.

"Ya know how Agnes is," Angela whispered. "If she catches ya eating before the others, she'll pitch a fit."

If there was enough time to argue, Abby would have. Instead, she walked away looking strangely at Angela.

63

In the area in back of the main house there were long wooden tables with benches. This was where the overseers ate. When the workday was done, the overseers took their places. It was the kitchen staff's duty to serve them. The staff laid plates out on the table; Agnes ladled the thick stew into each. The staff served the plates to the overseers, with bread and jugs of cider. When the overseers finished eating, they retired to the bunkhouse.

"Nobody eats till we clean up," Agnes announced to the staff. As they were doing so, trying to make it look like an accident, Angela moved the pot of stew across the stove, dropping it to the floor. The brown liquid spread across the kitchen floor, steam floating up. The vegetables lay near the stove.

Agnes came running from outside into the kitchen, followed by the others. "What ya be doin', girl?"

"I was just movin' the pot over the hot spot; so, it'd be warmer for everybody. I'm sorry," Angela said, bowing her head in false shame, knowing she'd spared them.

Agnes let out a long sigh. "Oh well, looks like potatoes and eggs for supper." She pointed at Angela, "Ya, girl, are gonna clean up this mess."

"Yes'um."

The staff sat on the benches outside till Angela cleaned up. Later, Agnes and the others cut and fried potatoes with eggs and onions. They sat outside, eating. All through the meal, Abby eyed Angela with suspicious eyes. Angela paid little attention to Abby's stares. There was more to her plan that needed doing.

She planned her movement well. The dogs used for security and hunting slaves had just been fed. There were eight hounds in all. Angela took what was left of her concoction, pouring it over their food. Normally, the dogs would have barked when she approached, but they were too busy eating. They never came up for air, as they wolfed down their supper. Angela tossed the now empty jug into one of the fields.

The rest of the day continued like any other day. At sunset, though no one else was paying attention, Angela realized there were no overseers to be seen. She stole down to the kennel to find all eight dogs lying on their sides, completely oblivious to the rest of the world. She assumed it was the same with the overseers.

When the sun disappeared and night filled the world, Angela went to her room under the stairs. There she took one of the bedsheets; she also took the Bible that once belonged to her mother. In the kitchen, she rummaged through the pantry, collected all food that she could carry, items that would not spoil quickly. She placed the items in the center of the bed sheet along with the Bible.

"What are ya doin'?" a voice called behind her. Angela spun around. It was dark; all she saw was the outline of a woman. When she stepped forward, Angela breathed a sigh of relief – it was Abby.

"I'm goin' rabbit, Abby. I can't stay here any longer. I'm makin' a run for it."

"Where will ya go?"

"I'll know when I get there. I only know if I stay, it's goin' to go bad for me. Between the sisters, the madam, and worst of all, the master, I'll be dead before the end of the year."

Abby made no argument; she knew this to be true.

"They'll sic the dogs on ya."

"I put something in the dog's food, as well as the overseers' supper. They won't wake for a long time."

"So, that's why ya acted strange, tonight. That's why ya spilled the stew. So we wouldn't eat any of it," Abby said, sounding amazed, realizing it was all planned.

Angela tied the ends of the sheet, forming a sack. She tossed it over her shoulder, making for the backdoor. She turned once more to Abbey. "Why don't ya come with me?"

Angela could see Abby smiling from across the room, snickering, "It be twenty years too late, girl. I'd not only slow ya down, I'd get us both killed. No, ya go without me. I'll try to cover your tracks as best I can."

"Thank ya, Abbey," Angela said as she opened the door, stepping out into the world.

"God be with ya, Angela. I'll be prayin' for ya."

No one had ever prayed for her as far as she knew except her mother and father. It made her feel awkward, yet in a strange way calm. She turned, walking into the night.

****

Angela wasn't sure how many hours she had before they'd hunt her down. She wasn't taking chances, she ran across the fields and into the forest. For an entire day, she drudged deeper into the forest till the density of the trees nearly blocked out the sun. Only thin golden beams of sunlight cut through the dark every few yards. It wasn't till hours later there were no longer any shafts of light that she realized it was night. The entire day, not once had she stopped to rest. Though often she stumbled in the dark, she continued onward, wanting to get as much distance between her and the plantation.

Finally, exhausted, she allowed herself a few moments rest. She fell to the ground, placing her back against a large oak tree.

She miscalculated how tired she really was. The last thing she remembered was closing her eyes to rest for a few minutes. When she opened them again, sunlight was shining in her eyes. It was morning, or hopefully not later. She rose up; starting to run in what she believed was the right direction. Thankfully, every so often the forest would end and there would be an open field. Only then did she get her bearings from the sun, telling her what direction she was heading. Then the field would end at the edge of more forest. In she would go, loosing herself amongst the trees.

Again, as the day before, she hurried on until late into the night. The sack she carried over her back grew heavier with each hour. When she stopped for the night, she ate her fill of bread and hard-boiled eggs. The bread was already going bad. She had to eat around the mold. She had a small canteen of water, she'd been sipping at since she left the plantation, trying to make it last.

This night she knew better than hope for a short nap, she was too tired to care how long she slept. Closing her eyes, she drifted into a dream.

In her dream, Angela saw herself running through an open field of high grass. The sun was high, blazing white-hot, beating down like a hammer. The air was hot going into her lungs.

She heard sounds off in the distance behind her. Something was chasing her. As it approached she heard the sounds of dogs barking. It was the overseers and their dogs tracking her down. She ran as hard as she could, but the sounds grew closer.

When she got to the top of a high hill, she turned, looking back on the field she just ran through. She could see the heads of the overseers bobbing in the tall grass. She could not see the dogs that were low to the ground, but she could hear them. As they drew closer, she saw the men carried rifles. The hate in their eyes burned like little red hot coals. Every so often, she caught a glimpse of the dogs, a dozen, at least. There teeth were sharp like knives. They foamed at the mouth as madness ceased hold of them.

She was about to turn and run, but her feet were burrowed into the ground. Her eyes stayed fixed ahead, watching the group of men and dogs approaching.

When they were upon her, to her surprise they ran past her, as if they couldn't see her, as if she were invisible. She turned to watch them rush down the other side of the hill and into another patch of field.

Suddenly, the ground below them opened like a mouth of a mammoth sized wild animal. Flames shot up from the crevice; she could see hot red lava below. The group fell into the chasm. The dogs yelped in fear and then pain. The men screamed loudly to the sky, begging to be spared. Then the fissure closed. They were gone.

Shaking violently, Angela woke, her body covered with sweat. She realized it was only a dream, but she could not shake off the feeling of panic. She began running.

Eventually, she stopped to rest. She was completely turned around. Getting a quick look at the sky between the trees, she was able to see the sun, telling her what direction she was going. She turned, starting east.

An hour later, she came to a road. She followed it north. A mile or so up the road, she heard the sound of a wagon coming up from behind her. She hid behind some bushes on the side of the road, waiting for the wagon to pass.

The one-horse wagon moved slowly. Sitting on the buckboard was a lone driver. Angela recognized him, immediately.

"Tom-Tom," Angela shouted, coming out into the open.

"Whoa," said Tom-Tom, pulling back on the reins. "Miss Angela, I never done thought I'd ever see ya again."

"Are ya goin' to town?"

"Sure is, Missy. If ya needs a lift then hop on. Only, ya needs to hide in the back, so if someone comes up the road."

Angela threw her sack onto the farm cart, jumped up and laid in the back. It bothered her to think that for all her traveling she hadn't gone even as far as town. She must have been moving in circles.

Tom-Tom kept his eyes on the road as they spoke. "Sur nuff didn't think I'd ever see ya again, Missy," he repeated. "Ya sure caused a stir, like nothin' I ever seen or heard."

"I guess they're all out looking for me."

"The whole world be lookin' for ya, after what ya did."

Tom-Tom's account confused her. "What ya mean? All I did was run away."

"That be part of it, Missy. But after killing all them folks, the county be out lookin' for ya."

"Killing…! What are ya talking about?" she asked, sitting up.

"Them peoples and them dogs. First off, all the dogs be dead. And all but two of the overseers be dead. One of them be Bunter. Lord knows why he be spared."

The tea she made was more potent than she was led to believe. She'd been used. In her mind's eye, Angela pictured the old woman, Ravenna, laughing at her.

"I didn't mean to kill nobody," Angela pleaded.

"Means to or not, they all dead. When the Abernathys came home in the mornin' and saw what happened, Aamon was mad as hell. When they found out it was poison, Aamon realized the only way to poison them was to put it in their food. So, before anybody could say a word, he killed Agnes. Shot her dead right there in the kitchen, him figurin' she be the one to do the poisonin'. But when they caught wind that ya was gone, they knew different. They got the whole county out looking for ya."

"How's Abby?" Angela asked.

"She fine, but she would have got it next after Agnes, if they hadn't found ya missin' and turnin' the blame on ya."

"Stop the wagon," Angela ordered, taking her sack and jumping off the wagon. "I don't wanna put ya in danger."

"Heck, I don't care."

"I appreciate it, Tom-Tom. Just do me a favor. Don't tell anybody 'bout this for a week or so."

Tom-Tom sat silently, holding the reins. It was all too complicated and confusing for him. He even got teary-eyed. "All right, Missy. I don't say a word. Peace be with ya, child." With that he shook the reins and started off again toward town.

Angela watched till he turned the bend. Throwing her sack over her shoulder, she crossed the road, heading once again deep into the woods.

****

Days later, Angela was lost, still she moved onward. The food in her makeshift sack was gone. She was thankful she no longer carried the burden, but it also meant she was without food. Living on only roots and berries, she remained hungry all the time. There were many streams where she could drink and fill up her canteen. As well, she still clung to her mother's Bible, as if clinging to her mother herself.

Angela avoided any human contact. If she saw a house, a farm or plantation, she took the long way around, keeping her distance. Even going passed a field being worked by black slaves, she feared taking a chance, and would sneak by unseen.

Though she no longer knew what day it was, she knew it had been weeks since her escape. She continued north.

Then one day she heard a noise. It was like no other noise she'd ever heard. It was so loud it shook the air around her and the earth under her feet trembled. The sound repeated again and again.

Coming over a high ridge, she looked down into a valley. There was a long bridge spanning across a river. The booming sound she heard was the thundering of dynamite. Hundreds of men with guns were running in all directions on and off the bridge, dressed in uniforms, some in gray, others in blue. They fired at one another, and then fought hand-to-hand. Many men fell wounded or dying. There was so much bloodshed; the grass on both sides of the bridge was now red. The screams of men suffering filled the air, nearly as loud as the gunfire and explosions. It was a horrible sight.

Angela tightened her arms around her mother's Bible, and began running downstream. She wanted to get as much distance between her and the battle.

She ran till the sound of the gunshots sounded like a storm far off in the distance. Tired and hungry, she collapsed to the ground, leaning against the trunk of a large tree. She took a sip from her canteen, then placing it down. She stretched out flat on the ground, putting her mother's Bible under her head, closing her eyes.

In time, the sounds of the battle stopped. It was at the end of the day when the sun is nearing the horizon with just enough light to still see in the world, enough to barely make out shapes and colors. That was when she heard it. She lifted her head, listening intensely. She heard nothing. Perhaps, it was her imagination? She put her head back down. Then she heard it again. She sat up. She heard it once more and then again. There was no mistaking it. It was the sound of a man's voice, not speaking words, but moaning – moaning as if in pain.

Fearfully and with caution she followed the sound. She came to a large willow tree, its low hanging branches and leaves hid its trunk. She pushed aside the branches, slowly walking forward, like pushing aside a curtain to enter a small dark room. The moaning was loud. Moving toward it, she was close. When her eyes adjusted in the dim light, she looked down. That's when she saw him on the ground at her feet.

Part II

His Story

One

A Blessed Event

The Parker Plantation wasn't the largest or wealthiest in the county, but it was the quintessential Southern Plantation, seeped in tradition. It possessed four hundred acres of the finest soil in the South, twelve overseers, and one hundred and fifty hardworking, healthy slaves. The main house that could be seen from the road was a mansion with its two-stories, fifteen rooms, and four enormous Greek columns out front.

Samuel Parker, third generation owner of the Parker Plantation, could trace his family tree back to the old country, England. His relatives were documented as far back as Henry Parker, well-known secretary to Cromwell and author of many books on religion and politics. Though most of the Parker clan remained in Browsholme Hall in Lancaster, near Clitheroe, a small part of the family (the poorest of the clan) moved to various parts of Scotland to start farms. It is from this offshoot of the Parker family that Arthur Parker, Samuel's grandfather, came from.

Arthur, a young man in his teens, was a discontented farmer who set out on his own for the Americas. There, he became involved in the slave trade from Africa. By the time Arthur was in his thirties, he was a very wealthy man. He met and married a Southern beauty named Aniela Mitchell. Wanting to settle down, Arthur purchased some farming land next to property belonging to Aniela's parents. With his connections in the slave trade supplying cheap labor, the plantation was a success within two years. Though many other neighboring plantations raised tobacco, Arthur had the good foresight to plant cotton.

When Aniela's parents passed on, their land was willed to her, their only child, who turned it over to her husband, Arthur. Converting the connecting Mitchell Plantation to cotton, within ten years, the very wealthy Arthur Parker doubled his capital.

Arthur and Aniela had two children, the oldest a girl they named Pricilla, after Aniela's grandmother. The other child was a boy, Arthur's pride, that they named Travis, not after any family member, but for the French origin of the name. Knowing that one day Travis would inherit the Parker Plantation, and exporting cotton was usually done out of New Orleans' harbor, a French name made good business sense.

Little more is known about the Parker family other than the daughter, Pricilla, married a preacher, the Reverend Melvin Runt. They left for parts unknown, some say out west, and were never heard from again. Aniela Parker died during a flu epidemic. Arthur

Parker died a few years later from complications brought on by heavy drinking. His son and heir, Travis, took over the plantation at the age of twenty-two. He ran it in the same manner his father had taught him. At the age of twenty-five, he married a local girl, Bethany Hilbert whose father ran a slave auction, through which Travis obtained slaves at a very low price. Years later, after the passing of Bethany's parents the company fell into the hands of her brother, Douglas Hilbert, and later his son, Nathanial Hilbert. The association between the Parker and Hilbert families remained constant over the years and generations, supplying the Parker Plantation with slaves at below market prices.

Travis and Bethany had only one child, a son, Samuel. As with his father before him, Travis taught the child everything he knew about running a plantation. When Bethany and finally Travis passed on, Samuel took control of the plantation as smoothly as getting in or out of bed.

Samuel was a handsome cut of a man, with his wavy dark hair, thick, long sideburns framing his strong, square face, and a muscular frame like the depicted warriors in paintings during the Renaissance. His mind was sharp, his decisions well thought out, though sometimes marred by a quick and hot temper.

It was Samuel, who in his fist year as landowner, built the magnificent mansion that now sits on the property. He considered it a wise investment, believing it good for commerce, as it would make him the envy of the county and seemingly a man one would want to do business with. He also supposed it would be a way of attracting the right woman to marry, someone of quality and substance. This later proved to be true. And lastly, though he would never admit it even to himself, it was just a large and grand structure to house his inflated self-worth.

In the ways of a slaveowner, Samuel was deemed a saint by many blacks. Not that any man could own another man and be considered for sainthood, but in his treatment of his slaves. They were well-housed, well-dressed, well-fed, and treated well, or as well any slave could expect to be treated. It wasn't from a merciful heart, but out of good business sense. He'd learned early in life that you can attract more bees with honey than vinegar. Though too much honey is bad for the teeth and digestion, and vinegar is an essential in life's recipe and must be applied to a situation when necessary.

As with all the Parker men before him, for Samuel marriage was a necessity not always rooted in love. There was much to be considered. A candidate for a Parker wife needed to be pleasant to the eye, not only for his own delight, but to outshine others. She should be gracious and elegant in private as well as in public, more importantly, in public. Lastly, and most imperative, was her family background, both in status and in wealth.

Ida Gannon was the perfect candidate, fitting all criteria. She was a willowy beauty with golden hair, porcelain skin, and cobalt eyes as lucid as the skies on a summer's day. Possessing a fine mind, she never spoke before thinking, and would rather not speak if it created friction between speaker and listener. Her manners were without flaw. The head of the Gannon family was Drake Gannon, her father, the president of the County Seat Bank. A mating of the Gannon and Parker families would insure Samuel with loans at low rates, savings at high interest, and insider information on potentially good investments.

Ida and Samuel met at church. Though not a religious man, Samuel was a committed and avid attendee every Sunday. Being a parishioner had its benefits. It kept Samuel in good standing with the community, allowed him business contacts not available to nonchurchgoers, and lastly putting him in contact with all eligible unattached women in the county.

The wedding was an elaborate affair. The ceremony was held at the church to standing room only. The reception was held at the Parker Plantation with anyone of prominence in the county in attendance. Large tents were erected where the guest could mingle, eat, and dance. Everyone agreed the marriage of Ida Gammon and Samuel Parker was a mating of eagles.

****

Three months later, Ida was with child. Samuel was beside himself with joy and anticipation. To have a son meant the world to him. Of course, there was no way to predict it being a boy or a girl, which kept Samuel on edge for the next eight months. He was taking no chances. The entire staff of the main house was at her beck and call. Ida needn't lift a finger. If there was a way he would have convinced Ida to allow the male staff to carry her around, so she would be in no danger of stumbling, he would have made it so. And in one way, he did. He had all their belongings moved from the master bedroom on the second floor to a not-so-large guest bedroom on the ground floor. He forbid her any stair climbing, horseback riding, or buggy rides, which meant no visits to her family and no Sunday church service attendance. Normally, Ida would have protested such treatment, but Samuel would never budge, and she knew it. She made use of these restrictions by using them as the reason for having her family visit the plantation more frequently than usual and by weekly visits from the pariah reverend.

Samuel even went so far as hiring the best doctor in the county, Doctor Jasper Fairchild, with his nurse assistant, Alice Kinsley. Samuel paid them not only for their services but for them to reside in the main house for the duration of the pregnancy, as well as one week after. They put the doctor up in the upstairs master bedroom and the nurse in a smaller adjoining bedroom, the room they planned to be the nursery.

It became the habit that the daily meals, especially the evening suppers, were held in the main dining room with Samuel, Ida, Doctor Fairchild, and Nurse Kinsley in attendance. Much of the dinner conversation circled around Ida's condition and baby care. It was on one particular evening Doctor Fairchild became more open with the exchange, asking a question that seemed proper at the time. He was wrong. He'd unwittingly opened Pandora's Box.

"So, what baby names have the two of you been thinking about?" asked Doctor Fairchild, looking from Ida to Samuel and back again.

Ida smiled; her face lit up with enthusiasm. She placed her fork down, about to announce her thoughts on the matter. Before she could utter a word, Samuel with his head bowed down, staring into his plate, not stopping eating, made his announcement. "Travis...his name will be Travis...after my father...Travis the second," he declared this like a preacher shouting out the commandments. "That's how I see it and nothing will change it." So says the gospel according to Samuel Parker.

The smile left Ida's face; she looked at her husband, her mouth gapping. She and her husband never discussed names for the child. This was a surprise that she didn't see coming.

Fairchild sipped his wine, waiting for the other shoe to fall. Nurse Kinsley, not realizing the depth of the water they were sailing, nor its feverish temperature, posed another question. "That's a boy's name. What if it's a girl?"

Though wanting to speak, Ida looked to her husband, first.

"His name will be Travis," Samuel proclaimed as fact. He looked up from his plate at his wife.

She was just about to throw caution to the wind, but it was Samuel's stare that stopped her. She'd seen that look before. There would be no dialogue. Even the idea that the child might be a female was not opened for discussion.

The quartet went silent. Samuel continued shoveling food from his plate into his mouth. Fairchild nervously filled his glass with wine, swallowing it all in two quick gulps. Nurse Kinsley, finally understanding the gravity of the situation, put her head down, going silent. Unable to stay within the awkwardness of the moment, Ida excused herself.

"If you don't mind, I'm not feeling well. I feel a headache coming on. I'd like to be excused to my room." This was more of a request than a statement directed to Samuel.

"You're excused," Samuel said, as if granting permission to a child.

Ida placed her napkin in the center of her plate. She rose, bowing to her guests. Walking to her downstairs bedroom, she knew what she just escaped. If not for Samuel's concern of the child within her, there would have been hell to pay.

****

When the day of the blessed event neared, Samuel sent word out to all his friends and business associates within the county. They all received an open invitation to celebrate the birth of his son on whatever day that might be.

No one so much as uttered the question of the child being born female. If his wife, Ida, couldn't question it, it was wise to leave well enough alone. Samuel's closest friends always spoke of the child as *him*. Some even went so far as to call the coming child by his name, Travis. Many of Ida's lady friends as well as most of the women in the county, secretly, of course, felt pity for Ida.

All the preparations were made. Barrels of Kentucky Bourbon and Hard Cider from Maine were shipped to the plantation. Two prized Hereford cattle were purchased. The Hereford were kept in a pen away from all the other animals, fed the finest grains to fatten them, to be slaughtered within an hour of the newborn babe's first cries. A pit was dug out behind the main house for smoking the meat to be served as true Southern Barbecue.

It was Doctor Fairchild who made the call. The night had arrived. He and Nurse Kinsley waited at Ida's bedside throughout the night. The entire kitchen staff remained at their post keeping Doctor Fairchild supplied with hot water and clean towels, which he constantly demanded. Samuel withdrew to the house library with two other nearby plantation owners, Dan Owens and Stuart McDonald, Samuel's closest friends and drinking companions. They sampled the new shipment of Kentucky Bourbon, singing and laughing the hours away.

Late in the night, the house remained silent. At the turn of a new day, the clock in the hall chimed twelve times, the silence seeped again through the house. Then, a tiny voice cracked through the quiet like a hammer to an egg's shell.

"Hush," Samuel said to his comrades, placing his index finger vertically across his lips. "Do you hear that?" he whispered.

Again, the child's cry of new life echoed throughout.

"My son...I have a son!" Samuel shouted, tossing his full glass of bourbon in the fireplace. The flames burst over the mantle. Samuel ran out of the room and down the hall toward his wife's bedroom. Just before he was about to open the door, out stepped Nurse Kinsley, closing the door behind her.

"Is it a boy?" was Samuel's only question.

"Yes, it is a boy, but…" she hesitated for a moment. "I'm sorry, Mr. Parker, now is not a good time," she said, blocking the entrance to the door.

The child's crying bleed through the door.

"What do you mean? That's my son in there!" he insisted, trying to push her aside.

She pressed her hands against his chest, she spoke softly but firmly, "Please, Mr. Parker, listen to me. Something's not right. Now's not a good time."

"Nurse Kinsley, I need you!" Doctor Fairchild shouted from inside the room.

She shot a serious look at Samuel. "Stay here."

Opening the door, she slid in, closing the door.

"What goin' on?" a voice asked. Samuel turned to see his two friends, Dan and Stu.

Samuel was angry, "They won't let me in." Still drunk, his anger quickly turned to rage. He pounded on the door. "Hey, let me in or I swear I'll kick this door in!"

There was no answer from the room.

Samuel made a fist and began to punch the door again and again. Finally, the door opened. Doctor Fairchild stood before them, looking worn and tired.

"I'm sorry, Mr. Parker. We did all we could." Fairchild murmured.

"What are you saying? Is my boy all right?"

"It's not your son I'm talking about. It's your wife. She died giving him life. We did what we could, but it was not in our hands."

Pushing Fairchild aside, Samuel rushed into the room. He looked around. On the bed was his wife, motionless and pale. At the foot of the bed was a bassinet. He stepped forward, looking down at the child.

He turned to Fairchild," Is he all right?"

"He's fine, sir."

A smile grew on Samuel's face. He picked up the child, holding him close. "My son…my boy," he chanted, clutching the child in his arms. "Welcome to the world, Travis. Everything I have is yours."

Fairchild moved closer to get Samuel's attention. "I'm sorry about your wife, sir. I hate to bring this up, but I must. Yes, your son is fine, but he's going to be hungry soon. We need to secure a wet nurse for him, soon."

"Yes, of course," Samuel replied, never letting go of the child or taking his gaze off him. Samuel walked out of the room, still holding Travis. He showed the bundle to his two friends. "See, boys, this is my boy. Travis, these are my good friends, Dan and Stu."

"Sorry about Ida, Samuel," said Dan. "I guess we best be goin' on home."

Finally taking his eyes off his son, he smiled at Dan and Stu. "Go home, what are you talking about? I promised this county that when my son was born I was going to throw a fete like they never seen before. I want you boys to ride out to town and all the local farms. Tell them to be here this evening. Tell them to bring dry throats and empty stomachs."

"What about Ida?" Stu asked.

"Yeah, that is a shame," Samuel said. "We'll have a funeral and a burial in a couple of days. But a promise is a promise. You boys, do me that favor."

"Sure 'nough," said Dan, the smile returning to his face. The two men dashed off, out of the house, to the barn. In no time, they were galloping away on horseback, hooping and a hollering.

"You need to put the child back down," Fairchild gently warned, pointing to the bassinet.

Reluctantly, Samuel placed his son down. He turned, ran out of the room and out of the house. He kicked the door of a small shack.

"Who the hell is it?" an angry voice shouted from within.

"It's me! Open up and get out here, you old mule skinner."

The door opened, Sherman the head overseer, a tall lean man with a long dark beard and a balding head stood in his long johns. "I'm sorry 'bout that, Mr. Parker. How can I help ya?"

"My son's been born."

"Congratulation, sir."

"Listen, Sherman, you need to do everything I told you about. I want those two Herefords slathered, butchered, and cooking over a slow pit by this afternoon. Also get the kitchen folk making all the fixings. And tap those kegs and get them set up."

"Yes, sir, right away," Sherman replied, standing at attention like a soldier, looking foolish in his long johns.

Samuel turned, walking toward the main house. He stopped, looking back. "Oh, Sherman, there's two other things I need you to do. Have some of the boys go around back of the main house and dig a grave."

"A grave, sir?" asked Sherman, a little confused.

"Yeah, a grave, but not too close to the house, you understand?"

"Yes, sir, I understand, right away, sir."

"Most of all, I want you to find me a wet nurse, and bring her to me within the hour."

"Did ya say wet nurse, sir?" Sherman questioned, no longer a little confused, but very much so.

"That's right. My wife will not be nursing my newborn son," Samuel announced, not wanting to go into a full explanation just then. "My son will be hungry soon. Bring me a wet nurse."

"Mr. Parker, sir, only wet nurse on this here plantation is goin' to be a slave girl, a darkie."

"I don't care. My son's going to be hungry very soon. Milk is milk. I don't care if her skin is black, as long as her milk is white. You understand, Sherman?"

"Yes, sir, Mr. Parker, right away, sir."

Two

The Bonding

To everything there is a season, and a time for every purpose under heaven. A time to weep, and a time to laugh; a time to mourn, and a time to dance…for Pamela it was a time of tears.

Born a slave on the Parker Plantation, now at the tender age of seventeen, Pamela saw no light in her life and no future worth living. Her only thought was to go down to the river and throw herself in.

It should have been a love story, not a story of woe. Love was the reason, love was the answer, but love can be cruel.

Pamela lived in a one-room shack with her parents. As far back as she could remember, she worked on the plantation with the other slaves. There was little joy in her life till William. Of all the young black men on the plantation, he had shone brightly above the rest. William was tall, strong, and handsome, with a winning smile that melted hearts.

Pamela, on the other hand, at sixteen was just coming into womanhood. She was lanky and awkward, with much of the child look about her. She could never seem to get her hair manageable, no matter how she tried. She was darker than most, a sign of true African beauty. She couldn't help noticing the slave girls with lighter skin got more of the attention.

For this reason and other insecurities a young black girl may have at sixteen, Pamela felt sure she would never be attractive enough to men, least of all William. That's why it confused Pamela when William started to show interest in her. She was sure he was just playing with her – an unkind thing to do. When his advances became frequent and clear, she was at his beck and call. She followed him around like a starving puppy. She would have done anything for him.

In the evenings, the couple went for walks, hand in hand, sneaking into the shadows now and then to steal a kiss. Pamela had fallen head over heels in love. For her, the relationship grew deeper and more serious with each passing day. It was not so for William. It is interesting how two people can look at the exact same thing and have two completely different views. For William, this was just a moment in time like so many other moments with other women. Pamela hoped to be the one in William's life; sadly she was only one of many.

The night she confronted him about her situation, she hoped it would please him, and they would soon marry.

"What makes ya think it's mine?" he asked, wearing a wide smile.

"Why would ya ask that? Ya know I ain't been with nobody else," she responded, sounding shocked by his question.

"It's my word against yours. I just ain't ready for this," was his answer. His smile left his face, as he began to walk away.

"William…?" she pleaded, but it did no good.

She learned the hard way that it truly was her word against his. All he needed was to deny her accusations, and walk away. Meanwhile, she was in the family way with no one on her side or there to help. Her parents disowned her, kicking her out of their home. Pamela was forced to live in the communal barn that was set up for single folks without family. Her girlfriends were commanded by their parents to have nothing to do with her – a marked woman. No midwife would so much as speak to her in her hour of need. The entire slave community of the Parker Plantation would have nothing to do with her. That is except for some of the young men who now saw her in a new light – a dim light.

The next few months were hard on Pamela. The overseers didn't pay any mind to her condition. She was still expected to work a full day, giving her all. Without the help of a midwife, she had no idea if all was well or not.

Some call it coincidence, others call it fate. The same night the mistress of the manor went into labor, so did a young slave girl. Both went through the same experience with different results, yet both ending in tragedy.

The night of the delivery, there was moaning in the corner of the community barn. When the moans turned to cries of pain, some of the women took pity on her and did what they could to help her, which was little.

For hours, she wriggled in pain. Her body burned with fever and covered with sweat. Finally, the time came, but there were no sounds of life.

"It be born dead, dear," one of the women said softly.

Pamela reached out. "Let me see!"

"No, child, ya don't need to be seein' such things," another woman announced. "Ya just rest. We be takin' care of it, for ya."

Inwardly, Pamela wanted to do something – anything, but she was still in pain and too exhausted to do or say anything. They never even told her if it was a boy or a girl.

****

Two births on the same night, Sherman couldn't believe his good fortune. His boss told him to get a wet nurse within the hour, and he was about to deliver. Surely, this would be a feather in his cap.

Sherman heard from one of the other overseers about what happened the night before to one of the slave girls. He found Pamela in the corner of the community barn. Still in shock, she stared into the nothingness before her.

"Get up, girl, ya got work to do," Sherman laughed, helping Pamela to her feet. Others in the barn watched, saying nothing, not getting involved. Sherman guided Pamela out and up to the main house. She moved as if in a dream, all around her a distant blur of movement. He took her in through the kitchen door in the back of the house. Walking through the house, as they past the staircase, they heard young Travis crying from his nursery on the second floor. Sherman paid little to no attention, where as a baby's cry, grabbed at Pamela's soul. She looked up the staircase, wondering, was it her child calling for her from heaven. She feared not.

Sherman guided her to the home library. He figured Samuel would probably be celebrating with a bottle of bourbon. He was right.

"Sorry to bother ya, sir," Sherman said coyly as they entered the room. "I brought ya the girl ya asked for."

Samuel looked at them through a drunken haze. "...girl, what girl? I didn't ask for any girl. And if I did, I wouldn't want one that scrawny."

"No, sir, she ain't that type girl. She's the wet nurse ya wanted."

With the door of the library open, they could hear the child crying from upstairs. Samuel walked across the room. Standing in the doorway, he looked up the staircase. "Yes, he is hungry. Send her up to feed him this instant."

"Yes, sir," Sherman responded, taking hold of Pamela, leading her out of the room.

As they past by Samuel, he stopped them. He spoke to Sherman, as he gave Pamela the once over. "When she's done feeding my son, there's a small room next to the nursery, I want her staying in it. She's to see to my son at anytime, any hour." He moved in closer to Pamela, taking a whiff of her. "He needs feeding right now. But before she moves into her room, I want her cleaned, scrubbed, and in fresh clothes. Now, go!"

Sherman grabbed Pamela by her wrist, pulling her quickly up the stairs. It wasn't difficult to find the nursery. All they need do was follow the child's cries.

Finding the child in a bassinet, swaddled in a blue blanket, they both stood looking down at him.

Michael Edwin Q.

"Well, I guess ya can take it from here. Ya don't need me. When ya done, come on out that door. I'll be waiting for ya," Sherman said, sounding a bit embarrassed as he walked out of the room, shutting the door behind him.

Pamela looked around the room. It was finer than anything she'd ever imagined. Travis started crying, again. Her gaze was drawn to him.

She looked down on this perfect newborn child with his fine dark hair, blue eyes, and cream colored skin, though his face grew red as he fussed over his hunger.

"Why are ya alive, child?" she asked. The sound of her voice taking the child by surprise; he stopped crying. "Why are ya alive, child?" she repeated. "My baby was born tonight, too. But it's gone...dead. Why are ya alive, child?"

She thought of the unfairness of life. For just a moment, she thought of smothering the child with a pillow. Perhaps then there would be fairness and justice in the world. Then the child cried out again in hunger.

"Don't cry, baby, it's gonna be all right," she whispered, taking him up in her arms. In that instant, Travis stopped crying.

There was a rocking chair in the corner of the room. She walked over and sat down. She unbuttoned, and put the child to her breast. The child suckled loudly. Pamela looked to the ceiling, weeping deep tears of great sorrow. "Oh, Lord, oh, Lord," she cried out.

In that moment, a bond was formed between the child who had no mother and the mother who had no child.

Three

Pound Cake

It was a lonely life for Pamela, disconnected from any of the other workers on the plantation, including the house staff. Still, she wasn't mistreated, far from it. Her room was clean and comfortable. Her clothing was well-made and new. The food they offered was plentiful and nutritious.

Pamela became more than just a wet nurse to Travis, she became his caregiver. Each day, Samuel visited his son, more to gloat over him than anything else. But it was Pamela who spent the most time with him, keeping him fed, clean, and happy. Not only was it an easy post, but a joyous one for Pamela, and in time, done with love.

A few months later, Travis began eating soft foods as well as being nursed. It was clear when the boy turned one it was time for him to be weaned. At that point, it was discussed that Pamela return to the core slave population. It was also obvious and understandable the connection between child and nurse was a deep connection. Travis was never as content, calm, or obedient with anyone other than Pamela, including the boy's father. So, it was decided Pamela would stay on, no longer a wet nurse but as a nanny, or as those in the South termed it – mammy. From then on, she would be known as Mammy Pam.

It's true you cannot spoil a small child; a pound of feathers is as much interest to them (if not more) as a pound of gold. Once Travis began to comprehend what he liked and what he didn't, that was when Samuel began indulging him. This upset the house staff. Spare the rod and spoil the child was well understood by slaves. They'd seen it before. When the master of the house turns the world on its head to pander to his son and heir that child will grow to be far worse than the father. It would seem Travis was destined to be a monster, both as a child as well as a man.

As a young boy, Travis terrorized the house staff. He pushed people out of his way; food not to his liking was tossed to the floor; every object was a weapon and could be thrown at anyone or anything at anytime. It all depended on the child's mood, which most often was foul. There was no reason to hide his behavior from his father who not only turned a blind eye to it but seemly encouraged such conduct. Strangely enough though, Travis never acted in such a manner in the presence of Pamela. For whatever reason, perhaps he didn't want to displease his mammy. Meaning he instinctively knew right from wrong, but no one gave him any boundaries. When Pamela learned what the boy was doing behind her back, she was determined to set the boy right. She had a plan. She carried it out in secret, away from others, especially Samuel.

Whenever Travis was eating alone, Pamela would quickly walk past, pushing his food off the table and onto the floor. The child never cried, he would look down staring at the splattered food. The first time Pamela did this, she feared Travis would tell his father, and there'd be hell to pay. But he didn't. Even at a young age, the boy knew Pamela would be punished. She was the one person he really cared for and respected. She was the one person who meant anything to him. He would do nothing to hurt her or shatter the bond between them.

There were times Pamela tossed something across the room at him, a book or a candle. Or course, it was only when the two were alone. Never did the article come close enough to harm him. It was the loud sound and the violence of the action that startled him. He was not a stupid child, he knew that Pamela was reenacting his tantrums and selfish actions, but to what end.

The last part of Pamela's plan was harsh, but went straight to the point. One afternoon, Travis was alone in his room, sitting on the floor, playing with tin soldiers. Pamela walked in the room, took a handful of the toy soldiers and tossed them out the window. Travis ran to the window, looking down to see his toys spread on the grass. He turned to Pamela, just staring, a large question mark on his face.

Pamela got down on one knee to be at eyelevel with him. "Ya don't like it, do ya? It don't feel good, do it?" She reached out for him and held his arms with caring. "There are things in everybody, called feelings. Everybody got the same feelings, some got more than others, but they all got the same kind. What hurts ya, hurts other folk the same way. It'd be a better world if everybody remembered the other folk's feelings. Now, I know ya to be a smart and good boy. Ya don't wanna be bad, do ya?"

Travis shook his head in shame. Pamela pulled him in close, hugging him. "I love ya, boy, very much." She whispered in his ear, "Come on, let's go outside and find your soldiers."

****

When Travis turned eight, his world changed. It became bigger. Three years earlier, his father had hired a series of local school teachers to tutor him. Being an intelligent child, he learned well and fast. At eight years old, his father enrolled him at the local school in town, believing the boy needed the company of others his own age, to learn to interact. As well, at the age of eight, Samuel kept Travis at his side whenever possible. The boy was either at school or with his father. Samuel's plan was to see his son grow to be a strong and wise man that would someday inherit and run the finest plantation in the county.

Each day one of the overseers drove Travis by carriage to school in the town. At first, it was difficult for the boy. He was an outsider. The other children made sure he felt it as well as knew it.

It was somewhat understandable. The other students began school much younger. They all grew up together. Being schooled at home, Travis was trying to enter a fraternity that took years to form. They had their own ways and rules that none of them felt obligated to share with him. It would be a slow process of trial and error. As well, though many of the children came from wealthy families and plantations, they all heard how the Parkers were far more affluent then they. If they were born with silver spoons in their mouths, Travis' spoon was gold. They saw this new boy being driven to school each morning. His lunch was brought to him fresh and hot by a white man on horseback, and they watched him being driven in a carriage back home at the end of the day. This caused an air of jealousy in the classroom.

To make matters worse, Travis' school knowledge far surpassed his classmates. The home tutoring advanced him beyond the others. The once blessing was now a curse.

"I don't want to go back to school," Travis announced to his father, one night over dinner.

"Why not?" his father asked, knowing that would never happen, but he was interested enough to want to hear the answer.

"The other children don't like me."

"I see," Samuel said, he stopped eating to think long and hard. Instead of giving his son sympathy and or advice, he gave him his own view of the world. "They're all a bunch of losers. Don't worry; someday most of them will be working for you."

Nothing else was said. Samuel returned to his meal, as did Travis. The boy thought about what his father said, not understanding it fully or thinking it of any use.

Before bedtime, Pamela cornered the boy, bringing him into the kitchen. They were alone. Travis was confused, but he always trusted her. So, he silently listened to her instructions.

"We gonna make a Pound Cake," Pamela announced.

Though the prospect of cooking one of his favorite deserts excited the boy, he remained confused. Why a pound cake and why now in the middle of the night?

"Do ya know why they calls it a Pound Cake?" she asked.

Travis shook his head.

"They calls it a Pound Cake 'cause ya needs a pound of everything to make it, a pound of butter, a pound of flour, a pound of sugar, and a whole mess of eggs."

She placed all the ingredients into a bowl, mixing them well. After greasing a deep pan, she poured the batter into the pan, and then put the pan into the oven. They sat at the table waiting."

"Mammy Pam, why are we doing this?" Travis asked.

"Why, don't ya like my Pound Cake?"

"I do, but why are we cooking one at night?"

"'Cause ya goin' to take it to school tomorrow."

Travis thought about it. He realized Pamela had a plan, but he couldn't understand what it was. "Am I supposed to give out Pound Cake to the other children, so they'll like me?"

"No, child," then she thought about what she just said, "Not really. Ya gonna take this here cake and eat it in front of everyone. If anyone looks at ya with their mouth open, like they wants some, offer 'em a slice. Once they starts eatin', ya ask who they is and what they likes."

After the cake cooled, Pamela cut it into small slices, and then putting the slices into a makeshift bag made of parchment.

"Take this up to ya room, but don't eat none till tomorrow."

Travis found it difficult to sleep that night. The temptation to sample one of the slices tormented him. But trusting his mammy, he did what he was told.

The next day, Travis waited till lunch break. He sat in the schoolyard alone, as he'd done many times before, all the other children ignoring him. It was when he started eating a slice of Pound Cake did he get any attention.

"Is that there Pound Cake?" asked a small boy, standing before Travis, looking forlorn.

"Sure is! Would you like a slice?" Travis asked, offering a slice.

The boy snatched it as fast as a chicken pecks, pushing half into his mouth.

"What's your name?" Travis asked.

"Toby," the boy replied through a full mouth. "You're Travis, ain't ya?"

And so it went. One by one, children came to Travis. Once he gave them a slice and asked their names, everything seemed to fall into place. All was going smoothly until Travis looked up to see four of the larger boys standing before him.

"Give us the cake," the largest boy and leader demanded.

"Why?" Travis asked, sounding confident.

"'Cause if ya don't, we're gonna break your head."

Thinking fast, he wondered what Pamela's advice would be. She'd not considered a negative. Then he remembered the advice from his father.

"I'm sure you could," Travis said. "But I won't give up without a fight. I'll lose, but I'll put some hurt on you, first. And before I start to fight, I'd sooner stomp on this cake before you get a bite. So, I'll be hurting, and you'll be hurting, and no body will be eating cake."

The leader looked carefully at Travis, trying to figure it all out.

"There is a way we can all have cake?" Travis proposed. The boys waited for the answer. "I can give you each a slice, if you just ask for it."

The leader thought about it for a long time. It made sense, but it didn't quite sit well with him. He looked at the slice of cake Travis offered, his mouth watered.

"Can I have a slice?" the leader asked in a calm manner.

Travis handed him a slice. "So, what's your name?"

****

It had been a good day for Travis. He was now well on his way to fitting in at school and making new friends. But it was a confusing day, as well. Though he loved and respected both his father and his mammy, he was aware, even at his young age, how different they were, mostly in their approach to life.

There were times he tended to believe his mammy over his father. Pamela was far gentler than his father, always willing to listen before she gave her advice. Though he hated to admit it, he was much more comfortable with Pamela than with his father. In fact, he was more comfortable with Pamela than anyone.

Travis feared his father, but not in a bad way. He feared him like one should fear fire, with respect. The good things about fire: it warms you, it cooks your food, and it gives you light. His father offered many good things, but like fire, if not used wisely it could destroy you.

Often, the advice he received from Pamela and his father differed. He was never sure which advise to take. Here was a truly deep dilemma. During the same situation, he'd followed the advice of both his mammy and his father, and gotten good results.

When he told Pamela the outcome of her Pound Cake plan, she smiled, hugged him, telling him how proud she was of him. When he told her about the bullyboys in the schoolyard, she looked worried as she listened, and then relieved with the results.

"That's usein' your head," she proudly said to him.

When he told the story to his father, Samuel congratulated him on his handling of the bullyboys, telling him how proud he was of his son. As to the part about sharing slices of

Pound Cake, his father was less impressed, though he did comment, "You are a good-hearted lad, in deed."

That's when it all became clear to Travis. It dawned on him like a bolt of lightning. There was no reason to place the advice of either his mammy or father above the other. Sure, they were different; but now he understood how they differed.

Pamela would be his heart, and his father would be his head. Heart and head, neither one more important than the other, both are needed. But all in all, the last say would always be his. This would have been quite a revelation to anyone at any age. To learn it at such a young age was a blessing.

Four

Tears and Ashes

Travis' life was the life of a prince. He wanted for nothing. Horses, guns, clothes…nothing was denied him. Yet despite it all, he was a good lad, a bit mischievous but what boy of eleven isn't'?

He was well-liked by all his schoolmates, though he was especially close to some of the boys his age. There was Toby, the first boy Travis made friends with. Gunter, the bully Travis met the same day as Toby, along with Gunter's mates, Mark, Stanley, and Richard. All of them came from wealthy families. Their fathers knew and did business with one another. When they weren't attending school or working with their fathers, they would meet to go fishing, hunting, or swimming. They became a brotherhood of five. They had their own secret handshake, code words, and whistle calls. In school, they were given a summer assignment to read *The Three Musketeers*. This seeded a strong need for the thrill of adventure. In secret, they would use makeshift swords of sticks, fighting duels; the winner would declare he was *d'Artagnan*. They became more roguish from that summer on, committing misdemeanors none of them would dare alone.

The relationship between father and son continued as it had for years. Samuel was the wizard and Travis was his apprentice. All communication was nothing more than Samuel instructing Travis on life as a man of pride and family honor, on running a plantation, and not much else. Any communication on life's problems, heartbreaks, and confusion, Travis brought to Pamela, who not only gave good advice but was a good listener.

For this reason, it shocked Travis when his father took the boy into his confidence. It was a sunny day; the two went horseback riding, just for the shear fun of it. Stopping at the top of a hill, they looked down on their plantation.

"Do you miss your mother?" Then Samuel corrected himself. "What a silly question. Of course, you don't. You never knew her. What I mean is, do you miss having a mother?"

Travis thought about it for a moment. "I don't think so. I suppose I don't know what it is I'm missing out on."

"Would you like to have a mother?"

Travis just looked at his father, wondering what was coming next.

"I've asked one of the women at church to marry me. She said, 'Yes'."

"Do I know her?" Travis asked.

"She's in the choir. She's tall with dark hair, kind of pretty."

"Is she the one with the high voice?"

"Yeah, that's her. What do you think?"

The problem was Travis didn't know what to think. Not knowing how to respond, he asked "When's the wedding?"

"In a week," Samuel responded.

Travis thought it strange that his father would ask how he felt about it when everything was already planned.

Samuel sat up in his saddle, waving his right arm across the view below. "Don't worry, son, one day this will all be yours. Wife or no wife, when I die, she'll be taken care of, but this will all be yours." He turned to look at his son. "So, what do you say? I think it will be good for you, finally having a mother."

"I can hardly wait," Travis said, unsure of the statement, but not wanting to disappoint his father.

****

The day of the wedding was sunny and warm. Samuel made all the arrangements to have the ceremony at the plantation. An arch covered in white roses served as the altar. Rows of tables filled with food and drink for the guests. One long table for deserts – mostly baked goods. The kitchen staff worked for three days, getting everything perfect. As well, barrels of bourbon and hard cider stood ready and tapped.

Everyone who was anybody in the county was invited. They slowly started pouring onto the plantation an hour early, dressed in their best clothes and bearing gifts for the newlyweds. No one turned down the invitation. There were all of Samuel's friends, business associates, and even one or two enemies he was still on speaking terms with. It was best to go, and not get on Samuel's bad side.

Travis dressed in his finest clothes as did his father. They went down to the garden in the back of the main house where the ceremony would be held. All the guests were assembled. Reverend Pike from the local church stood in the center of the arbor. Samuel took his place before the minister. Then the sound of horse hoofs echoed in the distance. A one-horse carriage slowly came from the edge of the plantation all the way to the ceremony site, stopping a few feet from the nervous groom. Samuel watched; his smile larger than Travis ever saw it.

Belial Thompson, soon to be Belial Parker, stepped out of the carriage, taking her place next to Samuel. He took her hand. The couple smiled a lover's smile to each other. It was in that instant Travis recognized her.

She was a dark-haired, middle-aged woman, slender and tall, perhaps as tall as Samuel. She wore a white flowing gown. Her hair was done up high with tiny *Baby's Breath* woven into her locks. Travis didn't think her a very attractive woman. If she made his father happy, he was for her.

It was the prospect of having a mother for the first time in his life that swayed him. For the first time since knowing of his father's wedding plans, he was excited. He wanted so much to connect with this woman, to make her his mother. He'd do whatever it took to make her like him. Once they were bonded as mother and child he would love her and dedicate himself to her for the rest of his life.

Reverend Pike, known for his elegance, preformed a ceremony that brought tears to the eyes and smiles to the faces of all. When he pronounced Belial and Samuel man and wife, Samuel kissed his bride. Cheers filled the air. Those who carried pistols shot them in the air. It was an exciting moment, and no one was more excited than Travis.

The celebration was grand. Folks drank and ate, sang, danced into the night. Travis and his mates ran through the crowd sampling everything offered. When the sun set, the house slaves lit torches all around, giving light so the party could continue late into the night. It was then Travis finally got a chance to speak to his father.

"Congratulations, father," Travis said, offering his hand.

"A handshake?" his father questioned. "Come here," Samuel said throwing his arms around his son. They both laughed. Samuel looked deep into Travis' eyes. "How does it feel to finally have a mother?"

"It's good...it's good," Travis said, not knowing for sure, but thinking it the appropriate response.

"She's a wonderful woman," Samuel continued. "I want you both to get along and be happy."

"Where is Belial? We haven't spoken. I'd like to welcome her and congratulate her."

Samuel was pleased to hear such talk. "She's gone back to the house for a moment. She wanted to take those silly flowers out of her hair," he said with a laugh.

"May I go and speak with her, father?"

"Yes...yes...I think that would be just the thing. She'd like that."

So, with his father's permission and blessing, Travis ran back to the main house. He rushed up the stairs to what was his father's bedroom, and would now be his parent's bedroom. He rapped gently on the door.

"Who is it?" Belial called out from within.

"Travis, ma'am, I'd like to talk with you."

"And I with you, come in, Travis."

Travis found her standing in front of a mirror in the last stage of taking the Baby's Breath from her hair. She turned, looking at him with a vacant stare.

Travis' heart was beating as fast as his mind was racing. He wanted to make a good first impression. He decided to not hold anything back, saying what was on his mind.

"I want to congratulate you and welcome you to the family. I promise I'll do everything I can to be a good son, mother."

He stood for a long time waiting for her response. She continued staring without expression. Finally, she took a step toward him.

"Listen, you spoiled little brat. Let's get everything crystal clear. I'm not your mother, and wouldn't want to be. I married your father, not you. We may have to live under the same roof, but that doesn't mean anything. Just stay out of my way, and we'll get along fine."

Travis' mind went blank. He felt a need to say something, but nothing came out.

"You may leave, now," Belial ordered.

In a daze, Travis turned, leaving the room.

"Shut the door, please," Belial said coldly.

Not wanting to face the woman, without turning, Travis reached behind, closing the door.

Travis' heart was shattered. He needed someone to talk to. Returning to the party, he sought out his father. He found him drunk with his friends. Any effort to talk with his father would be useless.

Drunk! Perhaps, that was the answer? Travis found a tall, empty drinking mug. He moved around the outskirts of the men drinking with his father. Whenever he was sure none of them were watching, not that it mattered, they were so far gone; he'd pour a sip from their mugs into his. Not too much that it would be noticed; but in a short time he held a full mug of bourbon, nearly up to the brim.

Moving slowly through the crowd as not to spill a drop, he found his mates by the barn.

"Open the barn door," Travis said. Toby was the first to move, pulling open the barn door. Travis entered.

"What'cha got there?" Gunter asked, following Travis, the others followed Gunter.

It was dark inside the barn. Slivers of light cut through the slits in the slates of wood, just enough light to make out shapes.

Stanley lit a match, holding it up against the darkness.

"There's a lantern by that stall. Light it," Travis ordered.

When the lantern was lit, the entire barn was bathed in a dull yellow light. Their shadows danced across the floor, walls, and ceiling

Again, Gunter asked, "What'cha got there?" as he pointed his chin at the mug in Travis' hand.

Travis' eyes went wide, the whites of his eyes glowing, reflecting the lantern's flame. "It's bourbon," Travis said in a grave whisper. He put the mug to his lips, taking a deep, long swallow. It burned going down, but he did his best to hide his distain for the burned woody taste. In turn, each boy took a long drink from the mug. As with Travis, they hid their loathing of the liquid. Only Toby gave his honest opinion.

"That's terrible! It tastes like kerosene."

"How would ya know?" Mark laughed. "When did ya every taste kerosene?

They all laughed.

After making three more passes, the mug was still half-full.

"Ain't so harsh after the second and third sip," Richard commented. They all nodded in agreement.

Standing became uncomfortable; as well, their footing was becoming unsure. So, they sat down on the ground using hay for cushions. They continued passing the drink around. The last thing Travis remembered was looking down into the mug and seeing only a sip left.

Suddenly, Travis woke with a jolt. He felt strong hands and arms carrying him. Looking up, he saw the ceiling of the barn. Shadows danced on its surface, mixed with the yellow-orange glow of flames. Outside the barn, the men placed him down. Travis could barely stand. His mates were there, next to him, all of them lying on the ground.

"Their fine," someone said, "just dead drunk."

Travis looked to the barn. Flames danced along the outer walls. Rows of black slaves and white men relayed buckets of water, throwing them on the flames. It was useless. Finally, using shovels they dug a trench around the barn to keep the fire contained. Everyone stood watching it burn to the ground.

The crowd standing around Travis parted. Samuel with eyes blazing marched up to him.

"Father…" was all Travis could say as he stood before his father. Samuel swung his fists at him. Blow after blow hit him till he fell to the ground. Still, his father pounded him, mercilessly.

"That's enough, Sam. He's just a boy," said one the men trying to hold Samuel back. But he continued punching Travis.

"On my wedding day….on my wedding day," Samuel shouted over and over between each blow.

When some of the men finally contained Samuel, Travis struggled to his feet, starting for the main house. Looking back, he saw the fire dwindled to red ambers. He ran upstairs to his room. Still in his clothes, he fell facedown on his bed, burying his face in the pillow.

Long gone were the effects of the bourbon. His thoughts were clear, but his mind was crammed with too many of them. Nothing went right that day. Between his confrontation with Belial and her rejection of him, getting drunk and burning down the barn, letting down his father, it was the worse day of his life.

Try as hard as he could not to, he began to cry, sobbing deeply into his pillow. His body quivered, his pillow was sopping with tears in just a few minutes. Just when all felt hopeless and he hadn't a friend in the world, he felt a loving hand move across his back. He didn't have to look up. He knew that touch. It was Pamela.

He felt so ashamed, crying like a baby, but he couldn't stop. However, he also knew that his Mammy Pam would be the only person in his life who would not judge him. She spoke softly over him.

"There, there, never ya mind, child, never ya mind."

Five

Questions

Travis lived a solitary life on the plantation. In his teens, long after the memory of his father's wedding day had diminished, a dark cloud still hung over him. His connection with his stepmother was a sour and distant one. She warned him to stay out of her way, or there would be trouble. True to her word, there was no trouble between them. They lived within the same space, but they didn't live with each other. As for his relationship with his father, which was never close or warm, it remained as bitter cold as a business association between two strangers who had no other choice than to meet and discuss relevant topics.

The only close and lasting bonds in his life were between him and his schoolmates and, of course, his Mammy Pam. As close as he was with his mates, their relationships remained only skin deep, never going into the muscle of the matter, fearing showing weakness. Besides, graduation was nearing; Travis planned to go to university far from home and friends. As for his Mammy Pam, just as being overly close with boys your own age was considered weakness, being overly close with a black woman would be looked on as foolishness. Travis trusted and loved Mammy Pam, but there was a bridge separating whites and blacks, neither one was allowed to cross. The word *Allowed* being a poor narrative; the word *Forbidden* being the true and clear description.

His father's instructions as to how to properly run a plantation was a daily ritual. Travis knew all about cotton growing, as well as its sales, shipping, and storage. He understood how to hire and fire overseers, what to expect from them, and how to handle them. Animal care was a top priority. Not to mention the upkeep of farm equipment and running the main house like a smooth sailing vessel. All this was passed on from father to son. Only one subject remained a mystery to Travis: the buying, selling, and keeping of slaves. Samuel purposely held back this part of Travis' education till last, as he felt it the most important. He was determined to enlighten Travis on such matters before he left for university. The two walked down to the property set aside for slave quarters.

"What do you see?" Samuel asked his son.

Travis thought for a moment. He wanted to be precise in his observation, to avoid being teased and ridiculed by his father. Encouragement was never a part of Samuel's teaching, but mockery was.

"I see rows of rundown, one-room, shacks. I see vegetable gardens. I see a well in the center of the quarters."

Samuel made it sound like a dare, "Go on; what else do you see?"

"I see black folks, slaves, walking about, men, women, and some children."

"Can they see us?" Samuel asked.

"Of course, they can," Travis answered, thinking the question strange.

"Can they?" Samuel replied. "Not one of them has looked our way. How can they see us, if they don't look at us?"

Travis realized the truth of the statement. Every slave looked to the ground as they walked by. Within the next two minutes, the area was deserted. Every slave retired to their home. Travis and his father stood alone.

"Not one of them raised their head to look at us. They've all scattered back to their houses," Samuel observed. "Why?" he said, strongly, demanded an answer of Travis.

Again, Travis was torn. If he didn't answer, his father would chastise him. If his answer was wrong, he'd belittle him. Finally, Travis decided to take a stab at it. A wrong answer was better than no answer.

"Respect…?" Travis answered, his tone sounding more like a question.

Samuel continued staring forward, not at his son, and smiled. "I knew a boy who respected his father, but he still burned down his father's barn."

This took Travis by surprise. The barn burning incident hadn't been mentioned in years. This was far worse than chastisement or belittlement, it was derogation.

Samuel continued, "No, they don't act this way or do what they're told out of respect." Samuel waited in a moment of silence, wanting to be sure every word sunk into his son's mind. "Fear…! Fear is what makes them do what they're told, to act right, and keep in their place. Fear is the only weapon you have. Don't be fooled; these people are animals. Let down your guard for just a moment, they will turn on you like a pack of wild dogs. Just like dogs, they can smell fear, so don't ever fear them. Always make sure they fear you, and you'll never have any trouble with them. At the first sign of trouble you must snuff it out like a fire that will burn you if you don't. Punish them severely, if necessary. Kill them if need be, if not only for you and the family's good name, but for them, as well."

This last statement confused Travis. How was it for their good?

Samuel ignored his son's bewildered look. He continued, "If you are to be the master, you keep the animals in fear. Once that fear takes hold, the animal is tamed. You must treat a tamed animal with a gentle hand, only raising it when they disobey. You must always give them a little, so they remain hopeful. Take away their hope, and they will turn on you at any cost, even their own lives. Do you understand?"

Travis just nodded.

"Good! Now, let's get back to the house, it's near suppertime."

As they silently walked back to the main house, Travis was more perplexed than ever. He considered what his father told him. What about Pamela, what about Mammy Pam? She did so much for him over the years. Certainly, she didn't do it all out of fear. Mammy Pam feared no one, least of all him. It made no sense. Was Mammy Pam the exception? Was his father wrong? Travis needed to find out.

Six

Flapdoodle

It was the end of spring of the last year of their schooldays. For Travis and his mates, this would be their last summer together. They promised themselves it would be a memorable one, starting with the night of their graduation.

They all met at Gunter's family's plantation. Though not as large as the Parker Plantation, it was sizable. Gunter took them behind the main barn. Reached down into some high weeds, pulling up a bottle of whiskey he'd hid there.

"It's my father's," Gunter remarked. "He has so many he won't even know it's missing."

"Didn't any of ya learn from the last time we did this?" Toby questioned, rolling his eyes and shaking his head.

"Don't be such an old maid," Richard remarked.

Toby continued, "Oh yeah, this time we can burn Gunter's father's barn down."

Gunter opened the bottle, taking a long pull, and then looking to Toby, "Listen, no one said ya have to drink. The more for me, I say. If ya want to remain a momma's boy for the rest of your life…"

Toby snatched the bottle from Gunter, taking up the challenge. "We'll just see who's a momma's boy," he said, taking a long swig.

Within an hour the bottle was empty. They all staggered about the property.

"Now, what do we do?" Mark asked, his words slurring over his teeth through his lazy mouth.

"I got just the thing. Follow me," Gunter announced, walking off with the rest of them following.

When they got to the edge of the slave quarters, Gunter hid behind some of the bushes. He motioned for the others to do the same. From their concealment, they held a clear view of the well that the slaves used.

"She should be here soon. She gets water about this time every evening," Gunter said, pointing to the well.

The others had no idea what Gunter was talking about until someone stepped out of one of the shacks, heading to the well. It was a young, black, slave girl, perhaps in her midteens. She wore a small blue kerchief on her head with her hair tucked under it, a tan blouse buttoned to the neck, and a bell-shaped dress to the ground with a white apron around her waist. Her frame was petit; she couldn't have weighed much. What little light there was shown on the side of her face emphasizing her high check bones and smooth coco-shade skin.

When she was a few feet from the well, Gunter jumped out into the open.

"Come on!" he called to the others.

Before the girl could take in a breath to scream, Gunter grabbed her from behind. His right arm went around her torso, keeping her arms in check; his left hand was over her mouth, muffling her cries for help.

Struggle as she may, she was no match for Gunter, still she continued to fight back.

"Come on!" Gunter called out once more.

They all ran to him. Immediately, Mark, Stanley, and Richard grabbed hold of the girl on all sides. Now, her struggling became useless. Travis and Toby stood to the side, watching. Gunter looked at them sternly.

"If you two think you're in for a free ride, you're mistaken. Come here and help!"

Travis was speechless, remaining motionless.

"What the hell do ya think you're doin'?" Toby shouted.

"Keep your voice down!" Gunter grunted at Toby. "Let's take her to the barn," he told the others.

They dragged the girl to the barn. She fought all the way, though it was clear she was tiring. Travis and Toby trailed behind.

In the barn, they threw her against a post. Before she could catch her breath, Gunter tore the apron off her and stuffed it in her mouth. With only one hand he held her in place against the post.

Her eyes were wide with fear, looking from face to face. Her breathing was quick and deep. Her body shook in terror.

"Let's see what we have here," Gunter said. Using his free hand, with one swift motion he tore the front of her blouse open. She stopped trying to scream and began crying.

Once more, Toby spoke out, "What the hell are ya doin'?"

"What does it look like we're doin'? What are ya, a flapdoodle?" Mark laughed. They all laughed, except Travis.

Gunter pointed his finger in Toby's face. "If ya don't like it, ya can just leave."

"Then I will," Toby grumbled, heading for the door.

"What about ya?" Gunter asked, looking to Travis. "Are ya a flapdoodle, too?"

Travis didn't say a word; he turned and walked toward the door. Just before leaving the barn, he looked back over his shoulder. He saw Mark, Richard, and Stanley holding the girl to the ground as Gunter undid his belt and unbuttoned his trousers.

Outside, Travis and Toby sat on a bale of hay, staring at the barn door.

"Do ya believe those idiots?" Toby complained. "They make me sick."

Travis sat, silently listening to Toby's rant.

"This is so wrong," Toby continued. "It goes against the law of God."

Travis looked to Toby, questioning, "What do you mean?"

"It's in the Bible," Toby argued.

"It is?"

"Yes, it is," Toby stopped for a moment to call up the Bible verses he'd memorized, that he felt concerned the situation. "Now, I remember: Leviticus 18:23. *Neither shalt thou lie with any beast to defile thyself therewith,*" Toby quoted verbatim.

Travis looked confused. "What…what are you talking about?"

"It's in the Bible," Toby elaborated, "You're not supposed to do anything with animals."

Travis still looked puzzled

"Don't ya get it? Blacks ain't nothing more than animals. Well, maybe on a higher level. I mean, they can reason some, as far as their little minds will let 'em. But they're still animals." Toby repeated himself, "*Neither shalt thou lie with any beast*! That's what those idiots are doin'." Toby shrugged his shoulders and shook his head. "Well, they can all burn in hell. See if I care."

This was not what Travis expected from his friends, be it Gunter and his followers or Toby with his self-righteousness. Between the drinking, confusion, and uneasiness, Travis' head began to spin as did his stomach. He felt sick. Standing, he ran behind a wagon and heaved. When he was done, he wiped his mouth across his sleeve. He looked up just in time to see Gunter, Mark, and Stanley leaving the barn. They were laughing, as they tucked in their shirttails.

"What about the girl?" Travis grunted.

"What about her?" Gunter said. "Don't worry about her. She knows her way home." His smile grew large. "This ain't the first time." His smile grew larger. "And it ain't the last."

Seven

Venom

Travis planned to go to university in the fall to study business as well as agriculture, two subjects needed to run a plantation. His excitement was mixed with uneasiness. The plantation and the local school were his only world. Now, that world was to become larger, it made him apprehensive, though he never showed his anxiety to any one, not his friends, especially not his father, not even to Mammy Pam.

The summer passed slowly for Travis. After graduation night, he spent little time with his friends. The incident that night in the barn with the slave girl left him uncomfortable with their friendships. He didn't ignore them per se, but always had an excuse not to spend time with them.

Surprisingly, Samuel's approach toward his son was different that summer. Normally, he delegated Travis' chores and studies, focusing mostly on studies than chores. Wisely and with pride, Samuel allowed his son to while away his summer leisurely, knowing that in the fall Travis would need to apply himself like never before. He expected Travis to not only do well at university, but to excel. The pressure would be on in the fall, so Samuel loosened the leash, allowing Travis to spend the summer freely and frivolously.

Most days, Travis slept late. After washing and dressing, he'd go downstairs to eat breakfast alone or with Mammy Pam, which was just as he wanted it. He avoided his parents as much and often as possible. His father, though friendly, was often facetious in his manner and speaking with him. As for his stepmother, the least contact the two made the better.

Often, after breakfast, he'd take one of his father's rifles, saddle up one of the horses, and spend the morning shooting pheasant. He liked to ride past the fields where the slaves worked, to the empty fields beyond where he could be alone.

It was on a day that started no different from any other day, though it was destined not to be. While Travis slowly road off to the far end of the plantation, he could hear the slaves working the fields off in the distance. The sky was clear, full of flying birds, the bright sun blinded him. He held his hand over his eyes for shade.

Then, without warning, his horse reared up on its hind legs, winnowing loudly in straining fear. Travis slid out of his saddle, falling face down. Before he even hit the ground, his horse ran off in terror. His rifle flew out of his hand into a bush a few yards away. Once he got his bearings, he lifted up slightly. That was when he realized what spooked his horse. Not three feet in front of him was a diamondback rattler, coiled and ready to strike.

It was a big one, bigger than any he'd ever seen, at least five feet long and as thick as your fist.

The snake slithered closer. Its cold lifeless eyes aimed at his face. Travis remembered his father once told him that rattlers couldn't see well, they hunted mostly by smell and hearing. If he could just stay still enough, long enough, perhaps it would go away? He held his breath, trying to stay as motionless as possible, but it was useless.

The serpent's jaw opened wide, exposing long needlelike fangs an inch long, dripping with venom. Before Travis could make a move in any direction, the fangs sunk deep into his left hand, into the flesh between the thumb and forefinger. The dagger-teeth remained imbedded as the serpent continued to bite down. Travis had to wave his arm wildly, to loosen the beast's grip and tossing it away.

Instantly, blood gushed in thin streams from the pinpoint wounds. A pain like being gorged by red-hot knitting needles filled his hand, and then shot up the arm to his shoulder. He rose to his feet, turned, starting in the direction of the workers in the fields off in the distance. They now seemed so very far away.

He didn't get farther than ten steps when he stopped and buckled over from intense sharp pains in his gut, like razors sloshing around inside him. The sound of his heartbeat pounded in his ears, getting louder but slower with each passing second. Not able to withstand much more, he fell face down in the dirt.

With all his strength, which he felt leaving him at an alarming rate, he screamed for help. He waited, there was no one around. He screamed again for help, and again. His eyes were closed; the red dust under him flew up his nostrils with each labored breath. Then, a miracle happened, an answer to his prayers. He heard footsteps.

"So, what we got here?" said a man's voice.

The sound of the footsteps came from two different directions. It was at least two people.

"Looks like the Massa's brat son," said another male voice.

They rolled him over onto his back. He tried to focus his eyes, but he could do so only for a moment. In that instant, he saw the faces of two black men. He recognized them as two slaves from the plantation. He felt one of them take hold of his arm. His hand was beginning to swell, it was now twice its normal size, and was pulsing with pain.

"Looky here; the boy got a snakebite." The man pressed down hard on the wound. Travis screamed out in pain. "Does that hurt, Hobbadehoy?" the man asked pressing harder on the injury.

"He gonna be dead for sure," the other announced.

Then one of them began kicking him in his side over and over.

"Don't kick him. That gonna leave bruises."

"I say, so what. They think it be when he fell off his horse."

The other man thinking it a logical answer, they now both began kicking him.

"Please, help me," Travis struggled to get the words out.

"Help ya?" laughed one of the men, who then pressed his foot down hard on Travis' aching hand.

They stopped for a moment. Travis heard them circling around him.

"Well, looky, looky, what's this?"

Travis could tell by the sound that one of them found the rifle. The next moment, Travis felt the mussel of the gun pressed to his forehead.

"Don't shoot 'em. He be dead soon enough. If they find him shot, they gonna search all through the slave camp till they find who done it."

"I don't care," said the man holding the rifle.

With the cold steel still pressed against Travis' head, he could feel and hear the man pull back on the trigger, as it clicked in place. Travis was a finger flinch away from his brains being blown away.

Suddenly, the sound of a gunshot shattered the air. The man standing above him dropped the rifle, falling on top of him. He was dead – shot dead.

The sound of someone running toward them grew louder.

"You get one too, you black bastard!" the runner shouted. Travis recognized the voice – it was his father.

Another gunshot exploded. Travis heard the body of the other man hit the ground.

"Don't worry. It's going to be all right," his father said as he lifted his son up in his arm, placing him over the back of his horse. Samuel mounted the horse, as well. He raced back to the main house.

Samuel carried Travis up the stairs of the porch of the main house. Some of the house slaves rushed out to help him. They brought him up to his room and placed him on his bed. Some of the male slaves took off his clothes.

By now, Travis was weaving in and out of consciousness. The next time he opened his eyes it was dark. Mammy Pam sat on the edge of his bed, cooling his forehead with a wet towel.

"Ya got to hold on, child. Just ya hold on," Pamela whispered. "Close your eyes, now, and get some sleep."

"I'm afraid," Travis said. "If I close my eyes, I may never wake up."

"I ain't gonna let that happen, no way, no how," Pamela said softly.

Travis believed her. Mammy Pam had never lied to him. Feeling reassured, he closed his eyes and fell asleep.

****

Travis woke to a bright sun-filled room. He felt weak and woozy. His head was throbbing as was his arm. He looked at his hand; it was still swollen.

"The worst is over. I believe ya gonna make. Thank God."

When Travis' eyesight cleared, he saw Pamela standing at the foot of his bed. She walked to him, and held a cup of water to his lips. It surprised him how thirsty he was, as he drank it all down.

"How long was I out?" he asked Pamela.

"It's been three days. It was touch and go for a spell. We feared we'd lose ya there for a moment. But the Lord's been good. Would ya like something to eat?"

"I don't feel hungry," Travis replied.

"But ya gotta eat something. I'll go get ya some clear broth. It'll be good for ya."

Just then the bedroom door opened. In walked Samuel.

"That'll be all, Mammy Pam. Leave us. I want to speak to my son, alone."

"I'll be back in a tick with some clear broth," she whispered to Travis. With her head bowed, she made her way around Samuel and out of the room.

Samuel moved in closer. "How are you feeling, son?"

It was strange to hear his father call him, 'son'.

"I feel a might weak, but I'll be all right."

"Of course you will. You just rest and get your strength back."

Again, it was odd to hear his father show concern for him.

"I was afraid I was going to lose you, son," Samuel admitted, his voice cracking with emotion. "Your stepmother sends her best," he added.

This almost made Travis laugh. He realized there was no point in saying anything about it. Besides, he was bathing in his father's newfound concern.

Samuel moved in closer until his face hovered over his son's. Looking down into Travis's eyes, he spoke softly. "Now, you understand what I meant?"

Travis had no idea what his father referred to.

Seeing the questioning look on Travis' face, Samuel began to clarify his statement. "About the slaves, about the darkies, those black bastards. You must never trust them. Never turn your back on them, because they'll stab you in the back, for sure. They're nothing but animals, and you have to treat them as such. You can't love them, so, you might as well hate them.

"You can love a horse, treat it proper, but then one day it rears up and kicks you. That animal needs to be put down. It's the same thing with darkies. Don't ever be afraid to put a darkie down, just like a disobedient animal.

"I know you care for Mammy Pam, and you should. She's done many a good thing for you. But never forget, when push comes to shove she'll be just like all the rest. Don't you ever forget this, Travis."

"I won't, Daddy."

The door opened slowly, Pamela walked in carrying a tray. On it was a napkin, a spoon, and a bowl of hot clear broth.

"I brought ya something to get ya to start eatin'," she said, wearing a smile.

"Thank you, Mammy Pam," Travis said coldly. "Just leave it on the nightstand. I'll get to it later." He hesitated for a moment. "Thank you, Mammy Pam; you may leave, now."

Eight

Moving in the Wrong Direction

Only three times in his entire life did Travis travel outside the county, and that was when he was a boy. Those three times were when he accompanied his father to a slave auction, and even then it was only to the next county.

On the day he left, there were mixed feelings. His father beamed with pride, assuring him not to worry about anything other than his studies. Anytime he needed money, any amount, for any reason, it was just a telegraph wire away.

His stepmother's sentiments were the easiest to read. It was clear she was pleased for him to go, being out of her sight. It was one of the rare times she smiled at him, as far as he remembered.

His Mammy Pam, Pamela, was a mystery to him. He could tell his leaving affected her, but he wasn't sure in what way. There was a look of concern mixed with pride, and dare he think it…affection. She was the only one to hug him good-bye.

Originally, he planned to make the trip by horseback, but he knew that once he settled in at the university, the care of a horse would only be a burden and an unnecessary expense, so he went by train.

Of course, Travis had seen trains traveling through the land many times, but he'd never been on one. He always thought of trains as loud and powerful machines, but that was nothing compared to riding inside one. The hissing of the engine and clattering of the metal wheels was deafening. He could barely hear himself think. The bouncing and swaying was so drastic that he was sure at any moment they would jump the track and crash. Looking around, none of the other passengers seemed concerned, so he tried not to show his. But, inwardly, his nerves were frazzled, as he bit his lower lip and tightened his fists till his knuckles shown pallid.

****

Atlanta, Georgia was like traveling to a foreign land, or even another planet. Travis never saw so many buildings and people in one place. The hustle and bustle made his head spin. He spent the day exploring. He ate at a restaurant where the servers were all men – a very strange experience. Stopping in a few bars for a drink was an experience. Most of them had entertainment. Not just a piano player like back home, but four or five musicians playing at one time. There were dancehall girls wearing the most flamboyant costumes you could image. Now and then, a group of them would entertain the customers with a dance, or one of them would get up and sing a song with the band. However, the most popular form of entertainment was gambling. There were dozens of gambling tables and house dealers. Travis was tempted to try his luck, but not understanding most of the games he feared making a fool of himself.

He got a room at one of the better hotels. Atlanta was not the end of his journey. His final destination was to the university in Athens-Clark County, thirty miles northeast of Atlanta. A carriage left from Atlanta to the university, once everyday, early each morning. Thinking it best, despite all the hoopla of the big city, Travis turned in early.

****

The university was like a city unto itself. It was on hundreds of acres with dozens of buildings. Some designated for education, other for the amenities needed for the students and staff.

Once registered, Travis settled into his dorm room. It was a small room at the corner of the second floor. It had two windows, one looking at the grassy area in front of the building, the other overlooking at the barns to the right of the building that housed horses and carriages.

There were two single beds, against separate walls. There were two study desks, at the foot of each bed. Two dressers stood next to each desk. The remaining walls were covered with empty book shelves, anxiously waiting for new deposits.

Having never met him, all Travis knew of his roommate was his name: Philip Cary, the son of a wealthy tobacco merchant.

Travis, realizing he'd preceded his roommate, took the liberty of selecting the bed, desk, and dresser of his liking. He placed his belongings down, and spread out on the bed, placing his folded hands behind his head.

Just then, the door opened; a young man pulling a steamer trunk behind him entered.

"Travis Parker?" the young man asked.

"That's me," Travis replied, smiling and holding his head up to take a good look at his new roommate.

"Good, that means I'm in the right room," Philip surmised as he lugged his steamer trunk to the foot of the unoccupied bed. "The name's Philip Cary," he said, also stretching out on his bed.

Philip Cary was a gangly, long-limbed youth with curly brown hair, large wooly sideburns, sharp green eyes, and a protruding pointed chin.

Philip reached into his inner coat pocket, pulling out a whiskey flask, and offering it to Travis.

"Not quite now," Travis said, sounding thankful.

Philip shrugged, opened the flask, taking a long hard drink. He balanced the open flask on his chest, careful not to breathe too heavy or fast, as to not spill any. He stared up at the ceiling as he spoke.

"You know, Travis, we're going to get along just fine." Philip said, in a lackadaisical manner.

"Oh, and how is that?" Travis asked, also speaking in an easygoing tone, staring at the ceiling.

"Because I get along with everyone, and everyone gets along with me," Philip proposed. "I'm a very likable chap."

"Funny you should mention it," Travis replied. "I'm a very likable fellow, also."

"That's great!" Philip answered back. "We'll get on swimmingly."

They both burst into laughter. The open flask fell off Philip's chest, pouring onto his bed. He jumped to his feet, trying to salvage as much whiskey as he could.

"When you said '*swimmingly*', I didn't know you meant swimming in whiskey," Travis said, dryly.

"You're all right, Parker," Philip announced, toasting the last few drops in his flask to Travis, drinking it down in one swallow.

****

Like anything you do, do it often enough, it becomes routine. There were classes to attend; followed by late night studies. This left little time for entertainment, Other than afternoon horseback rides through the surrounding fields on horses hired through the university, and late night walks alone, life was all work and no play.

Yet, it was different for Philip. He could read faster than anyone on campus, as well as retain everything he read, and recall at will. He was the envy of every student; especially Travis. Philip had more free time than anyone on campus. His study regiment was an hour of study a day. If he studied a full day, he would be ahead by weeks.

For this reason, Travis suspected, was why he saw little of Philip. The top grade student was often out somewhere gallivanting. It wasn't until one night that Travis learned where Philip spent most his time. Travis was at his desk burning the midnight oil.

"I need your help, Travis."

Travis turned in his chair to face Philip. "You need my help?" he laughed. "You who can read an entire textbook in two days, who passes every exam like it was child's play, need my help?"

"I know you wonder where I go when you don't see me for days. I ride into Atlanta. At first, I went from saloon to saloon, mostly gambling. One night I went to a saloon called *The Piccadilly*. It was there I met the most beautiful woman in the world. Her name is Estella Post."

"So, where do I fit in all this?" Travis asked.

"She barely pays me any mind. If you could come with me to the Piccadilly, talk to her; tell her of all my better qualities."

Travis laughed even harder, now. "I don't understand. You've got a silver tongue, especially when it comes to telling the world of your *better qualities*."

"That's here with you and the other fellows. Only when it comes to Estella, I'm tongue-tied. I'm an absolute buffoon. You've got to help me, Travis."

Travis shook his head. "I'd like to, Philip, but I've got a test in a couple of days that I can't afford to fail."

An impish grin formed on Philip's lips. "I'll help you pass. Come with me one night to meet Estella. Do this for me, and I'll guarantee you'll pass your test."

Travis took up the open book from his desk, offering it to Philip. "Show me."

****

Though similar to many of the other saloons, the Piccadilly was unique in many ways. It was the largest saloon around with more gambling, women, and drinking. It was so loud inside that Philip needed to scream at Travis to be heard.

"That's Estella over there," Philip said, pointing to one of the dancehall girls standing at the bar. She held a whiskey glass in one hand; her other arm was slung over a man's shoulder, as she smiled, looking into his eyes.

"Doesn't look like she's been missing you," Travis said, being facetious.

"Don't make fun. This is important to me," Philip pleaded. "Isn't she beautiful?"

"I wouldn't know," Travis replied. "She doesn't look my type."

As if on queue, the man standing with Estella tipped his hat to her, bowed, and walked away.

"Come on, let's go talk to her." Philip was off toward her before finishing his sentence.

As they approached, Travis began to understand Philip's infatuation. Of all the dozen dancehall girls, Estella was the most beautiful; more attractive than any woman Travis could remember. Her shoulder-length black hair seemingly cascaded like ocean waves to the shore. With glowing violet eyes, flawless porcelain skin, and a shape only Michael Angelo could have carved from marble, Travis began to understand Philip's out of control passion for this woman. Though he knew better, the fever that inflicted Philip, Travis had caught. There was no stopping it.

"So, if it isn't my little schoolboy," Estella said, with a hint of aloofness.

It didn't bother Philip. He was glad just to be remembered.

"Well, aren't ya goin' to buy me a drink?" she questioned Philip.

"Yes, of course," said Philip, and then ordering three whiskeys. "This is my roommate, Travis Parker."

Estella didn't respond; she just looked Travis up and down, as if she wasn't very impressed.

Handing out the glasses of whiskey, Philip motioned to Travis to start a conversation, something that would highlight his attributes to Estella.

"So, when did you and Philip meet?" Travis asked Estella.

She laughed at the question. "That's like asking me when was the last time I was bitten by a mosquito, it's not that important to remember." She took a sip from her glass, nearly draining it.

Travis continued, "Philip's one the top students at the university."

"Well, hurray for Philip!" she shouted, raising her glass high and fast, spilling all its contents. "I need another drink," she said to Philip who jumped at the chance to do anything to impress her.

It was then Travis noticed something very important about his companions. As for Philip, Travis never saw his roommate and friend so vulnerable. Philip was not only a good student; he was a force to be reckoned with. He could hold his own with the best of them. But concerning Estella, he was a begging puppy at her feet.

Regarding Estella, in that moment, Travis understood her. For one thing, he knew she was drunk, far drunker that he first suspected. She was a woman of the streets who wheeled her beauty like a sharp knife, cutting anyone who came too close. She knew how to handle men. The whiskey loosened her lips. If she were sober, she would have treated Philip kinder, but only to manipulate him.

But most important was the realization that no matter how much a fool Philip made of himself, or how vulgar Estella was, he wanted her more than anything or anyone in his entire life.

"I bought you something," Philip said, handing her a small velvet box.

Estella opened it, taking out an ivory broche, examining it. "Why it's beautiful," Estella proclaimed, tossing it across the room. She laughed in Philip's face. "Ya think ya can buy me off with some cheap trinkets. Come back when ya willin' to spend some real money on me."

Philip turned, starting for the exit with Travis close behind.

"Philip, wait up!"

Stopping in the doorway, Philip stopped and sadly addressed his friend. "She's drunk. She doesn't know what she's saying. She's usually not like this."

"Let's go back to the university," Travis whispered soulfully.

"No, not now, I need to be alone. I'm sorry, Travis." With that, Philip walked out onto the walkway and was lost in the crowd before Travis could stop him.

Travis went back inside, walked up to the bar, standing before Estella.

"That wasn't very nice…what you said to Philip."

Estella just smiled, swaying back and forth in her drunken stupor.

"When was the last time you ate anything?" he asked, truly concerned.

"Buy me a drink," was all she could say.

Frustrated, he took hold of her by the arm, guiding her out of the saloon.

"Hey, watch who you're pullin'," she slurred her words, trying to break free of his grasp.

He paid her no mind, pulling her down the street, and then inside one of the many better restaurants in Atlanta

"I'm sorry, sir, but I'm afraid you can't bring that woman in here," whispered the Maitre d', not to let any of the guests hear.

Travis reached into his pocket, took out a bill of a large denomination, handing it to the Maitre d'.

"Will a booth be to your liking, sir?"

After a few minutes of eating, with a full stomach, Estella became more coherent.

"Do you remember what you did?" Travis questioned. "You weren't very nice to my friend, Philip."

"When I drink too much, I move in all the wrong directions. Worse part is I do it too often."

"Philip loves you. . .you know that?"

"That's his problem." Estella slowly rose to her feet. "Listen, I appreciate ya helpin' me get my head on straight, again, but I gotta get back to work."

Travis didn't know where the words came from; they just seemed to float out of his mouth. "May I see you, again?" he asked, against his better judgment.

"If ya like," Estella replied.

"That's not an answer. Don't brush me off like that. I'm not like Philip. I'm not like the others. Again. . .may I see you, again?"

She smiled knowingly, "Yeah, I'd like that." She turned, walking off.

He knew it was a move in the wrong direction, and he was cold sober.

Nine

Like Candy

The friendship between Travis and Philip remained strong, but it was not an honest friendship. Philip continued to call on Estella every chance possible. He doted on her in everyway possible, to the point of obsession. He bought her priceless gifts, gave her money. When Estella was sober, she treated Philip well, but no more than any other man in her life, whom she used and abused freely. When she was drunk, which was often, she treated him horribly to the point of heartbreak. Philip hid his feeling and relationship with Estella from Travis as well as his other friends at the university, knowing they would disapprove and think him a clod for his actions. Nevertheless, Philip was a fool in love, unable to stop.

Travis was just as deceitful, but for a different reason. He too made the long ride to Atlanta to call on Estella. He foolishly did what he could to find favor in her eyes, lavishing her with gifts and money, with the same results as Philip. If she was sober, she'd spend the night in his arms, giving his heart false hope. If she was drunk, it was nothing short of painful hell.

Travis hid his feelings and ties to Estella from everyone, not because it would make him look foolish. He understood it to be foolish behavior, but didn't care who knew would see it as so. No, he hid his affection for Estella because of Philip who adored her beyond measure. He felt he was betraying his friend. Yet, he knew that someday the truth would be known. He lived in dread of that day.

It was over the Christmas Holidays, when most students left for their homes to spend time with their families, except neither Philip nor Travis left campus. They stated they wanted to remain to keep ahead of their studies. The true reason was neither one of them could bear to be far from Estella.

"I have a confession to make," Philip admitted to Travis early one evening. "I've been seeing Estella whenever I can."

Travis said nothing, just listening.

Philip held up an engagement ring to Travis. "I'm going to ask Estella to marry me."

"Are you sure about this?" Travis asked, sounding truly concerned.

"I've thought it over. I have to make a try for it."

Travis could think of many arguments why Philip shouldn't propose. He remained silent, selfishly knowing she would turn him down. For this, Travis felt more ashamed. Only if Philip was out of the way could he pursue Estella openly and freely.

Philip rushed from the room, off to Atlanta to seek his destiny.

****

Travis was suddenly wakened in the middle of the night. He sat up in his bed, leaning on his elbows. The room was dark with dull moonlight seeping in through the windows. The door flung open. Philip came staggering in, obviously drunk.

"Philip, are you all right?" Travis asked.

Philip pulled his arm back, quickly brought it forward, tossing something across the room. Even in the dark, Travis knew what it was. From the sound of it, he knew it was the engagement ring he intended for Estella.

"She turned me down," his words were slurred.

Before Travis could say anything, Philip ran out of the room, slamming the door behind him. Travis lay back onto his bed, closing his eyes. Again, a wave of great shame washed over him as he fell back to sleep with the relief of knowing Estella turned down Philip. He couldn't help but feel relieved and hopeful.

Again, Travis was awakened. How many hours passed, he didn't know. There was a dreary glow of sunlight entering the room from the windows. It was early morning. There were voices coming from outside, shouting of men. Travis went to the window to see what the cause was. There, below, in front of one of the barns was a group of people. Travis dressed quickly, and then went out to investigate.

There was foreboding in the air. Travis instinctively knew something was wrong. As he approached the barn, friends warned him to turn back, gently placing their hands on his shoulders. Looking into their eyes, Travis understood the gravity of the situation. Fearing the worst, he continued forward.

Inside the barn, from a rope tied around the center ceiling beam dangled the body of Philip Cary. On the ground below, lay the ladder he'd used to hang himself. Using the same ladder, they cut the rope, gently lowering the body down. No one spoke.

Travis looked on in disbelief. His mind filled with mixed feelings of shame and deep sorrow. He fell to his knees next to the body, covering his face, crying into his hands.

****

The wind blew hard across the station, as Travis and many others watched the train pull away carrying Philip's body back to his home and family. In the midst of all those people, Travis felt alone. It was all too late to make anything right.

Travis hired a horse from the stables, and started for Atlanta. He wanted to speak with Estella. Perhaps, if he did, he might make some sense of it all. He doubted it, but he felt he needed to give it a try.

When he got to the Piccadilly, it was late afternoon. Estella's one room living quarters on the second floor of the Piccadilly was empty. All her belongings were gone. Everyone he spoke with told the same story. She quite her job, packed her things, and left town. No one knew why she left or where she left to. Travis rode back to the university, confused and dismayed. It broke his heart that she was gone, but part of him was relieved.

****

A month after the death of Philip, they still hadn't assigned another roommate for Travis. He lived alone. Thoughts of Estella and Philip haunted him. He threw himself into his studies to keep such thinking at bay. In all that time, not once did Travis visit Atlanta.

One late afternoon just as the sun headed toward the west, Travis' studies were disturbed by a knock on his door. His face flushed and his body trembled when he opened the door.

"Estella?" he questioned his own eyes.

She was sober. Travis could always tell when she was or wasn't. She looked at him with sorrowful eyes. "I need help," she said, shyly.

"Philip is dead," he said.

"I know." She pointed to a space beyond him. "May I come in?"

He moved aside, letting her enter, rays of sunlight coming in from the window shown on her, making her glow. Seeing her in the flesh, in his room, was a dream come true.

"I need ya help," she repeated.

"How…?"

She hesitated for a moment. "I'm gonna have a baby."

The first question to come to Travis' mind was whose baby was it, but he feared asking, still, something inside him forced him. "Whose baby is…?"

Before he could finish, Estella answered," I don't know. It could be yours."

The vague answer was like a bullet to his heart. "It could be yours," meant there was a possibility it wasn't his, it could also be Philip's, or dare he think it, someone else's, perhaps one of many. The way of the conversation was too much to bear. He changed the subject.

"How can I help?"

She bowed her head in shame. "I have no money. I have no place to stay."

"Well, you can't stay here. Do you have a horse?"

She nodded that she did.

"Good. I'll take you to Atlanta. First, we'll get you a place to live."

Travis hired a horse from the stables. They rode slowly to Atlanta without a word said.

In Atlanta, Travis got a room for Estella at one of the clean and moderately priced hotels. While she settled in, he went out for something for them to eat. He came back with enough food to keep her for a few days.

Against his better judgment, Travis spent the night with Estella. Her true personality shined in her sobriety, deepening his feelings for her. In the morning, as he prepared to leave, they spoke low and soft. Travis took what money he had left, handing it to Estella.

"Here, take this. Just don't go back to the Piccadilly, or anything to do with that way of life."

"What am I supposed to do, sit in this room day and night waiting for ya to come?"

"There's plenty to do in Atlanta. I'll be back in a couple of days. Don't worry I'll take care of you."

He kissed her good-bye. Already, he could feel the coldness setting in.

Before leaving Atlanta, Travis went to the telegraph office. He telegraphed his father for more money. He would need it.

****

Travis visited Estella in Atlanta as often as possible. Perhaps, a bit too often, his grades suffered. He treated her like a queen, besides paying her rent and giving her spending money, he showered her with lavish gifts, dinners at expensive restaurants, clothing, jewelry, anything her heart desired. There were shows at the local theater, concerts, and plays. He did everything in his power to keep her amused; fearing a moment of boredom would send her running back to the Piccadilly and her past way of life. The only solution was to spend large sums of money – Travis' father's money. He was grateful his father never questioned the pleas for more money by telegraph. Though there were a few telegraph responses asking for him to write more often and perhaps consider a visit in the near future. Travis wrote his father, lying about his life and his true situation.

It was to be a long weekend, Travis was caught up on his studies for the moment, and he would not have a class until the coming Tuesday. He decided to ride into Atlanta to spend the weekend with Estella.

Running up the flights of stairs and down the hall to her room, Travis was stopped by a large crowd of hotel guests standing outside Estella's door. Pushing the people aside, he made his way into the room. Standing on one side of the bed were the hotel manager, two police officers, and the local doctor, packing his little black bag. Lying in the center of the bed was the cold, motionless body of Estella. Her flimsy nightgown was torn as if she'd died in anguish. Her hair was slicked back and glued to the pillow with sweat. Her skin was no longer porcelain white, but was pale with an unnatural blue tint to it. The doctor took up his black bag, walking toward Travis.

"Did you know her?" he asked.

Travis nodded.

"I'm sorry, son" the doctor said, trying to step around Travis.

Travis stopped him. "How did it happen?"

"Opium..." he replied, "Nasty stuff, some folk smoke it, while other's eat it like candy. Your friend here just ate a little too much." Again, the doctor maneuvered around Travis, heading for the door. "I'm sorry, son," he repeated.

"What about the baby?" Travis asked.

The doctor looked at him strangely. "Baby...what baby?" the doctor asked.

"The one she was having," Travis answered.

The doctor shook his head as he walked around Travis to get to the door. "I'm sorry, son, but there was no baby."

Riding his horse beyond the limits of endurance, back to the university, Travis blamed the tears in his eyes on the strong, quick wind to his face. Back in his room, he sat motionless in his chair. For a while he stared at Philip's well-made, empty bed. Then he looked out the window till the sun came up. After packing his things, Travis hired a carriage to take him to the train station in Atlanta. He was going home.

Ten

Much Is Required

It felt strange to Travis to be back home on the plantation. He hadn't been gone very long. Not much on the plantation changed. It was the changes that happened within him that made it no longer feel like home.

Thankfully, his father never questioned Travis' return, nor did he ever show any disappointment in him not finishing his studies. In fact, the opposite was true. He would brag on his son who'd gone to university to anyone who'd listen, like it or not. Belial, Travis' stepmother was a different story. Over dinner, she'd make remarks about his quitting school. She never commented straightforward, having a sharp and quick tongue; she was the mistress of sarcasm.

Travis saw little of his old schoolmates. Richard, Stanley, and Mark all went off to school; Toby and Gunter were busy working for their fathers. When they did get together, they would enjoy reminiscing their school days. After that, they found they had little to talk about and now even less in common.

It seemed the only constant in Travis' life was his Mammy Pam. Her concern for him was always obvious. Her treatment of him was always fair and caring. Now, more than ever she perplexed him. He remembered the two black slaves who tried to kill him, how they acted in hatred toward him because of what he was and not who he was. Also, now, he could see in the eyes of the other slaves their hatred for him. The two men were killed because of him. Not taking into account their actions, he was the cause and that was all that mattered, and they hated him for it. Because of their hatred, Travis felt inclined to respond in kind. Still his relationship with Mammy Pam was good, which blurred the lines, leaving him confused about the matter and skeptical of everyone but her.

****

It all started out as small talk, outside the church after services, or at the counter of the dry goods store. Over time, the small talk became more frequent. Word heard by a friend of a friend, and then passed on to another. Until, small talk became rumor. It being a suspicious rumor spoken over cigars and brandy in the study, over tea cakes in the parlor, and supper in the dining room. More than ever, folks became more interested in goings-on.

They listened for word from the telegraph office, reading not only the local newspaper but those from out of the county or even out of the state.

Finally, it was announced: there would be a war. A war the likes of which this country had never seen before. The southern part of the country would fight the northern. Many reasons were given for the war; most would agree it was about the choice of everyday life. For the South, the center of that life was *Slavery*.

At first, the prospect of war was a running joke in the South. The North would be no match for the South. It would be a quick and painless victory, taking only a few months, at the most. Still, every southerner knew it would take a mass effort on everyone's part. This meant each of them pulling their weight, starting with the young men. Hundreds enlisted daily. Travis held no doubt what he needed to do.

Though Samuel agreed wholeheartedly with his son's decision, he saw matters in a different light. Travis was the son and heir of the most wealthy and powerful man in the county, and well-known in higher circles throughout the South. To enlist as a common soldier or even in the infantry would be a disgrace to the family's name and honor. No, leadership was in the Parker flesh and blood, right down to the marrow of the bone.

Though Travis protested against it, Samuel pulled every string within his grasp. He wrote letters to those he knew in the Confederacy. Within two weeks, it was declared Travis was to report for duty, taking up the rank of captain.

This was a major problem facing the Confederacy – a two-folded one. There would be no problem recruiting fighting men. As for leaders, there was a great need. Of course, there were many qualified officers to choose from, many of which learned their soldiering trade in northern states – some even at West Point. These were few and far between. The second problem was that in their need for officers, they filled these positions with friends, family members, men of wealth and power, and even some who purchased their rank. Though usually possessing leadership qualities, these men lacked in military savvy. Travis would be one of these.

Samuel made arrangements for Travis to be fitted for a captain's uniform. Not only would this take the financial burden off the Confederacy, it ensured Travis would look the part of the hero, rather than a rank-and-file officer wearing a dilapidated uniform issued by the military. The material was the customary gray. Custom-fitted with a double row of gold buttons, a saber and sash at his side, knee-high boots polished to a mirror finish, and a wide-brim hat with one side cocked and a white plum in the other.

As well, Samuel spared no expense purchasing the finest white steed in three counties.

On the day Travis left home, his father hugged him (a rare sentiment, indeed), his stepmother shook his hand (even more rare), and Pamela hugging and kissing him and burst into tears. She ran to the edge of the plantation to the main road, there she stood, crying and watching till he rode out of sight.

****

Travis was to report to, of all places, Atlanta. Actually, it was a large field on the outskirts of Atlanta. As he rode into camp on his white mount, dressed in his new custom uniform, all eyes followed him. This made him feel uncomfortable, till he learned that most of the other officers arrived in similar if not more flamboyant uniforms. The men watching him knew that perhaps he might be their leader. They were not impressed. Their stares were just to try to size him up.

Travis was assigned to bunk with three other officers in one large tent. Officer's tents were separate from those of ordinary soldiers. The differences between officers and soldiers were deeper and more complicated than just housing. When Travis fully understood these differences, he was then grateful for his father's efforts to secure him a position. All ill feelings over his father that haunted him were forgotten.

The area for common soldiers was as large as the area for officers, only there were one hundred times more soldiers than officers. The soldiers slept twelve to a tent. Their ill fitted uniforms were made of thick, heavy wool, making it a blessing in the winter and a sweat rendering curse in the summer. No matter what season, it was uncomfortable, making them itch. There were not enough uniforms to go around, which was a lucky thing for the few without, wearing their own clothing and preferring them. The shoes issued to them were neither a left shoe nor a right shoe. They were constructed straightforward. In time, the curve in a man's foot would designate right shoe from left, giving new meaning to the saying *breaking in a new pair of shoes*. They also received a haversack in which to carry their personal belongings. There was a belt on which they carried musket balls and powder, and of course, a rifle slung over the shoulder.

Food rations were plentiful, but varied from soldier to officer. A soldier lived on mostly beans and hardtack, not as good as what most plantation owners fed their slaves. Where as officers were served stews with some meat, hardtack, and some beans. It was not as good as the food they were used to, but they all understood with war comes hardships.

The main purpose of camp was to get the men to think as one. There were lessons in how to load, fire, and reload a rifle in the least amount of time. The acceptable minimum was one minute, with a goal of getting down to twenty seconds. Of course, there was target practice. Marching played a major part in their training. Once they learned how, they did it for hours each day.

Officers were taught how to command wisely over men, with just a brief hint of military procedures. Those officers who had studied war before enlisting were the lucky ones. The others would have to learn by trial and error.

It was planned and hoped for that this training period would last as long as ninety days, but war slows down for no man. There were battles to be fought, and soon. Training camp lasted only thirty days. The soldiers, like their counterparts the officers, would have to make due with on-the-job training.

****

Travis quickly learned how the military worked. They didn't call it the service for nothing, because that was the job of every soldier. There was service from the generals down the line, all the way to the private at the bottom. Generals in conference with other high ranking officers, colonels and majors, made all the plans of attack and defense. They would order those in service under them, captains and lieutenants, to put these plans in motion. These officers would order the men in service under them, sergeants, in conjunction with their corporals, to order the servicemen to prepare and act on the initial plan. Keep in mind, the lower the rank, the closer you were to the fighting, and nearer to death.

Travis was given leadership over a troop of two hundred and fifty men. This was considered a small fighting group. What was the purpose of such a small group was a mystery to him till he was informed of his first assignment.

Captain Travis received orders to march these men, these two-hundred and fifty, to Bedford County in Tennessee. As the first battles of the war were being fought more to the east and hadn't moved so far west, as of yet, the journey was a quick and safe one. Travis and his troop of marching men were placed under General Nathan Bedford Forrest, a native son of Tennessee. Forrest was in command of a cavalry battalion, which was his strong point. Still, upper command felt it necessary to round out his forces with foot soldiers. Travis not only delivered these men but remained with Forrest as commander over them.

All feelings of inadequacy Travis held were washed away in two waves. First was the realization that so many other officers did the same, no more worthy of the position than their pocketbooks. The other was on meeting General Nathan Bedford Forrest, and learning of his story to the rank of general.

Forrest was born and raised in Bedford County, Tennessee, to a wealthy family. He was a shrewd businessman, turning his family fortune into millions, owner of several cotton plantations and trading in slaves.

Having no previous or formal military training, he volunteered into the Confederate Army as a common private. After donating large sums of money to the *Cause*, and suggesting a cavalry corps that he would not only fund but head, Tennessee Governor Isham G Harris granted Forrest's wishes. He received the rank of general over his own cavalry battalion.

****

Once arriving, they remained in Bedford County for more training. Forrest had his own way of doing things. No one was to leave until his will was instilled in his men. It was a month later they were put on the move.

In the late fall of that year, they were on the march, moving freely according to Forrest's whims. The first fights they took part in were small in Kentucky. They marched from one small skirmish to another, winning every one of them. Right away, Forrest's style of warfare became immediately clear to all. He had a no-nonsense approach, striking quick, hard, and head on. In no time he had a reputation as a man to be feared, and an admirable foe. Even at the Battle of Fort Donelson in Tennessee, the battle where many Confederates were killed and many more surrendered, Forrest got many of his men out safely, as well as men from other units.

The part Travis played in these campaigns was notable. He led his men bravely. They respected him and would have marched into hell for him, if he asked. During battles, Travis could be found mounted on his white stallion at the frontlines, in the heat of the battle, wheeling a pistol in one hand and a saber in the other.

Something Travis never shared: he was never for certain if he'd killed anyone. He knew his marksmanship was good. He'd aimed at Union soldiers, pulled the trigger, and watched them fall down. When wheeling his sword, he knew when he hit his mark. He knew the feel of steel against flesh and bone, the pressure along the blade when it entered a person's torso, having to pull back to retrieve the weapon.

Inwardly, Travis hoped and prayed none of his victims were hit hard enough to die, though he always aimed his best and slashed with all his might. Never seeing one of his victims fall dead was a strange comfort to Travis.

Travis' bravery, his way with his men, and military savvy did not go unnoticed. The news was given to him by Forrester, himself.

"It seems you are destine for greatness, *Major*," Forrest laid strong emphasis on the word "Major". Forrest then handed an envelope. "Go ahead, open it," Forrest said, laughingly, after Travis spent too much time staring at it.

He opened it, reading it slowly. It was an official letter signed by the President of the Confederate States of the Americas, Jefferson Davis. It went on to say how his efforts as a soldier and leader were highly appreciated.

There was even a quote from the Bible: *He that is faithful in that which is least and is faithful in much* and *to whom much is given much is required.*

This part preceded the announcement that Travis was promoted to the rank of Major. He would be entrusted with twice the amount of men and horses, and to separate from Forrest's forces and proceed under his own command, following orders.

Forrest snapped to attention and saluted Travis. "Congratulations, Major Parker," Forrest relaxed, offering his hand in friendship. The two men shook hands. "Well…" Forrest said thoughtfully, "God bless you, sir, and God bless the Confederacy."

Eleven

Miller's Bridge

In fitting with his rank, as well as the inconveniencies brought on by war, Travis stopped shaving, growing a full beard, though keeping it well-trimmed with a scissor each night before bed.

Orders from his superiors directed Travis and his men to march farther south. This was both a blessing and a curse. The blessing being that while most troops were heading north where most of the battles would be fought, they would see little action, at least for the time being. The curse would be that if they did have a confrontation with the enemy they'd be on their own with no hope of help from reinforcements.

Also, they were not so far from the Parker Plantation, being so near Travis often considered visiting his family and friends, though he knew it would not be possible. He knew the area well, which was possibly why they had him march south to that particular region.

Travis was very familiar with the Chanteyukan River. In his teens, during summer vacation from school, often he and his friends would ride the hundred miles to camp out on the river's bank, spending their days fishing. Though he never crossed it, he held a vivid memory of the Miller's Bridge that spanned the Chanteyukan River. It was one-hundred and twenty-five feet high, and two-thousand five-hundred feet long. As well, Miller's Bridge was twice as wide as most. One side was for normal traffic: folks on foot, horses, and wagons. The other side was the pathway for the railway. Also notable, Miller's Bridge was made up of three different materials: stone, iron, and wood.

The importance of Miller's Bridge was that its railway was a lifeline to the Confederate troops for transporting food and supplies. To the west, there were no railways crossing the Chanteyukan River. To the east, there were many railways going north but they were hundreds of miles away, far from the bend in the river.

Through secret channels the Confederacy learned of the Union's plan to destroy Miller's Bridge. Travis' orders were to stop them, saving the bridge at all costs.

Travis marched his men over the bridge, going south. On the other side was a large open field, perfect for camping, but being out in the open was too obvious, leaving them vulnerable. Beyond the clearing were deep woods. They marched into the forest; just deep enough to be hidden yet still have a clear view of the bridge. Travis ordered no tents to be erected. Everyone would sleep on the ground. As well, no fires were to be lit. Thankfully, the weather grew mild, and the nights were clement. So, the long wait began.

More than the usual amount of men kept guard day and night, always watching in the direction across the field to the bridge. Travis knew there would not be many Union soldiers coming to destroy it. A small platoon could move quickly, be harder to spot, and still get the job done. It was presumed they would try to use dynamite to blow up the bridge. A good portion of the bridge was constructed of wood; it would be easy to burn it down. Only carrying large quantities of flammable liquid would not be easy or logical, whereas dynamite was lightweight. Burning down the bridge would take too long. Dynamite was instantaneous. It was the rational and simplest method.

The long wait continued as days became weeks. The men became antsy. Sleeping on the ground they tolerated, as well as the cold meals every day. No one dared complain. Compared to the rest of the Confederate Army who were farther north putting their lives on the line, battle after battle, they had it easy, and they knew it.

It was late one night that Travis was called to the edge of the woods. He bent low, hiding behind a rock with some of those on watch.

"What is it, Sergeant?" Travis asked.

The soldier handed him a pair of field glasses. "Here, sir, take a look. It's a Yankee."

Using the field glasses, Travis focused in on the bridge. There was a lone Union soldier on horseback riding to the most southern end of the bridge, back to the northern end, and then back to the south.

The sergeant put his rifle to his shoulder. "Say the word, Major, and he's a dead man."

Travis placed his hand on the sergeant's shoulder. "No, don't. He's just a scout. The others aren't far behind. A shot would tip them off."

The Union soldier stopped at the center of the bridge and dismounted. He looked over the side, down at the water below; he went to the other side, doing the same.

"He's figuring out the best places to plant the dynamite," Travis stated.

They watched the Union soldier remount and ride off going north.

"Be ready," Travis warned. "They'll be here soon, probably first thing in the morning."

Word of what had happened spread through the camp, putting them all on edge, waiting. No one could sleep.

Travis was right. At first light they heard the sound of horses off in the distance coming from a northerly direction. A small squad of twenty men appeared on the north entrance of the bridge. They rode across the bridge, two of them stopping every so often till there were a row of mounted Union soldiers on both sides of the bridge. They were to keep guard as four men dismounted and began to string dynamite on both sides of the bridge.

"Get the men ready," Travis ordered.

Travis ran back deeper into the forest where they had the horses tied up.

"Mount up, men," Travis told the others, as he mounted his steed.

Travis rode to the edge of the forest. He unsheathed his saber, and looked down and back.

"Are we ready, Sergeant?" he asked.

"Ready when you are, sir."

Travis rode out from the forest, into the clearing. He brought his saber up, pointing it at the enemy.

"Charge!" he shouted as he dug his spurs into his horse's sides. He galloped toward the bridge, the other horsemen at his side, the two-hundred plus foot soldiers running behind them, screaming like banshees.

The heads of the Union soldiers turned with a jolt to the oncoming onslaught. Those stringing the dynamite tried to work faster. When they realized it was useless, they light the fuses. They mounted up, rode to the north entrance of the bridge and stood their ground.

As Travis raced to the center of the bridge, the dynamite began to explode. The blast did little harm to the metal structure, but pieces of stone and wood flew into the air and at Travis and his men. The Union soldiers opened fire.

Within seconds, many Confederate soldiers fell. They returned fire to the Union side of the bridge; they were standing their ground, which was easier than trying to fire on the run.

The closer they came to the northern side, the more men fell. Travis could hear the shrill of the bullets whizzing past his head. The air was filled with gunfire and the smell of gunpowder.

Travis had the strangest sensation as if someone were tapping him on his right shoulder. He looked to see his coat ripped, blood pouring from it. He'd been shot, but had no feeling of it. His arm went limp, the saber falling from his hand. He felt a jolt to his side. There was no feeling of pain. The next moment, he was hit again in his other side. Blood shot from him like a Roman fountain.

The last stick of dynamite blew, sending splinters of wood in every direction. Travis' horse was hit hard in the rump, causing the animal to rear up on its hind legs. When the beast stood up straight, Travis was thrown from his saddle. He came crashing down onto the side of the bridge. His left leg slammed against the railing. He wheeled his arms franticly, trying to regain his balance. His efforts were too late and too slight. He rolled off the side off the bridge.

The one-hundred and twenty-five foot drop to the water looked more like a mile. In his mind, he couldn't understand why it took so long. Then, he hit the surface – hard.

The water was far shallower than he expected, no more than five feet. He hit bottom, the sharp rocks cut him like knives. When he rose back to the surface, he struggled to move his arms and legs to gain control. His limbs disobeyed and ignored his plea. All he could do was breath deeply and hold it to stay afloat.

Looking up, he saw the bridge spanning from left to right. The glare of the sun blinded him. He could hear the sounds of the skirmish, but those sounds were growing farther and farther away. The river's strong current was taking him away. He was hopelessly floating downstream.

In time, the sound of gunfire diminished and finally faded. All he could hear was the water rushing, his breathing, and the pounding of his heart.

How much time passed, he had no idea. Suddenly, he came to a dead stop. He opened his eyes, struggling to gain focus. He was lodged between two large boulders. Feeling the river bottom pressing against his spine, he knew he must have been on the riverbank.

He thrashed about, trying to sit up. It was futile to try. It was then he realized how many gunshots had found him. He had multiple wounds, one in his shoulder, his left side, and one in his right leg. The fall from his horse onto the railing of the bridge damaged his left leg; he felt certain it wasn't broken.

It was a great effort to keep his head above water. Whenever he relaxed his head fell below the waterline, sending the cold muddy water up his nose and down into his lungs.

To make matters worse, the pain that he should have felt when he was shot, swept over him like a wave of pure hurt.

He heard the sound of horses off in the distance. It could be his men looking for him, but then it could be Union soldiers. He couldn't take the chance. With all his strength and will he pulled himself out of the water and onto the riverbank. Inch by painful inch, he dragged his near lifeless body using his feet and his elbows. It took all his willpower not to cry out in pain.

There was a tall willow tree not far from the riverbank. Its branches hung low. He struggled passed the foliage toward the unseen tree trunk. The full branches hid him from the outside world. It was like being in a cave made of brushwood and leaves. Even the light of the sun was blocked out.

He heard the horses coming closer. There was no way to tell if they were friend or foe. Fear like he'd never known filled him, as he moved his tongue around in his mouth, sensing the salty taste of his own blood. He was bleeding internally.

His only regret was he would face death alone. No one would know of his passing. They would only assume it, when too long of no word from him passed.

He wanted so much to sleep, but he feared doing so. He needed to fight to stay awake, to stay alive. He wanted to live.

He heard the sound of someone walking outside, around the tree. Some of the branches were pulled back. Sunlight poured in. He opened his eyes. That's when he saw her standing over him.

Part III

Their Story

One

Meeting in the Grotto

They just stared at each other for a moment, Travis unable to speak, Angela taken aback by the sight of him. Their eyes met. She saw the fear and pain in his. Her head spun as she noticed all the blood, as she counted his wounds.

It was then the sound of horses grew near.

"I'll be right back," she whispered.

She placed her Bible and canteen on the ground, and left the shelter of the willow tree.

There, across the river was a small band of Union soldiers on horseback. She walked to the water's edge. They halted when they saw her.

One of the men shouted to her, "Say, girl, you seen any soldiers?"

"Ya mean the one that just floated by, here on the river?" she shouted back. "He must be a mile downstream by the way he was goin'. Don't matter much; he looked to be dead, for sure."

The soldier who shouted to her lowered his head as if in deep thought. When he came to a decision, he raised his head and looked at the others. "Come on, let's go back."

They turned around and galloped back upstream.

She waited till she felt sure they were well gone. She entered the willow tree grotto. He was out cold. She fell to her knees next to him. Rummaging through his jacket, she found little, just a watch and a good size hunting knife.

He opened his eyes. She placed the hunting knife against his throat.

"Don't worry, they's gone. I lied. Lord knows why. I should have let `em finds ya." She pressed the blade hard against his throat, nearly perching the skin. His eyes went wide. "I wonder if I should kill ya? It be better for both of us. Ya would be outta ya pain, and I get the pleasure of sendin' ya to your just reward. There'd be one less slavery-lovin' cracker in the world. If I ever do anything to make this a better world it'd be takin' ya out of it."

He needn't speak; his eyes told the story. She removed the blade from his throat. She took up her canteen, opening it. Placing her hand behind his head, she lifted him up and gave him a drink.

"I got to be the most foolish woman in the world," she whispered, mostly to herself.

He wondered if the Yankees were looking for him had they won the battle. His question was answered in the next moment. Six loud explosions could be heard in the distance. It would seem, though outnumbered, the Yankees had won. They were destroying Miller's Bridge.

She put the canteen down, turning her head toward the sound. "Good," she said softly, also knowing all too well what it meant. She placed his head back down. "Ya know, them bullets have gotta be taken out, or ya gonna die." She rose and walked to the outskirts of the branch edge. Before leaving she turned and looked down at him. "I'll take them bullets out. Ya may still die anyways, but that would be God killin' ya and not me." She turned and left.

He had no idea how much time had past. He opened his eyes to see her stoking a small fire next to him. The canteen was close to the flames. She was heating up water. She knelt next to him, carefully tearing his uniform where he was bleeding.

She placed a four-inch twig as thick as your thumb between his teeth. "The Yankees are camped upstream. You're sure to let loose screamin'. This here's gonna hurt like hell."

Using her skirt to protect her hand from the heat, she poured hot water over the hunting knife. She started with his leg; burrowing into his wound with the knife. He moaned, his teeth digging into the twig in his mouth. After what felt like an eternity, she dug the bullet out of the wound and tossed it aside.

Tears were running down Travis' face.

"Maybe, next time you'll think twice before ya figure what side ya want to fight on," she said as she poured more hot water over the blade.

As she tunneled into the next wound with the hunting knife, the pain became unbearable for him. He arched his back off the ground. After letting out a long sigh, fell back to the ground – unconscious.

****

He woke to find her fingers in his mouth. When she took them out, there was a familiar taste in his mouth.

"Chew it. What's the matter, don't ya like fish? Well, it's all we got," she said, holding a stick on which was a small roasted fish.

Before she could place another bite in his mouth, he struggled to speak, "Thank you."

She ignored him, stuffing more fish into his mouth.

"Thank you," he repeated.

She obviously didn't want to answer him, to even acknowledge him. She let out a long sigh, when she realized he wasn't going to let it go.

"What's ya name, soldier boy?"

"Travis."

"Ya were lucky. All them bullets never hit anything important. They all were in the fleshy parts. I got all the bullets outta ya. Ya may live, I don't know."

"You…?" he said softly.

She knew what he meant. He wanted to know her name.

"I'm Angela," she said, shoveling a large piece of fish into his mouth. "From the looks of your uniform, ya must have been somebody special."

He didn't answer.

When he swallowed the bite, she wiped his lips with the hem of her skirt. Then she rolled over on her back next to him. She spoke staring up at the roof of the grotto. "Get some sleep, ya gonna need it. In the next few days we'll know if ya gonna make it. Don't fret none, if ya die, I'll bury ya. If ya live, I'll take care of ya till ya can walk. After that, I'm gone."

Travis closed his eyes and gently whispered one more, "Thank you."

****

Travis woke to find he was sitting up with his back against the trunk of the willow tree. The branches pulled back; Angela entered carrying two apples. She handed one to him. It was difficult to hold it, but he was determined to feed himself. He bit into the apple; it was sweet.

"So, it looks like ya gonna live," Angela said in a joking manner as she bit down into her apple. She bent low and picked up a stick off the ground and held it to him. "I found this here stick, yesterday. It'd make a good crutch." The stick was long and sturdy with a Y-shaped configuration at one end. She placed it under her arm, walking around in a small circle. "Ya see," she said, offering it to Travis. "Ya gonna have to get up and start walkin' before ya can't and start gettin' sick, again."

Travis knew she was right. He pressed his back hard against the tree trunk, using all his strength in his arms and legs he slowly and painfully worked his way to his feet. Angela handed him the stick. He placed it under his arm, taking a few steps forward.

"Ya can do better than that," Angela teased

He tried again, taking a few more steps. He was in pain, but he was not going to cry out and give her the satisfaction of mocking him. He nearly toppled over. Angela reached out to catch him. Their hands entwined.

She looked at his hand in hers. "My, but ya got soft hands. I bet ya ain't never did a day's work in ya life." It was true, but he wasn't about to admit it. In contrast he felt the palm of her hand. The skin was taunt and rough from years of hard work. "So, what were ya, some kind of mama's boy?" Again, he refused to justify her question with an answer. "Bet ya had plenty of darkies kissin' the ground ya walked on. Ya like darkies waitin' on ya hand and foot, don't ya?" she scoffed at him.

He took in a deep breath, held it, and walked around the trunk of the willow tree. He pushed himself till he'd walked around it three times. He moved with determination. Now, he not only wanted to get better and walk, he wanted to be able to get away from Angela, despite being indebted to her.

****

Two days latter they were outside the shelter, standing on the riverbank. A storm was forming in the north sky. Dark clouds moved across the blue, slowly turning it to gray.

"What's your story?" Travis asked, trying to sound as gentle as possible, not wanting to seem intrusive. Angela looked as if the question didn't make sense to her. "I mean, what are you doing out here on your own?"

She gave him a side-glance with a hint of a smile. "Ya mean, what is a colored girl doin' out on her own? Ain't she need to be in the cotton fields on some plantation? Ain't she suppose to be doin' what Massa say, workin' her fingers to the bone for Massa, havin' his babies and raisin' them on her own? Ain't I supposed to be grovelin' at Massa's feet, like all good black folk?"

Realizing he'd hit a nerve, Travis stood silently watching the dark clouds in motion.

Angela stared far north at the storm. "I went rabbit. I'm a runaway," she confessed. Travis turned to look at her, she turned to look back. "Well, soldier boy, I've played the *Good Samaritan* long enough. I've done my share. It's time we went separate ways."

She went back into the shelter of the willow tree and came back out carrying her Bible and canteen.

"Well, don't just stand there. Ya can walk."

"I want to thank you for…"

"No more thanks. Just say good-bye and get goin'."

Her cold bluntness angered him, but he owed her, and if that's the way she wanted it, so be it. Leaning on his crutch, he started walking along the riverbank going upstream.

"Where the hell are ya goin'?" he heard her call from behind.

"I'm going back to the bridge," he replied over his shoulder.

"There ain't nothin' there but a blown up bridge and dead bodies."

He ignored her and kept on walking. There was a small grouping of stones in front of him. When he tried to walk over them, he tripped and fell.

Angela rushed to him and helped him up. "Ya is useless, ya know it?" she complained. "Ya ain't never gonna make it anywhere." She was at his side, the one without the crutch, putting her arm through the crock of his arm. "I best stay with ya awhile longer, before ya kill ya-self."

Two

Headin' South

Miller's Bridge was in shambles. More than half of it was demolished. Only two of the eight arches remained. Few stones were left and even less wood and iron. The train rails leading from south to north toward the bridge were uprooted. Obviously, the Yankees dynamited the tracks for a hundred yards south of the bridge.

The next moment the storm was overhead, the sky turned black and the rain poured down in sheets. The dark above lit up momentarily from bright, flashes of lightening, followed by ear shattering cracks of thunder. Angela began running across the field toward the forest.

When she was well into the wood, she shouted out to him, "Hurry up…before ya get struck down!"

Travis moved across the field as fast as he could. When he got to her, he was soaking wet. They sat on the rocks, looking at the rain.

It was then Travis felt something that he needed to air between them. Through all her kind caregiving, she never once spoke to him with a civil tongue.

"You don't like me, do you? In fact, you hate me." he whispered, just loud enough to be heard over the dim of the downpour.

She didn't look at him, she didn't want to. "It's not ya that I hate, it what ya are. I hate ya kind, all of ya are evil. I never met any white folk that weren't wicked and cruel. I hate all of ya."

The hair on the back of Travis' neck stood on edge, as his blood boiled with anger.

"And what about your people?" he snapped. "You're all lazy! You lie! You cheat! Just before the war, two of my father's slaves tried to kill me!"

"Why did they try to kill ya?" Angela snapped back. "I'm not sayin' killin' is a good thing. Only ya gotta understand, ya took everything from them, then ya surprised that they hate ya. What if someone took everything from ya? The Yankees are tryin' to do just that, and ya hate them. Ya understand?"

They both fell silent, knowing the conversation was taking them nowhere. Still, as they calmed down, they both felt shame. Angela felt it for taking her hate out on this young man whom she knew nothing about. Travis felt it for talking in such a way to the woman who saved his life. Besides, she had nothing to do with the two slaves who tried to kill him. Then he came to the realization, the cold fact that it was his father talking through him.

"If you hate me so much then…"

"I said that I don't hate ya," she interrupted.

"All right, so you don't hate me. Except, if you have so much hate for whomever, why did you help me?"

Angela took a long time to answer. Then she held up her Bible. "This used to belong to my mother. She gave it to me when she died. I've been reading it and…"

"You can read?" Travis asked.

"Yes, I can read," she countered, sounding insulted. Then she continued, "I've been reading it and tryin' to make some sense of it all. My mother lived by every word in it. Much of it I don't understand. But I do know this much, something my mother always told me. This world ain't never gonna get any better for anybody till somebody takes the first step and tries to cross the bridge we all made. I ain't sayin' I ain't angry, because I am. But one day it's all goin' to be all right, it says so right here in this book. Only it's got to start with somebody and it might as well be me."

The uneasiness Travis felt suddenly disappeared. "I'm sorry," he said ever so gently. He turned and looked at her waiting for a response.

For some reason unknown to her, Angela's stubbornness melted away. She smiled at him, "So am I."

As calming peace fell over them, they turned once more to watch the rain.

****

In the morning, the sky was clear, an ocean of bright blue with billowy clouds sailing across it. The heat from the morning sun was already drying the ground of yesterday's rain.

Leaning on his crutch, Travis stood near the railroad track. Looking down at the ground, something glittered at his feet. With closer inspection he saw it was a revolver. A Confederate issued pistol left by one of his men from the battle. He quickly placed it in his belt, hiding it under his jacket before Angela was out of the woods.

"So where are we goin' next?" Angela asked.

This question took Travis by surprise for two specific reasons. One: he was not expecting the word *we*. So, now they were together? Second: the tone of her voice had changed. There was concern and respect in her voice. Perhaps, their talk the night before had cleared the air. Strangely enough, her changed attitude had changed his. They saw each other in a new and different light.

Travis surveyed the train tracks at his feet; he looked north to the bridge and then south to the rail line that stretched to the horizon.

"Since the war, this rail line has only been used to ship supplies to our troops in the north. They don't do this too often, which is why we've not seen or heard a train all this time. But I need to warn them. I'm going to follow these tracks to the first town I get to. From there I can send them word about the bridge, before one comes barreling down here and derails."

"I know this area," Angela stated. "The next town is Colleyville. It's a might far up a ways. It's gonna take us maybe a few days."

We, and now *us*, for some reason the words sounded natural and good to Travis.

"You know, there's no reason you have to come with me. It might be dangerous," Travis warned her.

Angela laughed, "What's more dangerous than bein' a runaway slave in the south. Beside, ya need me."

He smiled at her. "Yes, I do," he admitted.

Travis started walking along the rail line going south. Angela hopped up on one of the tracks and began walking alongside him, her hand on his shoulder to keep her balance.

****

It was slow going. Looking south, the view didn't change – two train tracks, parallel lines, reaching out into infinity. The exercise was good for Travis. He started to not favor his crutch as much, and he was moving faster and more natural.

"Ya know, out here in the open, we can be seen for miles. If there's any Yankees around they'll see us," Angela warned.

"True," Travis replied, "but traveling in the woods would take forever. Besides, if a train is coming, we'd see it miles away and maybe be able to stop it."

Angela nodded in understanding; still it didn't stop her from feeling uneasy.

After walking together without saying a word, Travis struck up a conversation. "So, what's your story? Tell me about yourself."

Angela snickered, "What's to tell? Ya know the stories as well as I do. I was born a slave on a plantation. My parents didn't want me, so I was taken in by neighbors. To me, they were my real parents, and I loved them."

"Loved…?" Travis asked.

"Yes, loved, they're both dead, now."

"I'm sorry," Travis said, sounding sincere. "How did they die?"

"How do all slaves die? There's not many ways. I can tell ya most don't die of old age. That's a luxury no black folk can afford. That there's for white folk, only."

Inwardly, Travis knew she was speaking the truth; it made him cringe when she spoke that way.

She continued, "My father was hung for being disobedient, and my mother soon died after from a broken heart. If ya ask me, despite what it all might look like, all slaves die of a broken heart."

Finally, Travis asked the one question he truly wanted to ask, "Why did you run away?"

"Why did I go rabbit?" Angela contemplated out loud. "The Massa took a shine to me and put me to work in the main house. Oh, not out of the kindness of his dirty little heart, but out of the darkness of his dirty little mind. He had eyes for me. I got away with him not gettin' me for the longest time because his wife never gave him a chance. I figure she suspected his intention from the day I came to stay at the main house. We all knew the day would come when he'd have his chance, and one day he got it. I couldn't stay, so, I went rabbit."

"How did you get away? I'm sure they went after you," Travis asked, thinking it the most logical question.

Angela hesitated. "I had a long head start." She looked at him as she spoke. "Listen to the whole story before ya make a decision. I knew they'd sic the dogs on me and come after me. An old witch who lived on the plantation showed me how to make a sleeping potion, at least that's what she told me it was. I put it in the food of the overseers as well as what they fed the dogs. I figured once they were all asleep, I'd have at least a full day's start on `em. Only it didn't just put `em to sleep; it killed most of `em. That gave me nearly a week's head start."

Travis stopped walking, turned; his eyes went wide staring at her.

"I didn't mean to kill `em. Ya have to believe me."

Travis continued to stare at her.

Finally, in anger and half in tears, Angela shouted at him, "If I hated white folk enough to kill `em, ya'd be dead, now!"

Travis began to walk, again. They marched slowly south in silence, keeping to the railway.

A mile up the road, Angela broke the stillness between them. "Now, it's your turn. What's *your* story? Tell me about ya-self."

"What's to tell? You know the stories as well as I do," with a chuckle, he echoed her opening statement. "Like you, I was born on a plantation. Only, my father owned it. Biggest plantation in the county," he said with pride. His face grew solemn. "My mother died giving birth to me."

"I'm sorry," Angela interjected.

Travis continued, "I guess you could say I was born with a silver spoon in my mouth. My father could be strict, but there wasn't much he wouldn't give me, if I asked him. My father remarried. I don't much like my stepmother, but then she doesn't like me, either. We kind of stay out of each other's way, it's better that way.

"When I was young, I went to school, and then later to university. When I returned from school, the war broke out, so I joined up. I'm not sure why. I guess it was expected of me."

Angela rushed a few steps ahead of Travis, turned around and walked backwards so they could talk face-to-face as they walked. "Ya ever been in love?" she asked.

A bittersweet smile appeared on Travis' face. "Yeah, once, while I was at university."

Angela waited for more information. "So…what happened?"

"Let's just say it didn't work out."

"Ya still love her?"

"She's dead," Travis said coldly.

"I'm sorry," Angela responded.

The smile returned to Travis' face. "What about you? Were you ever in love?"

"Yeah, once, it was a long time ago."

"You still love him?"

Angela thought over her answer. "Come to think of it, I don't believe I ever really loved him. He was the best looking fella around, but he was an ass."

Travis laughed. Angela's next question made him somber, again. "Ya ever were friends with any black folk."

Travis nodded. "Yes, I have." He was amused by the shocked look on her face. "My mammy, Mammy Pam. She has been taking care of me since I was a baby. I love her." The shocked look on Angela's face grew larger. "That's why I'm so confused. All my life I've been told the worst about slaves, but she didn't fit the mold. Now you come along and save my life. It's bewildering to me." He looked at Angela, "What about you? You ever were friendly with any white folk?"

"Hell, no!" was her immediate response, then she caught herself. "That is until now! I guess you're my first. That is if we're friends. We are friends ain't we?"

"Yeah, we're friends," he said through a wide grin.

The next instant, the smile was swept from his face. He stopped walking, staring into the distance. Angela turned around to see what he was seeing. Off in the distance, at the end of the railway was a dark spot.

"Colleyville…" she whispered.

"Colleyville," he echoed. He started away from the rails toward the forest. "From here on we travel through the woods till we get there. I don't want to take any chances. Who knows what we'll find."

****

Colleyville was a large town, surrounded by plantations and farms. Before the war, it was the hub where cotton was shipped by rail going north, but now army supplies dominated the rail's use. The Colleyville train stop was the last on the line before Miller's Bridge. There were two other reasons that Colleyville was well-known. One was that their one church; *The Holy Sheppard of Calvary* had a choir like no other. Four years in a row they took first place in the state competition against other church choirs. The other reason was that on the first Monday of each month they hosted a large slave auction, right in the middle of town in the streets. Folks came from far and wide to bid on some of the finest slaves money could buy at the lowest prices.

It was nearing sunset when Angela and Travis came to the outskirts of town. They were still high in the forest, looking down on Colleyville. Travis stopped Angela before she stepped out into the open.

"Let's wait and see if it's safe, first," he whispered in her ear.

They got down low to the ground and watched from afar. Travis' suspicions were real. Marching about in the center of town was a troop of Yankee soldiers. At the railway station at the eastern end of town were Yankee guards posted every few feet. Colleyville had fallen and was now occupied by the Union.

"Let's get out of here," Angela whispered.

"No," Travis said, pointing at the railway depot. "If the telegraph is still working in that depot, I can send a message down the line that the bridge is down, and not to send any trains. If I only knew if it was still working."

"Ya can't just go waltzin' down there to scout it out," she told him. "But I can," Angela said as she stood up and walked out into the open.

"No, don't!" Travis hissed, trying to grab her and pull her back. But it was too late. All he could do was keep low and watch her climb down the hill and walk casually into the center of town.

Three

The Depot

Travis watched from the woods as Angela made her way through the town. Just another slave sent to town on errands by her owner. It was as if she were invisible. No one paid the least attention to her.

She stopped every black person she came across, obviously gathering as much information as she could. Who else to get it from than fellow slaves? These were the people who were constantly ignored. So much so that no one guarded what was said, speaking freely in front of them.

For whatever reason, which Travis didn't understand, Angela entered nearly every store on the main thoroughfare. She pranced in, as if on an errand. Five minutes later, she casually walked out empty-handed. Then she'd enter the next store. She was never approached or questioned by anyone.

Travis' heart pounded in his chest, as he watched Angela make her way to the back of the railway depot. There were four guards protecting the building, one at each corner. Again, as if invisible, Angela went up to the building, pressing her nose against one of the windows. No one stopped her. Travis assumed she'd return with her findings; but to his surprise she entered the building.

Angela remained in the depot for what seemed like an eternity. At least fifteen minutes passed by when suddenly the backdoor flew open with a slam against the building. Angela soared out the backdoor with a Union officer close behind her. While she was still trying to regain her footing, the officer kicked her, sending her to the ground.

Travis was too far to hear what was being said. By the officers motions he new he was cursing her out. The officer pointed one last warning at her, and then kicked her to emphasize its consequence. The officer walked around her, heading for the saloon at the end of the thoroughfare.

Angela slowly got up, dusting herself off. She walked about, nonchalantly, waiting for the moment she could leave completely unnoticed. Standing at the edge of town, she looked in all directions. When she was sure no one was watching, she rushed up the hill to the forest. She fell behind the large rock where Travis was hiding. She was gasping to regain her breath. Sweat poured down her face.

"So, what's going on down there?" Travis asked.

"Give me a minute to catch my breath," she huffed back.

Travis waited silently. Angela reached in the deep pockets of her dress, taking out various items.

"Ya like candy?" she asked.

On a flat stone she placed bits and pieces of candy; but there was also some beef jerky, a carrot, a potato, and a handful of turnips. Now, Travis understood Angela's visits to all those stores.

She picked up the carrot and took a bite, talking as she chewed, "I learned from some of the folk I talked to that the Yankees took over the town the same day they blew up the bridge. Some of the landowners pulled a raid one night, but they failed. Many of them were killed. Since then, nobody's puttin' up a fuss.

"There was only one soldier in the depot. When I snuck in, I hid behind some pews that were set up for a waitin' room. The telegraph is still workin'."

"How do you know?" Travis asked.

"Well for one…I seen it. There was a cot set up for the soldier, so he could stay at the telegraph, night and day. An officer comes in to give him orders about somethin'. I listened, and I heard and learned it all."

"Seems the Yankees are playin' like they's Johnny Rebs. The next town up the line don't know that the Yankees got control of Colleyville. They keep tellin' 'em up the line that the bridge is still there and the rails are clear.

"Then I learned there's a shipment of supplies comin' through in two days. It's sure to be destroyed when it tries to cross the bridge. Then the officer saw the top of my head behind one of the pews."

"I saw how he kicked you out of the depot. Why did he let you go?" Travis was confused.

"I just give him what he wanted."

Travis was afraid to ask. "And what was that?"

"A dumb, stupid colored girl…I just acted as stupid as he believed I should be…just the way they like it. He paid me no mind and kicked me out."

Travis hoped Angela wasn't including him in that *they* she spoke about.

He looked down at the depot. "I've got to get down there and send a telegraph message to the depot up the line, warning them that the bridge is out."

"And how do ya plan to do that?" Angela laughed. "Ya just gonna hobble on down there. Even if ya was walkin' right without a crutch, ya still got that gray uniform on."

Travis thought long and hard. He picked up a slice of jerky, pointing it at her. "I got an idea," he said with a smile, and then bit off a piece.

****

Sometime after midnight, the town of Colleyville slept, save for the four guards around the depot. Travis and Angela went down the hill to the outskirts of town. Angela left Travis in hiding, making her way around the buildings along the main thoroughfare, at the end of which was a large barn. It was a public barn used by the citizens of Colleyville. Angela slowly opened the barn door and entered.

Inside, Angela found a lantern hanging from a hook on a post. The lantern's flame was low, giving just enough light to make her way around. Taking hold of the lantern, she walked to the back of the barn. There were only three horses, each in its own stall. She opened the stalls. The horses remained in place, unsure of what to do. Angela returned to the front of the barn, opening the barn door wide. With all her might, she threw the lantern at the back wall of the barn. It shattered, the kerosene dripping down. Immediately, the dry straw on the ground burst into flames. The fire grew high in seconds. The back of the barn was a wall of flames.

The horses whinnied in fear. Each reared up, fled their stall, running out the front door into the street. Angela ran off into the darkness behind one of the buildings.

In no time, the old barn was ablaze with a pillar of dark smoke snaking up to the stars. People came out of their houses, carrying buckets. They went to the horse troughs scooping up buckets of water and tossing the water at the barn. It was a brave but futile gesture. Clearly, the barn was destined to be ashes.

At the same moment, town folk rushed from their houses, the four guards around the depot deserted their posts, running to the barn to be of help. This is what Travis hoped for.

As painful as it was, Travis left his crutch behind. Moving as quickly as he could, Travis walked unsteadily to the depot. Inside, he found the one large room dark and the telegraph operator asleep on his cot.

Travis took his revolver, nudging the muzzle against the sleeping mans head. The Union soldier woke. At first, he didn't realize what was happening. When he did, his eyes went wide.

"Don't shoot, mister."

"Get up and start that telegraph," Travis ordered.

The man rose from his cot. He was dressed in his long johns. He walked to the telegraph and made a few adjustments.

"There…it's on," he said, his voice quivering.

"Put your hands on your head and get down on your knees," Travis demanded, never taking his aim off the soldier.

The man complied. Travis stood over the desk, one hand holding his gun to the man's head, the other on the telegraph key.

Travis wasn't an expert in Morse code, but he knew enough he could slowly get a simple message across.

Warning! Warning! Miller Bridge down!

He continued keying the same message over and over till he finally got a reply. Travis backed away from the desk.

"Don't make a move," Travis cautioned the man.

Lifting his hand high, Travis brought the butt of his pistol down onto the man's head. The soldier fell unconscious at Travis' feet.

Outside, they were still fighting the fire. The entire town was out doing their best, including the four depot guards. Other Union soldiers were now helping.

At the outskirts of town, Travis started back up the hill. At the summit, he hid behind the now-familiar rock, looking down on the scene below.

He half expected to find Angela waiting for him behind the rock. The plan was to meet back at the rock. It was understandable she would not be there. With so many people rushing about and her so close to the action, moving about would be slow and difficult.

They'd given up on saving the barn. They dug a trench around the structure in hopes of keeping the fire contained. They focused on throwing water on the other buildings in the surrounding area, fearing they too might catch fire.

Travis continued waiting for Angela. After a few minutes passed, he became concerned. A few minutes later, his concern turned to worry. Finally, his worry turned to fret.

He didn't know what to do. He thought of going down into the town, but he knew that to be foolish.

He stood up to get a better look of the goings-on below; still keeping crouched down behind the rock. That's when his worst fears were confirmed.

From out behind one of the buildings came two Union soldiers, one on each side of Angela, holding her by her arms. Both soldiers also carried a rifle in their other hand. They scurried her out into the open, past the burning barn, and down along the thoroughfare.

In the center of the line of buildings was one small building. The sign above the door read: *Sherriff Office*. The two soldiers guided Angela into the building. Inside, a light came on.

Travis could only think of one reason they had taken her. Someone saw what she had done and pointed her out.

Travis thought about what he should do.

Somewhere in the back of his mind he heard his father's voice, "You've done a great thing, my boy. You make me proud. You're a hero. You did what you had to do, so what if it causes some darkie's life? Now, get yourself out of there and come home."

"No!" he shouted in defiance to the voice in his head.

Four

Escape

Before sunup, Travis walked the outskirts of Colleyville. His decision to no longer use his crutch made going slow and painful, yet with each step he became more limber, feeling he was growing stronger. Coming to the back of a small home, Travis found what he was looking for. Someone left their laundry to dry overnight on a clothesline. Finding a man's shirt and pants was his good fortune. He quickly changed clothes, burying his uniform at the foot of a tree. He tucked his revolver at his waist, keeping his shirttail out to hide it.

The hoopla from the night before had stopped, though smoke still rose from the pile of ash that had once been a barn. The streets were empty, save for the four guards who had returned to their posts around the depot.

It was then the telegraph operator came rushing out of the depot, shouting to the guards, holding his wounded head, and still in his long johns. One of the guards ran off down the main lane, obviously to inform his superiors of what happened.

Travis went behind one of the buildings to hide. Being the only one out on the streets, and now with someone who could identify him - the telegraph operator – he had reason to hide. He kept hid, looking and waiting for an opportunity – anything.

Soon, the town came to life. Town folk scurried about to start their day. The noise around the depot was loud. Officers shouted commands at soldiers who scampered about like a swarm of warrior bees. They sent squads up into the hills and the fields surrounding Colleyville looking for clues.

They would look everywhere, not suspecting he was right under their noses. All he needed was to stay out of sight from the telegraph operator and he'd be safe.

Travis made his way around town via the back lanes behind the buildings.

He came on a young man chopping wood. Travis hid behind some bushes, watching. The young man took an armful of wood and entered the building, leaving the door wide open.

Looking in, Travis saw that it was a large kitchen, perhaps, the kitchen of a hotel or restaurant from the size of it. The smell of coffee and bacon cooking told him they were preparing breakfast.

Nearing the door, he heard men shouting and dishes clanking. Entering, he saw a man busy cooking at a stove, facing away from the backdoor. He caught a quick glimpse of a waiter, holding a food tray, going out a swinging door. This gave Travis an idea.

Leaning against the wall near the backdoor were some food trays. Travis grabbed one. In the center of the room was a table. On it were coffee cups, a coffeepot, and baskets of sliced bread. As quietly as he could, he went to the table, placing on a tray a coffee cup and saucer, the coffeepot, and one basket of bread. As he did this he never took his eyes off the man cooking who never took his eyes off his stove. Again, as quietly as he could, Travis went to the backdoor and left.

Holding the food tray as steady as he could, Travis walked to the front of the building, out into the open, onto the main lane. No one seemed to pay him much mind, as he hoppled toward the Sheriff's Office, the coffee cup and saucer clanging on the food tray.

Gently and carefully, using his foot, Travis opened the office door and entered.

It was a small room with rifles clinging to one wall. In front of the one window was a desk where two soldiers sat, one behind the desk, the other in front. Both leaned back in their chairs with their feet up on the desk. The moment the door opened, they both jumped to attention, fearing it might be an officer. They relaxed when they saw it wasn't.

"What the hell do ya want?" the one behind the desk asked.

"I brought food for the prisoner," Travis replied.

"Food....? I ain't heard nothing about no food."

"I don't know," Travis said, "I was just told to bring food for the prisoner."

"Did Malory tell ya to bring it?" asked the soldier in front of the desk.

"Yeah, that's who it was," Travis countered.

The soldier looked to his comrade behind the desk. "It's just like Malory to not tell us." He walked over to Travis. "Ain't much of meal," he commented, examining what was on the food tray.

"Well, you know..." Travis said, shrugging his shoulders.

The soldier took up a set of large keys from off the desk. "Come on, I'll let ya in,"

Travis followed the soldier through a door leading to a backroom. The other soldier returned to his seat behind the desk, putting his feet back up.

There were two jail cells in the backroom. The first was empty, and the second one looked to be empty, also. It wasn't until they came to the door of the second cell did Travis see Angela lying unconscious on the floor.

"There's a bed in this cell, why is she on the floor?" Travis asked.

The soldier laughed. "Well, she's had a hard night," he said as he opened the door.

Travis entered the cell, placing the food tray on the bed. He bent low, taking a closer look at Angela. She'd been battered. Her face was bloody. Her skirt was hiked up high to her waist. Travis reached down, pulling the hem down to cover her.

The soldier smiled. "I don't know how ya feel about it…doing it with a colored girl, I mean. But if ya wanna take a turn, be my guest. Have your way, we sure did."

Travis' blood was at a boil. He could feel the anger in him like hot lava flowing through his veins. He walked out of the cell. Before the soldier could close the door, Travis took out his pistol, raised it high over his head, bringing it down hard on the back of the soldiers head. He fell to the cell floor next to Angela with a thud.

Travis rushed to the other soldier in the office in the next room. He took a deep breath. He wanted to appear as calm as possible.

When Travis entered, the soldier took his feet off the desk and sat up in his chair.

"You have any rope?" Travis asked. "Your partner told me to tell you he needs a few strands of rope."

The soldier reached into the lowest draw of the desk, pulling out six lengths of rope.

"Now, what the hell does he need rope for?" the soldier complained, mostly to himself. He entered the other room, carrying the rope. "Duffy! What the hell do ya need a piece of rope for?"

Travis stood behind him, pressing his gun into the soldier's ribs. Instinctively, the soldier knew what it was and raised his hands high, still holding the rope.

"Don't do anything foolish. Just keep walking," Travis whispered.

When they got to the second cell, the soldier saw his partner motionless on the floor. "He ain't dead, is he?"

Travis ignored the question. "I want you to tie up your buddy. Go on, go ahead," Travis ordered, pushing his gun into the soldier's side.

Travis watched as he tied the unconscious soldier's hands and feet.

After Travis inspected the knots, he waved the gun back and forth as he spoke. "Sit on the bed and tie your legs together" The soldier did as he was told. "Now get down on your knees and put your hands behind your back." Again, the soldier complied. Travis knelt down behind him, placing his gun on the bed. He took a length of rope, and proceeded to tie the soldier's hands behind his back. "My guns right here on the bed, just inches away. One sudden move and I'll blow your head off."

When both soldiers were bound, Travis took the sheet off the bed, ripping it into four strips. He placed a strip inside each of the soldier's mouths. Then he used the other two strips as gags. Not wanting to take any chances, using his pistol, Travis knocked the soldier out cold. The two unconscious soldiers lay on the floor, side by side.

Travis returned his pistol into the waist of his pants. He bent down, taking Angela up in his arms. She moaned from the pain that being moved caused.

"It's all right," he whispered. "Everything's going to be all right."

One of Angela's eyes opened, looking up at him. "Travis?" she whimpered, in surprise.

He walked out of the cell, kicking the door closed. The keys were on the floor. He kicked them far away from the cell door.

In the office, Travis walked to the window behind the desk, looking out. There were few people on the street. Travis couldn't help notice two saddled horses tied up to a post outside the door of the Sherriff's Office. He could think of no other way. Stealing one of the horses and riding away was their only hope.

Travis waited till he saw fewer people on the streets. Still holding Angela in his arms, he struggled with the front door, getting it opened. Outside, he didn't waste a second. He rushed to the horses. He chose a white mare, the larger of the two horses.

Though he wished he could do otherwise, he had no choice but to toss Angela's limp body over the horse, in front of the saddle, near the horse's neck. He untied the horse from the post. With his hurt legs, it was a struggle mounting, but he made it.

Taking hold of the reins with one hand, he held Angela in place with the other. Not wanting to waste time, he didn't bother looking to see who was around. He pointed the horse west, leaving town. They galloped off as fast as the horse could manage.

After they we're well on their way and Colleyville was far behind them, Travis continued racing at a neck-break pace. It would probably be hours before they noticed what had happened, but he wasn't sure. Once they did, they would start tracking them down. He wanted to put as many miles between them and Colleyville that time would allow before the horse collapsed from exhaustion.

Hours later, the sun was on the horizon. Sunset colors stretched before them from north to south.

Finally, just before darkness, the horse began to faultier in its footing. More than twice it nearly stumbled and fell. Like it or not, it was no longer safe to continue. They could go no further.

As they came over the hill, he looked down. There was the western bend of the Chanteyukan River. He pulled back on the reins, halting the horse. The animal shook under them, its body oozing lather.

They slowly descended to the river. Travis dismounted, tying the horse to a tree near the riverbank. As gently as he could, Travis lifted Angela off the horse, placing her on the ground at the foot of the tree.

To give some relief to the mare, he took off the saddle. He placed it on the ground under Angela's head. He checked the saddlebag. There was a full canteen of water, some dry meat and hardtack, matches, a pipe, and a pouch of tobacco.

Holding her head in his hand, he put the canteen to her lips. She drank deep and fast.

"Whoa, not so fast," he warned, wetting his hand and cleaning the blood from her face.

She was shivering. He went off to fetch wood for a fire.

It was dark when he finally got a good fire going. He made it close to Angela, hoping the heat would warm her. But she continued to shiver. He placed his hand on her forehead. It was hot; she had the fever.

He lay down beside her, holding her in his arms to keep her warm. Her head was on his chest. She was aware of his breathing and his heartbeat.

Placing her hand on his chest, she began to cry like a child who woke from a bad dream.

He held her tighter. "You're all right, now. It's going to be all right."

She moaned into his chest, "My momma's Bible...they took my momma's Bible."

Five

I'll Never Let Go of Your Hand

When Travis opened his eyes, it was the middle of the night. The fire had died to a glow of red embers. Angela was fast asleep, still in his arms, her head resting on his chest. He looked at her face. She looked so peaceful. It felt strange to be this close, but it felt good. She was beautiful. More beautiful than any woman he'd ever known. Beautiful because of who she was. She was no longer a slave, no longer a colored girl, nothing but Angela.

As if in a trance, he brought his hand up to stroke her cheek. Her skin was smooth like the petals of a flower.

Her eyes opened. She looked up into his eyes.

Resting against his chest felt so natural. She'd never felt so safe in her life. She could not think of any other place she'd rather be or anyone else she'd rather be with.

Their eyes looked deep into each other's soul. Their eyes told stories, but their eyes asked questions: *Where is this place? Where are we going? Will you come with me?*

As natural as breathing in the scent of a flower, Travis bent low. Their lips met, softly at first, and then a passion rose, their kisses grew deeper.

She moved in his arms till her arms were around him. The entire world disappeared. There were no more wars, no more uniforms, no more north and south, slave and master, black or white, just Angela and Travis.

She cried as they made love.

****

"Can you ride?" Travis asked Angela as he saddled the horse.

"What about ya?" she asked. Those wounds must still be hurting."

"I'll get by."

"We'll get by," Angela adds with a smile. He smiled back.

Once in the saddle, Travis reached down. Grabbing Angela by the arm, she jumped up to help, and he lifted her up onto the horse, sitting behind him.

The river was low, low enough to cross. They moved slowly, much to the horse's relief. On the other side of the river was a steep hill. They rode upwards.

At the summit, they were up high enough to see far in all directions. The sun had started its journey across the sky. Everything was clear and bright.

Looking east, Travis saw them, a small squad of Union soldiers on horseback sent to track them down. From the bobbing of heads, he counted five of them. They were not far enough off for him to fell comfortable. Angela saw them, too.

"What are we gonna do?" she asked.

Travis pointed back down to the river, and moved his gaze to the north.

"There's another low-water bend in the river a few miles up that way, just north of Miller's Bridge. We could cross the river there, double-back, and cross back over here. Maybe, we can loose them."

Angela's arms were around his waist. She pressed her head against his back. Closing her eyes, she listened to him breath.

****

It took the entire morning to get to the bend in the river. They could see the demolished Miller's Bridge below as they passed it. Only remnants of its stone arches could be seen jutting out of the water. When they reached the bend in the river, they started downhill to the water's edge. Travis looked to the other shore, then at the rushing water separating them from it. The rains changed everything. The water was not only higher than normal; it was rushing and roaring passed faster than usual.

"Hold on," Travis said over his shoulder. Angela tightened her grip around his waist.

Into the water, a few feet from the shore, the water was saddle-high. If it got any higher, they would have to turn back. The speed with which the water hit them was strong, splashing up and soaking them.

Midway across, it was too late to turn back. The horse snorted as it struggled to get across. Suddenly, the mare lost her footing, toppling into the water. Hitting the water, Angela and Travis were separated. The strong current pulled them downstream. Angela went under time and again, first disappearing below the waterline, the next moment bobbing up, gasping for air.

Travis reached for Angela. Their fingertips touched, but he was unable to get to her. Finally, in one desperate effort, he took hold of her. He pulled her into him, holding her from behind with one arm. Using his one free arm and kicking his feet as hard as he could, he began swimming them to shore. They were only a few feet from the other side, but it could just as well been a mile. The current fought against them, pulling them downstream.

Without warning, they crashed into one of the destroyed, partial arches of Miller's Bridge jutting out from the water. They held onto it, trying to regain their strength and breath.

Travis shouted over the rushing sound of water around them, "I'm going to try to kick us off these stones toward shore. I need you to kick with me as hard as you can."

Angela nodded.

"You ready?" he shouted.

"I love ya!" she called out.

He looked at her as if all was calm and smiled. "I love you, too!"

With that he pushed his foot as hard as he could against the arch, pushing them in the direction of the shoreline.

"Kick…Kick!" he shouted.

The next instant, Travis felt his shoulder dig into the gravel shoreline. This stopped them from the force of the current taking them any farther downstream. Using all their strength, they worked their way out of the water. They remained lying on the ground next to each other, coughing up swallowed water.

Travis reached out, taking hold of her hand. "Are you all right?"

She nodded, tightening her grip on his hand.

Slowly, they worked their way to their feet. Travis looked downstream, and then upstream. The horse was long gone.

"We need to keep moving," he announced.

Angela looked across to the other side of the river from where they came from. "Well, let's see if they can track us, now, after all that."

Travis looked at her blankly, and then burst into a fit of laughter. Angela began to laugh along with him. It was good to be alive and together.

****

When night fell, their clothes were finally dry, which was a good thing for they knew they could not light a fire. Hopefully, they'd lost the soldiers who were tracking them down, and they had given up their pursuit. It was difficult to say, so it was best not to bring on any attention.

They walked out along the bank of the river. The sound of the river's flow mixed with the echoing of the cicadas.

"It's gonna be a hot one, tomorrow," Angela proclaimed. Travis gave her a questioning look. "They always says it's gonna be hot tomorrow when the cicadas get noisy"

Travis shrugged his shoulders, not knowing.

Angela stopped in her tracks, pointing a few feet ahead of them. "Look!" she shouted laughingly.

Travis' eyes followed her finger. It was the willow tree where they had first met and spent so much time together.

When they came to the tree, Travis held the willow's branches apart. Angela entered, followed by Travis. The familiar sent of green leaves surround them. It was too dark to see anything. They welcomed the darkness, knowing they would be concealed and safe at least for one night.

Travis reached around till he found her, pulling her close to him, and kissing her. They wrapped their arms around each other, falling to the ground, laughing.

****

Thin slivers of morning light cut through the branches of the willow tree. Rays of daylight danced about in their sanctuary. Angela's eyes flickered when a beam of light washed over her face, waking her. She opened her eyes to see Travis smiling at her. He was lying on his side, his elbow bent, his hand holding his head. He'd been watching her sleep.

"You are so beautiful," he whispered as he reached out and kissed her. He rose to his feet, reached down to help her up. "We need to go," he said, which was the cold truth. If the soldiers were still looking for them, they would be close.

"If they're still looking for us, they'll catch us. They're on horses and we're on foot. It's no contest." Travis stated as they walked along the banks of the river.

"So what should we do?" Angela asked.

"I know a place where we'd be safe, if we can get to it."

"Where's that?" she asked, feeling uneasy. There was an air of trepidation in the way he said the words *place, safe,* and *if*.

Travis hesitated before he spoke, and when he did it was in a slight stutter. "My father's plantation..." he said.

Angela stopped walking, looked at him, tilting her head. "Are ya kiddin'?"

Travis continued walking for a moment, going a few feet ahead of her. He turned to address her. "It's not that far from here. If we don't stop to rest we could be there in two days or less."

"And what will ya tell your father who I am?"

Travis' face went solemn. "I'll be honest. I could never tell him about us. I don't know if there's anybody I could tell about us. But if I told him you saved my life, he'd treat you right. We'd be somewhere safe, somewhere we can take our time and make some sense of all this. Where we can make plans for our future."

"Do we have a future?" Angela asked coldly.

Travis reached out, taking her hand.

"Do you feel my hand in yours?"

Angela nodded to him.

"I will never let go of your hand. Even if I'm not there, even if I'm dead, I will never let go of your hand."

She raised his hand to her lips and kissed it. There were tears in her eyes.

"All right," she said. "Let's go."

****

Perhaps, Travis and Angela eluded the Union soldiers, or they gave up, or maybe, just maybe, they weren't very good trackers, in the first place. Whichever, there was no sign of them.

This was a good thing, as Travis miscalculated the traveling time and distance to the Parker Plantation. Two days later, they were still walking south, with nary a sign of civilization.

There were a few shacks that spotted the countryside, but they were far and in between. They stayed as far as possible away from them, walking around them. There was no need to take unnecessary chances.

They ate what they could, gathering as they went along. Mostly roots, berries, and an occasional apple or peach.

Travis' plan to walk without stopping to rest, to get there all the quicker, was abandoned after the second day. They slept in tall grass to keep concealed from other travelers, of which they saw none.

"I know this place," Travis said, in recognition. "We're not far away, maybe another day or so."

The proposition didn't sit well with Angela. In fact, she was dreading it. Each mile brought her closer to what she feared, though she could not give it a name.

As they drew closer, Travis pointed out places familiar to him along with stories from his youth concerning each of them.

"What were ya like as a boy?" Angela asked.

"I don't know, like any other boy, I guess. What about you. What were you like as a child?"

Angela thought for a moment. "I couldn't say. Slaves don't have a very long childhood. As soon as ya can stand on your own, and your hands big enough to hold a wad of cotton, they put ya in the fields."

Travis regretted his question. Angela noticed his reaction.

"Don't worry," she said. "Things are better now."

****

It was sunset when they came to the crest of a high hill looking down at the Parker Plantation. It was larger than the plantation Angela came from, and larger then she imagined.

"There she is," Travis said with a hint of pride. "Come on, we're just in time for supper. Let's get some real food."

"Travis, wait," Angela said, standing as if she'd turned to stone and someone nailed her feet to the ground. "I'm afraid," she added.

He reached out and held both of her arms firmly. "Don't fret now. I promise I won't let anything bad happen."

She looked up at him. "Let's not go down, now. Let's go in the morning. Spend the night with me one more time before we can't. . ." her voice trailed off.

"Of course," he whispered, taking her by the hand.

They found some tall grass. There they would spend the night.

Six

Hell to Pay

In the morning, Travis and Angela walked down to the Parker Plantation to the main house. Many of the slaves were moving about the property, starting their day. They stared at Travis and Angela as they walked by, some because they recognized Travis, others because of their ragamuffin appearance. None of them said a word to them. For a slave, it best to be deaf, dumb, and blind.

At the front door of the main house, Travis knocked. Normally, he would simply enter, but he thought the situation, being the way it was, he'd best go slowly.

The door opened, a short, elderly, black man dressed in a dark suite opened the door. It took a moment for him to recognize Travis with his long unkempt beard and hair, dressed like a vagabond. When he did, his face lit up, his eyes went wide, and a crescent moon smile appeared on his face.

"Master Travis!" he exclaimed. "We didn't know if ya was dead or alive. And here ya are! Praise the Lord...praise to the Lord!"

"Good to see you, too, Sully. Is my father in?"

"He sure is, Master Travis. Both ya father and mother are in the dining room, havin' their breakfast."

At the mention of his stepmother, a chill rose along Travis' spine.

The old man opened the door wide for them to enter. His eyes remained on Travis as they walked passed him and down the hallway. Angela may as well have been too unimportant to see.

Going down the hallway, Angela walked close behind Travis. Looking about at what was grander a home than the one she served in. She had to consciously force her legs to move, she was so full of fear.

In the dining room, there was a long table. Travis' father sat at one end, his stepmother a long way off at the other.

"Travis!" his father shouted, rising from his chair and running toward him. "My boy...my boy," he repeated as the two men hugged.

His stepmother stood up from the table, tuned to Travis, offering her hand to shake. "Travis...," was all she said, as they shook hands. It was a politician's handshake, cold, pointless, and forced.

"Let me look at you," Samuel said, standing back to take stock of his son. "I don't understand. Why are you here and why are you dressed like that?"

"It's a long story, father," Travis answered.

Samuel looked over at Angela. "And what do we have here?"

It bothered Travis that the women he loved was referred to as *what*. But he knew better than to speak against it.

"This is Angela. I'd be dead, if it wasn't for her. She saved my life."

Samuel walked over and stood in front of her. Angela knew how the game was played. She remained standing with her eyes cast downward, and she would not speak unless told to.

"Well, missy, I thank you for my son," was all he said. He turned back to his son. "You must be hungry." Then he thought for a moment and laughed. "What a stupid question. Of course, you're hungry. Just look at you. Sit down, my boy, sit down."

"Shouldn't he clean up first?" his wife asked, already seated.

"Nonsense…! The boy's hungry, he needs to eat something. "Looking to Travis, "Sit down, my boy," he repeated. Then he shouted at the kitchen door, "Tessie….Tessie!"

A moment later a small, elderly black woman stood in the doorway. "Yes, sir?" she asked.

"Put out a setting for my son, and bring out a double portion of everything. Oh, and take this girl into the kitchen and see that she's fed."

"Yes, sir," then looking to Angela, "This way, girl."

As Angela walked to the kitchen door, she looked back for a second at Travis. Their eyes met in that moment. So much can be said without a word. It was like standing on the seashore, watching a ship that carried a loved one out to sea, finally disappearing over the horizon, on its journey to another land.

Travis' stepmother rose from the table, nodding as she walked past her husband and her stepson. "If you two gentlemen will please excuse me, I have things to attend to."

She left the room. Secretly, in both their minds, they thought this all the better, as both father and son sat down.

Over a large breakfast, Travis told his father about his exploits. Samuel beamed with pride over each and every word.

Samuel sat back in his chair, drinking his coffee. "Well, your room is as you left it. Go upstairs, clean yourself up, and put on some decent clothes. Do nothing for the next few weeks. Give yourself time to heal. And…when you've regained your strength, you can decide what you want to do. If you want to return to the army or remain here with us, it makes no difference to me. Either way, I'm proud of you, son."

"Thank you, father," Travis said. A serious look came upon him. "There is one thing, father."

Samuel put down his coffee, giving his son his full attention.

"Angela saved my life. I want her treated well."

Samuel laughed slightly. "Why, of course. I'm not as heartless as you think me to be. She saved my son, and she will be treated better than any slave that I have ever owned. We'll clean her up; give her new clothes, and something menial to do, perhaps, some undemanding job in the kitchen. And we'll give her a nice, clean space of her own to sleep in. Nothing large and glamorous, mind you. Something suitable and keeping with her status…that space under the stairs would be perfect.

****

After he cleaned up, Travis went to his room to dress. It felt good to be in his old room, to be in a safe and familiar environment. He had forgotten how much clothing he had in his closet. To be clean again and in clean clothes, to have a full belly, these were experiences he always took for granted – but not anymore.

There was a knock at the door. He walked to the door, but when he got to it, it flew open. There stood Mammy Pam, smiling at him. Travis smiled back.

"Ya ain't too big for me to hug and kiss ya, now, is ya?" she said, holdin her arms out wide. Travis ran into her arms like a child runs to his mother, and kissed her.

"Oh, Mammy Pam, it's so good to see you," Travis said, guiding her into his room.

"Let me look at ya," Pamela said, standing back to take a good look. "Ya turned into a fine man…a fine man, indeed," she announced with more than a hint of pride. "But are ya all right?"

"Oh, I'm just fine. I been shot up a few times, but I'm all right, now. I probably would have died, if it weren't for Angela. She's the colored girl who came back with me. She even helped me get back home."

"I heard all about her from the kitchen help. Gossip boils faster than water in the kitchen," she laughed, Travis laughed with her. "So, what are ya plans, boy?"

"Oh, I don't know. I think I'll wait a few weeks before I have to decide."

"Well, if I got any say in it, I say ya forget about war and the Confederacy, and stay home with ya Mammy."

Travis smiled and then hugged her. "Oh, Mammy Pam, it's so good to see you, again."

160

Slowly Pamela broke free of Travis and started for the door.

"I got to get back to work," she announced. "Since I don't have to take care of ya no longer, they find a world of things for me to do. They keep me busy, sure enough."

"Mammy…?" Travis asked with all seriousness.

"Yes, child?"

"Angela, the new girl…the one who nursed me and brought me home, could you see that she's treated well…for me, please?"

"The one who saved my boy's life?" she said with laughter. "That angel's goin' to be treated like a queen by everyone on this here plantation or they're gonna get what-for."

****

Tessie was a feisty old black woman who ran the kitchen like a sergeant at an army boot camp. She was one for screaming at the top of her lungs. But all her threats were empty ones. What it came down to at the end of the day was that she'd gotten the kitchen staff through another day without any mishaps, and that she cared for each and every one of them.

Tessie sat Angela down at the kitchen table, loaded a plate with eggs, bacon, and biscuits, placing them in front of Angela.

Tessie pointed and waved her finger at Angela as she spoke. "This here's a special day. Don't go puttin' it in ya head that ya gonna eat this good every day, and that someone's gonna wait on ya hand and foot. Ya understand me, girl?"

Angela nodded, and then pounced down on her food. It had been a long time since she ate any prepared food, cherishing every bit.

When she finished eating, Tessie had two other girls who worked for her take Angela out back of the main house. They already had a metal trough filled with hot water ready and waiting. They stripped her, scrubbed her down, dried her off, and dressed her in a new skirt, blouse, and apron.

Tessie put Angela to work for the rest of the day. All of it was simple kitchen work, mostly chopping and cutting ingredients for the midday meal and the evening's supper for the Master of the house and his family.

The kitchen help consisted of all women, except two young slave boys who worked at the stables. They would call for them whenever heavy lifting was needed, such as bringing in firewood or fetching sacks of potatoes from the root cellar.

The women who worked the kitchen treated Angela well. Though they weren't overly friendly, they weren't overly cold to her; in fact they weren't overly anything. They spent most of their day working with their heads down and their lips buttoned.

The day went by quickly. Angela enjoyed the work. It was a much-needed distraction from the thoughts that troubled her.

At the end of the day, she was tired. So, she retired to her cubbyhole under the stairs. Tessie had the two boys from the stables put a cot in her room, along with a nightstand and a lamp. It was all too familiar, just like being home – the one she ran away from.

She sat on the edge of the cot, bending over to take off her shoes. Just when she was about to close the door, she looked up and was surprised to see a middle-aged black women standing before her – smiling.

"Hope I didn't scare ya. My name's Pamela."

"Ya must be Travis' Mammy Pam. He told me all about ya."

"Did he, now? Well, I just wanted to welcome ya, and tell ya that if there's anything ya need, ya just come to Mammy Pam."

"I thank ya," Angela replied.

"And I thank ya, too," Pamela said, "for helpin' my boy come back home."

Angela was confused for a moment, and then it dawned on her. "Oh, ya mean Travis. It was nothing."

Pamela smiled and began to back away. "Well, ya just have a good night, and remember what I told ya. And thank ya, again."

"Good night," Angela said.

As Pamela walked away, she thought about not only what she just heard, but how it was said. Angela only said the name *Travis* two times, and both times her eyes lit up like two fireflies in the dark and her face glowed bright like a harvest moon.

Now, Pamela wasn't one to make a mountain out of a molehill, nor was she one to read anything into what might not be there. Still, she couldn't shake off the feeling that something wasn't right.

****

Days went by slowly. Travis and Angela hadn't spoke in all that time. There were mournful looks to one another from across the room, but no words. Then at some point, Angela no longer responded to Travis' gazes. She either looked at the floor or looked away. Clearly, she was avoiding eye contact.

Travis tried to find her and speak with her, but he could never find her alone.

Early one morning, while Travis was dressing for the day, there was a knock at his door.

"Come in," he called out.

The door opened, it was Angela standing in the doorway, holding a stack of men's shirts in her arms.

"I've brought Master Travis' shirts," she said, entering and placing the shirts on his bed.

He grabbed her by the arm. "Angela, what are you doing?"

"What I'm supposed to do. I cleaned and ironed Master Travis' shirts and here they are."

"Why are you acting this way?" he asked.

She pulled away from his grip. "I'm acting like any slave should act for their Massa."

"Angela, I'm not your Massa. It's me, Travis."

"Can I leave, now," Angela said coldly, "or does Massa want me to lie down on his bed."

"Angela, stop it! I told you how it would be before we came. I just need some time to figure out what we're going to do."

"And what would ya have us do?" Angela asked, being as blunt as she could.

"Just give me some time. All we need is some money, and we can go somewhere and start over together."

Angela's statements were cold and brutal. "Where are ya gonna get this money? And even if ya did, where would we go. No, I understand. I've got a good life, now. I don't' have to work hard. I live in the main house. I've got my own room under the stairs. What more can a colored girl ask for in life?"

"Stop it, stop it," Travis shouted. "I told you it wouldn't be easy. We just need some time, it will all work out." His voice changed. "I love you. I swear I love you."

The sound of his words melted all the coldness in Angela's heart. She began to cry. He wrapped his arms around her, pulling her in close.

"Just a little longer, and we can leave. We'll start a life together. Somewhere no one can touch us," he vowed.

He pulled her in close. Bending low, he kissed her. They kissed long and hard till there was no doubt in either of their minds what direction they were headed. Not that it mattered. Whatever direction they were headed, they were headed together.

"Don't stop believing in us," Travis whispered as he bent low and kissed her, again.

Not thinking, Angela had left the door to Travis' bedroom ajar. As they were kissing, someone moved in the hallway, stopping at the bedroom door. It might have been nothing. It might have been the wind. But it was not.

Travis took his lips from Angela's, turned his head and saw what he least expect and what he feared the most.

Standing in the doorway, watching intensely, was Belial, his stepmother.

Travis backed away from Angela. He looked to his stepmother, speechless, waiting for her to say something.

Their eyes met. She stood there, expressionless, the slightest whisper of a smile forming on her lips.

"Yes," Travis asked her.

"Nothing," Belial responded. "Nothing at all."

She turned and walked on down the hallway. They could hear her footsteps on the stairs.

Travis and Angela parted with a kiss. Angela held a newfound faith in the man she loved.

****

Travis waited, expecting the unexpected. Days passed, and there was nothing said by his father or his stepmother. She obviously hadn't told Samuel what she saw with her own eyes. Why did she keep such information to herself? Everyone knew she disliked Travis, even Samuel. Why was she not saying what Travis knew she wanted to say, to use the facts against him?

These non-actions made Travis fear her all the more. He assumed there was more hell to pay somewhere on down the line.

Seven

We Need to Talk

Travis was in the barn, grooming his horse. Not that he couldn't order the stable boys to do it, but because he enjoyed doing it. With a brush in each hand he combed the mare from shoulder to rump, all with long strokes in one direction. After doing one side, he switched to the other. That's when he saw Pamela standing and watching at the opening to the stall.

"Mammy Pam, I didn't hear you come in. How are you?" he said, and then continued his grooming.

"Travis, we need to talk."

All his life, Pamela called him by loving names she'd made up, or called him *Boy* or *Child*. She only called him *Travis* when something was wrong. He stopped what he was doing, put down the brushes, and then stood before her.

"What is it?" he asked apprehensively.

"What are ya doin'?" Pamela asked bluntly.

"What does it look like I'm doing?"

"That's not what I'm asking, and ya know it," Pamela said coldly.

The smile left Travis' face. He looked like a little boy who'd been caught with his hand in the cookie jar. Pamela was always the one to catch him, and only Pamela had a way of making him confess.

Pamela continued, "This Angela, the girl ya came back with, it ain't all what it seems, is it?"

Travis remained silent.

"I'm not blind. I she how ya look at this girl, and I see how she looks at ya back. Now, tell me the truth."

Travis lets out a long sigh, "I love her."

"Ya love her," Pamela echoes the words. "Are ya willin' to die for her?"

Travis looks at her, clearly not understanding the question.

"Because that's what is gonna happen to ya," Pamela explained. "And I hope she's willin' to die for ya, because if anyone finds out, they'll kill her in a heartbeat, before ya."

"I think my stepmother already knows," Travis confessed. "Why she hasn't told anyone, yet…?"

"Then ya need to do one of two things," Pamela warned. "Ya gotta give her up, and then send her off, or ya both gotta leave, and soon."

"Then we'll leave," Travis said with determination in his voice.

"Do ya know where ya gonna go?"

"There'll never be peace for us in this country. I was thinking we could go south to Mexico."

Pamela shrugged her shoulders, not knowing if Mexico was a good solution.

"If ya stepmother knows, then you're walkin' on thin ice. Ya need to leave…today, if possible."

"I've been putting all the money I can get my hands on aside. I should have enough in a week or two," Travis explained.

"That's not good enough," Pamela advised. "It needs to be right now."

Travis seemed lost for words. Pamela took a deep breath and gave out a long sigh.

"How much money do ya need?"

"One hundred more should do it."

Pamela spoke softly, "I'll make a deal with ya. If I get ya the money, will ya leave tomorrow?"

"Where are you going to get that kind of money?"

"Don't ya worry, I'll get it," Pamela said, it clearly being her last word on the matter, as she turned and left the barn.

****

The sun was shining and the air was warm. For this reason, Tessie thought it a perfect day to clean all the bedsheets in the main house. She had Angela strip all the beds, wash the bedsheets in a vat of hot water, and then hang them on clotheslines set up behind the main house.

As soon as Angela draped the first two bedsheets over the clothesline, the wind kicked up. The bedsheets furled like flags, and the sound of them fluttering in the wind was like the sails of a ship in the flurry of a gale.

"Angela…" A voice called to her from behind. She spun around to see Pamela.

"Oh, Mammy Pam, it's ya."

"Angela…we need to talk."

Angela put down the sheet she held, placing it back into the large wicker basket at her feet.

Pamela spoke matter-of-factly straight from the shoulder. "It's about ya and Travis." Angela's mouth opened, but before she could say a word, Pamela cut her off. "Don't deny it. I know all about it. I've just been talkin' to Travis about it. He's got plans of ya two headin' down to Mexico."

"If that's where he wants to go, then I'm goin' with him," Angela declared.

Pamela moved in closer to Angela. "If I give ya one hundred dollars, would ya leave by yourself, without Travis?"

"Not for the world," Angela replied.

Pamela laughed quietly, "That's what I though ya'd say. I always prayed for Travis to find a good woman. I do believe ya be her. When I was praying, I never specified what color she should be, but I guess it don't matter none. Especially now as ya both so determined. Oh well, when ya got the feelin' ya can't run away from it."

"Thank ya, Mammy Pam," Angela said, smiling.

"Don't thank me; just be ready for you and Travis to go rabbit first thing tomorrow morning."

****

Pamela casually walked up the staircase of the main house to the second floor. It was common to see her about the house so she wasn't secretive of her movements. She paid great attention to her surroundings. Because of what she planned to do, it would be better if she went unnoticed.

The door to the master bedroom was wide open. There were two clothes closets in the room, one for Samuel Parker, the other for Belial whose closet was understandably twice the size of her husbands, as she had twice the amount of clothing.

Samuel kept money on hand for emergencies. He felt proud of his initiative, keeping gold and silver coins hidden in a hatbox on the top shelf in his closet.

Little did Samuel know that everyone, literally everyone at the main house knew of his hiding place. His wife knew of his hoard, but as she got everything she wanted by just requesting it, she never mentioned it, allowing her husband his little idiosyncrasies. The house knew of it, the maids, butlers, the kitchen staff, and right down to the stable boys who carried in the firewood. Only what good would it do them to steal it. They would have no place to spend it, and if they were caught, it surely meant death.

Pamela took down the hatbox, the coins jingling within. Holding the box in one hand, she opened the lid with the other, taking out three gold coins and three silver coins, placing them in the pocket of her apron.

She replaced the lid, and just when she'd returned the hatbox to its place on the shelf, she heard the rustle of a crinoline petticoat, and then the voice of her mistress.

"Mammy Pam, what are you doing?" Belial Parker demanded to know.

Pamela closed the closet door, and then turned to face her.

"I'd rather not say, ma'am."

"You'd rather not say!" Belial shouted back in anger. "If you don't tell me this instant, there'll be hell to pay."

"If I tell ya, ya won't like it," Pamela warned.

Belial folding her arms in front of her, shooting daggers from her eyes at Pamela.

"All right, I'll tell ya," Pamela said. "I saw a mouse run across the room. When I went after it, it ran under the door into Mr. Parker's closet. I opened the door, and was just about to step on it and kill it when ya came in."

Belial unfolded her arms and held them straight up toward the ceiling.

"A mouse!" exclaimed Belial, in horror. She turned and rushed down the hallway.

"I told ya that ya wouldn't like it," Pamela shouted down the hallway to her mistress.

When she got to the end of the hall, standing at the top of the stairs, she looked back at Pamela standing in the doorway of the master bedroom. "Tell one of the boys to place a mousetrap in Mr. Parker's closet. Ugh, how I hate those filthy little beasts," she shouted back as she hurried down the stairs, cringing with each step.

Eight

I Thought Not

The bedsheets on the clotheslines were still damp, when they rode over the hill and onto the Parker Plantation. Every head turned to stare. They were a rough looking bunch. There were four men, in all. They were covered with the dust of the trail. Each man had the beginnings of a beard growing on their face. Their horses moved slowly and with great effort. Clearly, they displayed all the signs of being on the road for a long time. There were three men on horseback followed by a two-horse wagon driven by another man.

One of the overseers rushed into the main house, looking for Samuel, he found him seated at his desk in the library.

"Mr. Parker…Mr. Parker…!" the man called out, standing in the doorway of the library, trying to catch his breath.

"Buford…what the hell are you doing tracking mud into my home?" Samuel barked, looking up from his desk.

"Mr. Parker, there's four men ridin' onto the property!"

"Folk have ridden onto this property before, what makes these so special?" Samuel asked.

"I spoke with the leader," Buford explained. "He says he's a Sheriff."

Understanding the situation better, Samuel rose from his desk and out the front door, followed by Buford. Samuel stood on the front pouch, as the small group halted in front of the main house.

"Can I help you, gentlemen?" Samuel called out.

"You Samuel Parker?" asked the man mounted in front of the others, obviously the leader.

"That would be me," Samuel answered back.

"The name's Garland, Sheriff Garland. These here are my men. We're from Roister County."

"You're a long way from home, Sheriff," Samuel commented.

"That's true; we've been on the road for a long time."

"Well, state your business, Sheriff."

"I'm not gonna talk about it out here. Is there a place we could speak in private, Mr. Parker?"

"Yeah, sure, follow me."

Sheriff Garland dismounted and stepped onto the porch.

Samuel pointed at Buford. "Buford, I want you to see that Sheriff Garland's men get what they need. Make sure they get fed." He turned to Sheriff Garland. "…If you would please follow me?" They entered the main house.

Garland's men dismounted. Buford gave orders for their horses to be watered and fed. "Just follow me," Buford told them, intending to take them around back to the kitchen.

For no other reason other than curiosity, Buford walked to the back of their wagon to see what they were hauling. To his surprise, seating in the back of the wagon was an elderly black woman. She was small, gray-haired, and frail as dried twigs.

"Don't mind her," said one of the men. "She's a cranky, bitter, old crow. Don't get your hand to close to her, she'll bite it off," he laughed.

The men helped the old woman off the back of the wagon, and they all followed Buford around to the back of the main house.

As he and the Sheriff walked down the hallway to the library, it perturbed Samuel that his guest didn't have the good manners to take his hat off.

Sheriff Garland was an older man with more gray hairs on his head and in his beard than dark. He was slender and lean. In his filthy and worn clothes, he was the spitting image of a scarecrow. Only the sheriff's badge pinned to his vest over his heart looked clean and new.

In the library, Samuel pointed to a chair in front of his desk, "Sit down, Sheriff." Samuel took his place at his desk. Taking up a dark, wooden box from the corner of the desk, he opened it and offered it to Garland.

"…Cigar, Sheriff?"

"No thank you, sir; my smokin' days are far behind me."

"So, Sheriff, how can I help you?" Samuel asked as he placed the cigar box back onto the corner of his desk.

"Well, ya see, Mr. Parker, I don't know if ya heard any of this, but there was an incident at the Abernathy Plantation, in Roister County, a while back."

"No, I'm sorry; I haven't heard anything about the Abernathy Plantation."

"Well, it seems one of their female slaves, a young girl, ran off. Before she did she killed off most of the overseers and all of their trackin' dogs."

Samuel's face lit up, "Do tell? And how did she accomplish this feat?"

"Poison, Mr. Parker, she poisoned the lot of them. She put it in their food, killed all but three overseers and all of the dogs."

"The dogs, too, you say. Why that's monstrous. Nevertheless, it still doesn't explain why you're here, Sheriff."

"Well, ya see, sir, we've been out trying to track her down. We figure she never got out of the region. She got captured and sold to one of the local plantations, or she willingly placed herself on a plantation to elude detection. Mr. Abernathy was kind enough to lend us one of his slaves, an old woman that we got in the back of our wagon. She says she can identify this girl, no problem."

"And what is the name of this girl?" Samuel asked.

"Her name is *Angela*, but I doubt if she's using that name."

"Angela...Angela," Samuel repeated to himself until it dawned on him. "We've got a new colored girl named Angela. But I doubt she's the one you're looking for."

"It's a long shot, but she just might be. Tell me, Mr. Parker, what does this girl look like?"

Samuel laughed hardily, "Sheriff Garland, she's young, she's female, and she's colored. What more can I say? They all look alike."

****

Table and chairs were set up in back of the main house, under a shade tree. Garland's men, along with the old woman, sat feasting on scrambled eggs and potatoes – the fastest meal Tessie could whip up.

Angela walked out from the kitchen door with a wicker basket under her arm, off to fetch the clean, dried bedsheets. She was unaware of the guests sitting off a few yards away; she didn't even look in their direction.

Suddenly, the old woman began to scream. She rose from the table, pointing at Angela. "That be her...that be her!" the old woman shouted.

Caught off guard, Angela wasn't sure what to do. Her first thought was to run, but where could she run to, and how far would she get. She stood still as a statue as the old woman walked toward her.

"That be her...That be her," the old woman repeated as she drew closer to Angela. Two of the men came over to investigate, while one of them ran into the main house to tell Sheriff Garland what was happening.

A moment later, Sheriff Garland ran out of the house and up to Angela, followed by Samuel.

"That's her, all right," the old woman said, still pointing, only now a few feet from Angela. It was then that Angela recognized her. It was Ravenna, her mother.

"How did ya acquire this slave, Mr. Parker?" Sheriff Garland asked.

Samuel knew to give too much information might implicate his son. So, he kept the facts down to a minimum. "Not sure, Sheriff, my son found her out on the road somewhere and brought her here. She didn't say much. We had no idea she was a runaway."

Garland thought it a flimsy explanation, but he saw no reason to debate the issue.

It was at that moment that Travis came running out of the main house to investigate.

"Father, what's going on?" he asked when he came up to them.

Samuel turned to his son. "This here's Sheriff Garland and his men all the way from Roister County. It seems this girl you found is a wanted murderer, killed a few people at the last plantation she worked."

"There's got to be some mistake," Travis said.

"No mistake, son," Garland said. "This here woman worked the same plantation and has identified this girl as the killer." Garland looked to Samuel. "I'm sorry, Mr. Parker, but we're gonna have to take this girl away. Looks like ya out one slave girl."

"That's fine," Samuel said. "Take her away, good riddance, I say. I never paid for her, anyway. Who knows, maybe she'd kill us all in our beds, one night. It's best you take her away."

"Where will you take her," Travis asked.

"Well, I'm sure the folks at the Abernathy Plantation would like to see her hang. And I say they deserve to. But like it or not a judge has to approve a hanging. Not a trial, mind ya, just an approval. Or we might as well hang her here and now. Gotta keep the law, son, follow the rules. The nearest judge is in Colleyville, so I guess that's where we be headin'."

Two of Garland's men took hold of Angela, one on each arm. "Take her away, boys," Garland ordered. The other man helped Ravenna.

"I thank ya for your help and hospitality, Mr. Parker," Garland said. "Again, I'm sorry," he added.

Angela remained silent the entire time. As the men took her away, she looked back, her eyes locked with Travis' eyes. In the fleeting moment of that encounter, they told each other what needed to be said without words. He told her how much he loved her. She sent her love back to him. All fear left her and a smile appeared on her face. She knew he would come for her. He would rescue her or die trying.

****

Before Sheriff Garland and his company were off the Parker property, Travis was in his bedroom, preparing for his journey. He changed into his hunting clothes, not only rugged wearing but the colors of forest foliage for camouflage. He slung his backpack over one shoulder. Down in the kitchen he filled it with as much nonperishable food as he could find. In the library, his father designated one corner to house his gun collection. Travis took one rifle, two pistols, and ammo for all of them, stuffing the boxes of cartridges in his backpack. He tucked the two pistols in his belt, one on each hip.

Entering the barn, he was greeted by the two stable boys.

"Can we help ya, sir?" one of them asked.

"Yes, you can saddle me up two horses, the fastest we have."

"Two, sir?" asked the boy, thinking it strange.

"That's what I said. I want two horses ready as fast as you can."

They did what they were told. Fifteen minutes later, Travis was mounted and on his way. The two stable boys watched as Travis went over the ridge at top speed.

Thinking Master Travis' behavior a might peculiar, they reported what happened to Buford, the overseer. Buford, also thinking it strange, and being someone always on the lookout for a feather for his cap, went to tell Samuel. He found Samuel and his wife in their dining room, preparing to have their supper.

"Mr. Parker...Mr. Parker, sir," Buford whispered as he entered the dining room.

"What is it, now, Buford, that you have to disturb my supper? Can't it wait?"

"Sorry, sir, but I thought ya might like to know. Master Travis has just left the plantation with two horses."

"So, maybe he's going deer hunting, and he needs an extra horse to carry the carcass."

"But, the boys at the barn said he was armed to the tooth, two rifles and two pistols."

"That is strange," Samuel admitted. "Who knows what he's up to? I wouldn't make too much of it. Now, if you'd please leave so my wife and I can have our supper."

"Yes, sir, sorry, sir," Buford said as he left the room.

"I've got nothing but fools working for me," Samuel grumbled.

Belial leaned across the table toward Samuel, "And you're the biggest fool of them all."

He looked at her, questioning her statement, "What are you saying?" he asked coldly.

"I'm saying your love for your son has blinded you. You don't see it, do you?"

"What...see what?" he demanded.

"The colored girl...your son and that colored girl, they're in love."

Samuel let out a long hard laugh, "That's ridiculous."

"Is it?" Belial sneered. "She saves his life, they wander in the wilderness together for God knows how long, and you think nothing happened? And now, less than an hour after she's taken away to be hung, he rides off with two horses and enough arms to start a small war. Wake up, Sam; he's gone off to rescue her."

Samuel leaned low over the table towards his wife and whispered, "Do you really think so?"

"Oh, Sam, you're hopeless," she laughed. "What do you need…a brood of little black grandchildren on your knee before you believe it?"

Samuel slammed his fist down on the table, rose from his chair, and headed out the door.

"Where are you going, Sam?" Belial asked in a sarcastic tone.

Samuel didn't answer. He stormed out of the house. Standing on the porch, he shouted, "Buford!"

****

They bound Angela's hands and feet, and tossed her into the back of the wagon with Ravenna. They road for miles in silence, Angela staring at Ravenna, and Ravenna staring out at the road they left behind.

Finally, miles up the road, Angela asked the question that was on her mind, not in anger, but in sincere interest in the answer.

"Why?" was all Angela needed to say.

Ravenna understood the question all too well.

"I'm old," Ravenna replied. "I haven't much time left. Anything that would make these last few days of my life easier, I welcome. To point ya out to the authorities, gives me power, and with power comes security. I'll never live the life of a white women; I long since gave up on that dream. But I'll live my days out in comfort. And that's all a body can ask."

"…at the cost of the life of your own daughter?" Angela asked.

"What are ya talkin' about," Ravenna laughed. "Everyone is somebody's daughter or son. What's the difference? One lives, one dies, the world goes on. Make it the best ya can make it."

"That's a sad way to go through life," Angela commented.

"Is it?" Ravenna responded. "I'm not the one on her way to Colleyville to be hung, now am I?"

"That's true," Angela replied, "but it doesn't make it right."

"Oh, now you're talkin' truth now, are ya?" Ravenna said, laughing. "Well, dear, ya tell me what is truth and I'll bow down before ya."

"I don't know," Angela said.

Ravenna smiled at Angela's response.

"But I do know what it's not." Angela countered, wiping the smile from Ravenna's face. "I know it's not something inside me. Everything inside me is flawed. Anything that is truth, that is real truth, must come from outside me. Call it God, call it what ya like. If truth exists, it comes from outside me and ya, it comes from God. I don't see that in ya. I don't hear it in your voice. I just hear from ya what ya believe to be truth, which is no truth at all."

"Ya spin a fine web, my dear," Ravenna laughed "But like the spider's web it holds no weight."

"I don't care what ya think, "Angela said. "All I know is that I love and that I am loved. If ya can match that, I'll consider what you're sellin', if not, you're in my prayers."

Ravenna remained silent.

"I thought not," Angela said. "Everyone needs love in their life, givin' and takin', or they ain't got life. Like the Bible says, no matter what good ya do, if ya have not love, ya are a sounding gong. And ya, my dear mother, are a sounding gong. Have ya ever been loved or in love?"

Ravenna looked away, unable to answer.

"I thought not," Angela concluded.

Nine

Night

It wasn't a difficult trail to follow. Because of the wagon they were forced to stay to the roads. Also, the wagon is what slowed them down. So, it wasn't hard for Travis to catch up with Sheriff Garland and his men.

The trick would be to keep his distance and not be seen, biding his time for the right moment. Though he had guns, he wanted to avoid using them. Still, if it came down to a shootout, he was willing to kill or be killed.

They started out late in the day. It wasn't long before night fell and it was too dark to travel on. They found a small clearing on the side of the road. They made camp, started a fire, and cooked their dinner.

"Where's mine?" Ravenna complained.

"Relax old woman, you'll get yours," one of the men said. He turned to the others, laughing, "Cranky old crow, ain't she?"

Another man untied the bounds on Angela's hands, allowing her to hold her plate and eat on her own.

"Just because ya got ya hands back, don't get any bright ideas. Ya still bound at the feet. And though we want to keep ya alive, so we can hang ya…" his smile grew large and he directed it to Angela, alone as he said this. "But I wouldn't think twice about winging ya. Then I'd throw some salt on the wound, and that ain't no fun. So, just do what ya told. Go on, eat ya grub."

When she finished her meal, they tied her hands, again. They propped her against a tree trunk so she could sit up. Ravenna sat on the ground next to her. Sheriff Garland sat quietly on the ground far from the fire with his back up against a tall rock. The others sat in a circle close to the fire. They were loud and full of laughter, talking about what they were going to do once they got to Colleyville.

The night was all around. The glow of the campfire illuminated a large circle, beyond that the world ended and a dark world began. It was on the edge of that glow, just before you enter the abyss of shadows that something caught Angela's eye. Something moved from left to right, so quickly did it move that Angela wasn't sure she really saw anything. It moved quickly enough that none of the others saw it. When she saw it again, she knew it was Travis.

"We got a full day's worth of ridin'," Sheriff Garland announced, "Y'all best turn in for the night."

The man who had untied Angela looked at her and smiled. "Ya know," he said to the other deputy next to him. "In this light, ya can't tell if she's colored. And I ain't had any since we set off on this goose chase."

He stood up and started walking toward Angela.

"Say, Jim Bob...ain't she a might old for such doings?" one of the men said jokingly.

Jim Bob turned, "I ain't talkin' about the old crow. I'm talkin' 'bout the youngin."

They all laughed, knowing it was a joke.

Ravenna lay on the ground, turning her back on them all, wanting nothing to do with what was about to happen.

Jim Bob stood smiling, looking down at Angela. "Ya know, it might not be so bad if ya held ya breath and kept ya eyes shut."

All three men laughed.

Jim Bob placed his boot at the hem of Angela's skirt. Slowly, he moved his foot upwards, taking the hemline up, and exposing Angela's legs.

"Ya know, boys," Jim Bob said over his shoulder to the others. "I'm gonna tell ya something nobody knows, except for my wife. When she makes chicken, I always prefer the dark meat."

Again, they burst into laughter.

Fear grabbed hold of Angela, not a fear for herself, but for Travis. She knew he was watching from somewhere in the darkness. He could take only so much before he was pushed to the edge and forced to act. Four against one are dangerous odds. She feared for Travis.

Angela's thighs were exposed; the flickering of the flames sent light dancing over her dark skin.

Suddenly, a single gunshot rang out, cracking open the night's silence and echoing off the hills.

Angela closed her eyes. It was the end of Travis, and she didn't want to see it. He might kill one, two, or even three of them, but he was no match for four. Travis would be shot dead in the next minute, she just knew it.

When there were no more gunshots to be heard and the last of the echoes faded, Angela opened her eyes.

Standing over the campfire, with his smoking gun pointed to the stars, was Sheriff Garland.

His voice was calm but firm. "We got plenty of ridin' to do in the mornin'. Turn in." Garland lowered his gun, aiming it at Jim Bob. "I want a guard on this camp all nightlong. Ya can take turns."

"What the hell do we need a guard for?" Jim Bob protested.

"Because we got a prisoner and because I say so." Garland shook the gun muzzle at Jim Bob. "And ya can take the first watch."

"First watch, why me?" Jim Bob griped.

"Because, Jim Bob, you're the biggest ass I know."

The other two men laughed as they lay down for the night. Sheriff Garland returned to his place against the rock, tilting the brim of his hat down over his eyes. Jim Bob sat down, closer to the fire. Ravenna began to snore. Angela wriggled enough to get her hemline back down over her knees. Travis remained in the shadows, waiting.

****

Samuel stood on the porch of the main house shouting, "Buford!" A minute later Buford came running from the barn to the porch.

"Yes, Mr. Parker," Buford said, trying to catch his breath.

"Buford, I want you to select two other men besides you, and get ready to do some traveling." Samuel looked to the sky for a moment. "It'll be dark soon. No use in leaving now. Be ready to leave first thing in the morning. I want horses, guns, goods, you and your men to be ready at sunup."

"Yes, Mr. Parker. Can I ask what this is all about? Is it a hunting trip?"

"I guess you could call it that," Samuel smiled. "Buford, I'm going to take you into my confidence. Do you know what that means?"

Buford thought a moment before answering, "It means it's just between the two of us and I ain't suppose to tell anyone?"

"...Precisely! Samuel said. "The truth is my son Travis has got his heart set on that little colored the sheriff took away."

"The one they're gonna hang?" Buford asked.

"Yes, the one they're going to hang. As you know, my son left with two horses and plenty of guns and ammo. I suspect he's gone off to rescue her from the sheriff and his men."

"Then we're goin' to try to stop ya son?"

"No, Buford, we're going to take away his motivation. Give him no reason to stick his neck out. We're going to kill that colored girl."

Ten

One Solution

It was the middle of the night; Angela woke to a hand covering her mouth. Because she was bound hand and foot, she couldn't move, and now, nor could she scream. When her eyes adjusted to what little light there was, she saw Jim Bob's face inches from hers. She felt something pressing against her throat, something sharp. Then she realized he held a knife to her.

"Don't make a sound, or I swear I'll cut ya," he hissed softly. "I'm gonna take my hand away. Ya promise ya won't scream?"

Angela nodded.

He slowly removed his hand from off her mouth, keeping the knife pressed against her throat, nearly piercing the skin.

"That's good," he whispered. "If I gotta stay awake, I might as well make it worth my wild. Now, since we're both up, what do ya say we have a party?"

With his free hand, he started caressing her, moving across her like a snake over its prey. Then, his hand found the hem of her skirt. He slowly hiked up her skirt, the palm of his hand flat against her leg, first her shin, then her knee, and up her thigh.

Angela's body stiffened. She bit her lower lip, trying desperately not to make a sound. Still, no matter how hard she tried she couldn't stop from crying. Her face twitched as streams of tears poured from her eyes and down her cheeks. A soft moan escaped through her teeth.

"Now, ya promised me ya wouldn't make a sound," he said, pressing the knife into her skin, drawing a trickle of blood.

Just then, there was a deep resounding thud. Jim Bob's eyes shut, as his face cringed with pain. The next second, Jim Bob fell forward, landing on top of her. He was out cold. Before her Travis stood, holding a rifle in front of him. He'd knocked Jim Bob unconscious using the butt of his rifle.

It was a struggle, but Angela didn't make a sound, nor did she move. Travis bent down, took up the knife Jim Bob dropped, and began to cut Angela free, first her hands, and then her feet.

Taking her by the hand, he guided her into the darkness, to the horses.

****

Jim Bob's head was pounding when he woke. He placed his hand to the back of his head, feeling a lump the size of an apple.

It was just moments before sunrise; there was a dim crescent of light on the horizon.

"Wake up!" Jim Bob shouted as he rose to his feet.

The others were up in a blink. Ravenna rose up on her elbows.

"What the hell's goin' on?" Sheriff Garland shouted, looking at Jim Bob.

"Someone conked me on the noggin. I just woke up. Whoever it was took the girl."

Garland's first reaction was to slam Jim Bob in the teeth, and slap him up and down both sides of his head. But then, after thinking it over, it could have happened to anyone. It's just strange that it always seemed to happen to Jim Bob at the most inconvenient times.

"All right, everybody spread out, see if ya find anything, tracks, whatever," Garland ordered.

After a minute of circling the area, one of the men shouted out, "Sheriff, come quick, I think I found something."

Garland and the other men ran toward the voice. The man was pointing to the dust at his feet. Garland examined the spot carefully.

"I ain't no Injun, but I'd say there're two horses goin' that away," Garland proclaimed, pointing east. "Let's get back to camp and get ready to follow these tracks."

The big question, now, was what to do with Ravenna. She was too old to ride horseback; she needed to ride in the back of the wagon. The wagon moved slowly. They were pursuing two people on horseback; the wagon would slow them down.

For this reason, Garland made the decision for Ravenna to be taken to Colleyville by wagon. Jim Bob was selected to drive the wagon for no other reason than that Garland was tired of looking at him.

The sun was clearly up when they broke camp. Three of them mounted their horses. Jim Bob helped Ravenna onto the back of the wagon. Before he could get her up into the wagon, a shot rang out.

Ravenna fell dead to the ground, a bullet through the head.

****

The sun was still on the horizon when Samuel and his men set off. The tracks left by the wagon made it easy to follow. As the sun was coming up, they stopped. Looking up at a higher point above them, they could see Sheriff Garland and his men preparing to leave camp.

"I want you to take out that black witch," Samuel told Buford.

Buford was the best shot among Samuel and his men, so all responsibility fell on his shoulders.

Samuel looked through his field glasses. "They're getting ready to leave, make it quick," he informed Buford.

As they helped Ravenna onto the wagon, Buford took careful aim, held his breath, and pulled the trigger. The shot was to the head – instantaneous death.

Looking through his field glasses, Samuel knew a mistake had been made.

"You fool," Samuel shouted, slamming Buford on the side of his head. "You killed the old women, you idiot!"

"I saw a black women, I thought it was her," Buford said in his own defense.

Samuel watched through his field glasses as Sheriff Garland and his men took cover.

In time, not knowing what else to do, Sheriff Garland, had his men unbridle the horses from the wagon. One of them would be Jim Bob's mount. Throwing all caution to the wind, they took off following the tracks left by Travis and Angela, leaving Ravenna's body where it fell.

After observing what happened, Samuel knew he was wrong. Obviously, Angela was no longer under Sheriff Garland's arrest. He could only conclude his son had rescued her from her captures. A spark of pride shone in his heart for knowing how brave and ingenious his son was, but it was covered up by anger and prejudice.

He would pursue Travis and Angela. He would kill them both, clearing the family's good name. Erasing all signs of perversion and rot from the family tree, from the roots to the top branches. As much as he loved his son, there were things far more important than love, as far as he was concerned. Though it broke his heart, there was only one solution, the death of his son, Travis, and Angela, Travis' black unnatural love.

Eleven

For the Rest of my Life

Travis and Angela rode west as fast as their horses could travel. They heard a gunshot far off in the distance behind them. There was too much at stake to stop and listen, or to try to make sense of it.

An hour later, they came to a spring. It was time to give the horse a rest and something to drink. They dismounted, rushed to each other, falling into each other's arms.

Angela broke into tears at his touch, quivering in his arms.

"It's all right," he whispered. "I'm here. Nothing is going to ever separate us, again."

"I believe ya," she spoke to his chest.

"I'm sorry I put you through all this," he said, just before kissing her.

They kissed with great passion. They were as one. They breathe as one; their hearts beat as one. The separation between them was an ever disappearing line. The mystery of love was no longer a mystery. They understood it like a book read a hundred times over as many years. As clear as a summer sky after a long rain made everything new and clean, again.

"We need to go," Travis said, pulling the horses in close by their reins, helping Angela back onto her mount.

"Where are we goin'?" Angela asked as they galloped east.

"Not far," Travis replied. "We'll go west just long enough for them to believe that's the direction we're going. They'll think were heading for Texas or parts after that, maybe California. Then we'll double back for awhile, and then go southwest to Mexico."

"Mexico…" Angela echoed. "Will we be safe there?"

"I hope so. I just know we're not safe here."

"What if we go north to the Yankees?" Angela asked.

"I know what you're thinking," Travis responded. "The South is for slavery, and the North is against it. Maybe so, but nether the North or South tolerate blacks and whites together. It's just you and me from here on. I'm sure Mexico is the same, but there are plenty of parts where nobody lives. If we go southwest far enough, we'll meet the ocean. We could live by the ocean. Would you like that?"

"I don't know. I've only heard about the ocean. It don't matter none. I just want us to be together and live in peace."

They smiled at each other, dreaming a dream of an unpredictable future together, one most unlikely to come true.

After they spent half the day traveling west, they did an about-face, heading back east. A few hours later they were back at the stream they were at earlier in the day. Again, they dismounted, allowing their horses to rest.

"We'll give the horses a minute; then we need to start heading southwest. If we're lucky, those men are still following our tracks going west."

It all seemed to make sense to them. It would work. It would take only the will and the effort.

They rode into a valley, and then started upward. When they came to the summit of a high hill, they stopped, looking back.

"Look," Travis said, pointing at a cloud of brown dust some two miles behind them.

"What is it?" Angela asked.

"It's the sheriff and his men. By the way they're kicking up dust; I'd say they're riding hard. We don't have much of a lead. They'll be on us within the hour. We need to ride, and ride hard."

They looked forward down to the valley below. They saw a similar dust cloud as the one behind them, but this was ahead of them.

"I don't understand," Angela said. "Do ya think they split up and are comin' after us from both sides?"

"I doubt it," Travis replied. "That group below is much closer."

The dust cloud stopped suddenly. If they strained their eyes, Travis and Angela could see the riders below, four men on horseback.

"It's my father!" Travis shouted in relief. But then reality settled in on him. There was no reason for his father and his men to be looking for them unless they were hunting for them. A sad reality settled in Travis' heart.

Looking up, Samuel could see Travis and Angela on the crest of the hill. Taking his rifle from his saddle, he brought it up to his shoulder, aiming high. Even Buford looked at Samuel in disbelief. He would rather see his son dead than with *that* black girl.

Taking careful aim, Samuel pulled the trigger. The gunshot echoed against the hills and through the valley numerous times.

Angela was struck in the shoulder. The force knocked her off her horse, falling to the ground.

"Angela!" Travis shouted, dismounting and rushing to her.

"I'm all right," she said as he helped her to her feet.

The blast scared both horses. Travis' horse reared. He was able to keep hold of the reins, keeping it under control, but Angela's horse bolted off in fear.

Samuel began rapid-fire up at them. The other three men took up their rifles, joining him. The sound of bullets whizzing over Travis' and Angela's heads was like the buzzing of a swarm of bees. If not for the long distance and difficult angle, they would have been an easy target.

Travis took Angela up in his arms and lifted her up onto his saddle. When she was in place, he put his foot in the stirrup, and hopped up on the saddle with her. Just then, a bullet clipped him in the ear, slicing it in two. There was no time to see how badly he was hit. He kicked his heels into his horse's side and galloped down the opposite side of the hill, out of sight.

Halfway down, they could see the dust cloud being kicked up by Sheriff Garland and his men coming closer. There were only two directions left to go, east or west. Since Mexico was their aim, west was the obvious choice.

They turned west. Now with the two of them on one horse traveling on the side of the hill the going was difficult and slow. The slope was sharp and the ground was rocky. There were few trees, which meant there was no cover. They were out in the open and an easy target.

Travis held Angela close to him. His hand was red from the blood dripping from the wound on Angela's shoulder. There was a salty taste in his mouth. He realized it was the blood coming from his sliced ear.

In the midst of it all, Travis could not help thinking about his father. His own father shot at him, and was now in hot pursuit with intent to kill his own son.

A half of a mile onward, the slope steepened. It was difficult for his horse to move faster than a crawl. Finally, the beast stumbled over a mound of rocks, falling down on its side, throwing Travis and Angela into the air, landing five feet away.

Travis helped Angela to her feet. The horse got up and back onto its feet with great difficulty. Travis bent low, lifting the horse's front right hoof, inspecting it.

"It's broke," Travis declared.

He unstrapped the saddle, tossing it aside.

"This beast is in a world of hurt. Normally, I'd shoot it and put it out of its misery. But I don't want to call any attention to us. If we're lucky, they may not realize what direction we're heading till we're long gone."

"On foot…?" Angela said.

Inwardly, Travis knew it was true. They may have eluded their pursuers for the time being, but on foot their capture was inevitable. Travis looked eastward; he knew soon his father and his men would be coming over the hill. He looked downhill. Sheriff Garland and his men were still approaching.

If they were captured by Sheriff Garland, Angela would be taken to Colleyville to be hanged. Most likely, the same fate awaited him. If his father and his men were to get to them first, they'd both be shot on sight. It was hopeless.

"I love you," he said, reaching out to her.

She smiled up at him. "I love ya, too."

"Do you trust me?" he whispered.

"...with all my heart."

"I can think of only one place where we'll be safe."

"Take me there," she whispered back. "I'll follow ya for the rest of my life, no matter how long that might be."

Twelve

Were These Enemies

It was on the side of the hill that the two groups met. It surprised Sheriff Garland to find Samuel Parker and his men. They had detached the horses from the wagon for one of the men to ride. Leaving the wagon behind allowed them to move fast. Since time was of the essence, they left Ravenna's body unburied, lying on the ground near the wagon.

Both parties remained on their mounts as they spoke.

"Mr. Parker, what are you doin' here?" Sheriff Garland asked.

"I'll be straight with you, Sheriff; I'm out to get my son."

Putting two and two together, it all became clear to Garland.

"It's that colored girl, isn't it? You're son took a shine to her, didn't he? Well, he came into our camp last night, while we were asleep, and took her. We're trackin' `em down, just like ya."

"That's not what I said, Sheriff," Samuel countered. "I told you I'm out to get my son. He's dishonored me and our family name. When I catch up with them, I'm going to kill them both."

"Then it was you and your men who killed the old woman?" Garland surmised.

"I don't know what you're talking about, Sheriff," Samuel replied.

Garland knew Samuel was lying, but what could he say or do? There were no witnesses. It was Samuel's word against his. Besides, the killing of an old black woman was small potatoes, nothing to get up in a bind over.

"Go home, Mr. Parker. Let us handle this," Garland said, sounding more like an order than a suggestion.

"Sorry, Sheriff, my son has disgraced my good name. I'm honor bound to do what I have to do."

"Murder is against the law, Mr. Parker."

"Is it against the law to hunt down and kill a known criminal? He is a criminal, now, is he not, Sheriff?"

"Ya got me there," Garland admitted. "Well, if ya set on doin' this, we best work together, before we start goin' up and down these hills, shootin' at one another."

"What do you suggest?" Samuel asked.

"Well, we've been travelin' south, and we ain't seen 'em. Ya been travelin' north, and ya ain't seen 'em."

"Oh, we've seen them, all right," Samuel added. "We saw them not too long ago on the crest of this hill. We shot at them. They scurried back over the ridge."

"That means it's only one of two things," Garland said. "They're either headin' east or west. Since goin' east brings 'em deeper into Confederate territory, I'd wager they're headin' west."

Knowing this to be apparent, Samuel bit his tongue, rather than the idiotic stating of the obvious. Samuel didn't want to get on the sheriff's bad side. The sheriff and his men might be needed along the way. Many hands make for light work, the more eyes, the better to see with.

"Let's start headin' west and see if we can pick up their trail," Sheriff Garland announced as he took the lead. The others followed close behind, first Garland's men, and then Samuel and his.

Knowing Travis and Angela had turned to the west was a given to Samuel, which was why it frustrated him to travel so slowly. Garland was determined to find and follow Travis' and Angela's tracks, so they moved at a snail's pace. Again, Samuel bit down on his tongue – hard.

After traveling for nearly a half hour, which irritated Samuel to no end, they came on the couple's tracks.

Garland raised his hand for the group to stop. He pointed to the ground. "We found their tracks, except what I don't understand is there's only one horse; ya would think there'd be two."

"They had two horses," Samuel admitted. "When we saw them at the crest of the hill, we fired a few shots at them. The girl's horse bucked her off and ran. They were forced into using one horse."

"Well, let's just follow the trail. They can't be far off," Garland proclaimed, again taking up the lead.

The entire procedure was rubbing Samuel the wrong way. He couldn't understand why, since they knew what direction they were headed, they were traveling so slow and not galloping in hot pursuit. Only, Sherriff Garland liked to do everything by the book. He'd found the tracks, and he was going to follow them slowly, making sure not to miss a single one.

A short ways up ahead, Garland stopped them, again pointing to the ground.

"Something happened here," Garland said, looking in all directions. He dismounted and started walking down the hill.

"Where the hell are you going, Sheriff?" Samuel shouted, clearly annoyed.

Sheriff Garland ignored him as he walked on, disappearing behind some bushes. A moment later, a shot rang out, startling the horses. Garland stepped out from behind the bushes, walking back to his horse.

"What was that all about?" Samuel asked.

Garland pointed to the ground. "Their horse tripped and fell, breaking its leg. They left it here, and now they're on foot – see," he said, pointing out the tracks. "The poor animal stumbled down the hill to the bushes to die. I just put it out of its misery."

Garland remounted, signally for all to follow him. As before, determined to pick up on every track, he moved them slowly.

Once over the hill, they followed the tracks south. It didn't take Samuel long to realize what direction they were heading.

"This doesn't make any sense," Samuel declared.

"How's that, sir?" Garland asked.

"They're heading back to the plantation. It doesn't make any sense. Why would they go to the very spot where they could never escape from?"

Garland shrugged off the question, continuing to follow the tracks. If anything, he was a determined and patient man. All will become clear in time.

The footsteps continued at the Parker property, heading directly to the heart of the plantation. The footsteps led them passed the fields, right up to the steps of the main house, leading into the kitchen.

Garland dismounted, heading for the back steps.

"Wait one minute, Sheriff," Samuel called out, dismounting and rushing to the steps. "This is my home, Sheriff. You have no jurisdiction here, sir. I'm going in alone."

Being a man who lived life by the book, following every letter of the law, Garland backed off, letting Samuel pass.

Before entering the kitchen, Samuel drew his pistol. In the kitchen, he found Tessie sitting at the table, sobbing and whining into a dish towel.

"Tessie, what's the matter? What's wrong?"

"Oh, Master Parker….it's….it's…" Tessie couldn't finish her sentence or contain her sorrow, as she continued to cry into the towel in her hands. "Upstairs…upstairs…" were the only words she could force out.

Still holding his pistol in front of him, Samuel left the kitchen, entering the dining room. When he looked to his left, he saw his wife sitting in the parlor. He entered the room.

"Belial, what's going on here?" he asked.

She didn't answer, continuing to stare at the carpet at her feet.

"Answer me, damn it!" he bellowed.

She looked up into his eyes. They were empty eyes that gave him no answer.

"Upstairs..." she whispered.

Samuel left the parlor, heading for the stairs. He cautiously climbed to the top. There he saw the door to Travis' room wide open. He entered to find Pamela standing at the foot of the bed, staring down on it.

He moved to her side to see what she was looking at.

On the bed was Travis lying on his side. Angela was in his arms. They were motionless with their eyes closed as if they were sleeping.

Samuel placed his gun atop one of the dressers. The sound caught Pamela's attention. She turned to see who it was. Their eyes met, Samuel could see the sorrow in them, but there was something else – pity. Sorrow for what had happened, and pity for him, pity for the whole world.

Next to the bed was a nightstand. On it, next to the lamp, was a tray. On the tray were a teapot and two teacups. Samuel walked to the side of the bed. He lifted the lid of the teapot.

"Poison," Pamela murmured.

"They look so peaceful," Samuel exclaimed.

Tears flowed from Pamela's eyes, running like rivers down her cheeks.

"Were these enemies? I think not." Pamela said.

An unnatural and untimely cold wind swept across the plantation, trying desperately to blow away the past.

The End

Michael Edwin Q. is available for book interviews and personal appearances. For more information contact:

Michael Edwin Q.
C/O Advantage Books
P.O. Box 160847
Altamonte Springs, FL 32716
michaeledwinq.com

Other Titles in this series buy Michael Edwin Q:

Born A Colored Girl: 978-1-59755-478-4
Pappy Moses' Peanut Plantation: 978-1-59755-482-8

To purchase additional copies of these book visit our bookstore website at:
www.advbookstore.com

Longwood, Florida, USA
"we bring dreams to life"™
www.advbookstore.com

CPSIA information can be obtained
at www.ICGtesting.com
Printed in the USA
BVHW031700100921
616546BV00011B/989